ESCAPE
PLUS

"What kind of place is this?" Danny asked. "How come I'm not in a regular jail?"

Joe thought a minute before answering. "This is a new place. This Center has been set up for kids like you. Kids who are going to kill somebody – or get themselves killed – unless we can change them. Our job is to help you to change. We think you can straighten out. There's no need for you to spend the rest of your life in trouble and in jail. But you've got to let us help you. And you've got to help yourself."

"How . . . how long will I have to stay here?"

Joe's face turned grim. "Like I said, a couple of years, at least. But it really depends on you. You're going to stay as long as it takes. If you don't shape up, you stay. It's that simple."

Also available
by Ben Bova
in Methuen Paperbacks

Test of Fire
Winds of Altair
Colony
Voyagers
Voyagers II
The Starcrossed
The Exiles Trilogy
Orion
Privateers

BEN BOVA

ESCAPE PLUS

A Methuen Paperback

A Methuen Paperback

ESCAPE PLUS

British Library Cataloguing in Publication Data

Bova, Ben
    Escaplus
    I. Title
    813'.54[F]   PS3552.084

    ISBN 0-413-16010-6

First published in Great Britain 1988
by Methuen London Ltd
11 New Fetter Lane, London EC4P 4EE

Copyright © 1984 by Ben Bova

Printed in Great Britain by
Richard Clay Ltd, Bungay, Suffolk

Escape!, © 1970 by Ben Bova.
A Slight Miscalculation, © 1971 by
Mercury Press, Inc; 1973 by Ben Bova
Vince's Dragon, © 1981 by Ben Bova.
The Last Decision, © 1978 by Random House, Inc.
Men of Good Will, © 1964 by Galaxy Publishing Corporation;
1973 by Ben Bova.
Blood of Tyrants © 1970 by Ultimate Publishing Co.; 1973 by
Ben Bova.
The Next Logical Step, © 1962 by The Condé Nast Publications
    Inc.; 1973 by Ben Bova.
The Shining Ones, © 1975 by Ben Bova.
Sword Play, © 1975 by the Boy Scouts of America.
A Long Way Back, © 1960 by Ziff-Davis Publishing Co.
Stars, Won't You Hide Me?, © 1966 by Galaxy Publishing
    Corporation; 1973 by Ben Bova.

This book is dedicated to my Number-One Fan
and good friend, David Rosenfield

Contents

FORECAST:
THE WORLDS MODELER

It is called FORECASTS. It was created for the Joint Chiefs of Staff, the generals and admiral who head the U.S. Army, Navy, Air Force, and Marine Corps. It has cost more than a million dollars to develop, and will cost still more before it is fully tested and operational.

FORECASTS is a computer model of the whole world. It is a highly complex program that contains enormous amounts of data about global political trends, natural resources, and social and economic factors. The Joint Chiefs will use FORECASTS to help them make the predictions that go into their Joint Long Range Strategic Appraisal, in which the JCS evaluate what the world in general, and certain nations in particular, will look like over the next thirty years.

Science fiction writers have been making such predictions for generations now, and because the accuracy of the forecast is only as good as the quality of the information being used, the predictions of science fiction writers have generally been better than those of anyone else's—including the complex computerized "world models" of the scientists who call themselves futurists.

For example, futurists such as the late Herman Kahn have consistently missed the major turning points in recent history. No futurist predicted the Arab oil embargo of

1973 and the resulting panic of the energy crises which depressed the economies of the industrialized nations for a decade. The Club of Rome's much-heralded study, *The Limits to Growth*, failed utterly to understand that the Earth is not the only body in the universe from which the human race can extract energy and natural resources. The Presidential commission which produced *Report on the Year 2000* was equally medieval in its view, and failed even to see the vigorous growth of living standards in the small industrializing nations of the Far East, nations such as Taiwan, South Korea, Malaysia, and Singapore.

Science fiction's record of predicting the future is much better. Atomic power, space flight, organ transplants, population explosions, the changes in social mores that we now call "the sexual revolution," genetic engineering—all these changes in human capabilities were described in science fiction stories at least thirty years before they took place in reality. What is more important, science fiction writers also predicted the social consequences of such changes: the Cold War stalemate that has resulted from atomic weapons; the urban sprawl that came from increased mobility and growing population; the breakdown of traditional family values and morality that has accompanied the new sexual freedoms.

Why is it that science fiction writers have seen farther into the future than all others—and more clearly? Is it because they are trained in the sciences? Hardly. Although many writers of science fiction have degrees in the physical or social sciences, very few of them are actually practicing scientists. Isaac Asimov, for example, has not engaged in scientific research for nearly three decades, despite his doctorate in chemistry and his title of professor of biochemistry at Boston University School of Medicine. Ray Bradbury, on the other hand, has no scientific training at all. Yet both Asimov and Bradbury are world-class science fiction writers, and both have graced the literature with scores of powerful and predictive stories.

The thing that makes a science fiction writer better at predicting the future than anyone else is not scientific knowledge, although an understanding of science is very helpful, even necessary. Nor is it a mystical, arcane extrasensory perception of the future. No writer that I know of claims to be in contact with the Spirit of Christmas Yet To Come.

The science fiction writer's secret can be told in two words: *freedom* and *imagination*.

The professional scientists who try to predict the future with computerized accuracy always fail because *they are required to stick to the facts*. No futurist is going to predict that a semi-accidental discovery will transform the entire world. Yet the invention of the transistor did just that: without the transistor and its microchip descendants, today's world of computers and communications satellites simply would not exist. Yet a futurist's forecast of improvements in electronics technology, made around 1950, would have concentrated on bigger and more complicated vacuum tubes and missed entirely the microminiaturization that transistors have made possible. Science fiction writers, circa 1950, "predicted" marvels such as wrist-radios and pocket-sized computers, not because they foresaw the invention of the transistor but because they intuitively felt that some kind of improvement would come along to shrink the bulky computers and radios of that day.

The professional futurists labor under this enormous handicap; they are not allowed to consider the "wild cards," the crazy things that can and usually do happen. They are restricted to making more-or-less straight-line extrapolations of the facts as we know them today. Science fiction writers have the freedom to use more than the facts. They can use their imaginations. They can ask themselves, "What would happen if . . .?'' and then set out to write a story that answers the question. They can use their knowledge of the human soul—for that is what fiction is all about—not merely to describe the marvelous invention or the strange discovery, but to portray how real people—you or I—might react to these new things.

That is science fiction's great advantage, the freedom to employ human imagination to its fullest. The science fiction writer is not required to be accurate, merely entertaining. Although the writer need not have a professional knowledge of science, he or she should understand the basics well enough to know what is impossible—and how to move at least one step beyond that limit. The rule of thumb in good science fiction is that you are free to invent anything you like, providing no one else can *prove* that it could never be. Even though physicists are certain that nothing in the universe travels faster than the speed of light, they cannot prove that it is utterly impossible for a starship to circumvent that speed limit; therefore science fiction writers can create interstellar dramas, with merely a slight bow to acknowledge that their faster-than-light starships are using principles that were unknown in the 20th century. In creating such stories about some future times and places, the writer often creates an inner reality that eventually comes true.

You don't need a million-dollar computer program or a team of Pentagon scientists. All you need is that strange and elusive quality called talent, plus the fortitude to work long and lonely hours, together with the freedom to let your imagination roam where it will.

The stories in this collection are examples of how *my* imagination and creative freedom has led me to build worlds that do not exist—yet. From an electronically guarded prison that could be built today to the farthest ultimate reaches of interstellar space, these stories present eleven different answers to eleven different phrasings of that question, "What would happen if . . .?" One of these tales, *The Next Logical Step*, deals with the kind of computer that the Joint Chiefs of Staff might find themselves facing soon. Another, *A Long Way Back*, was my very first published short story; it dealt, in a way, with the basic factors of both the energy crisis that erupted a dozen years after the story was published and the aftermath of a nuclear war—a subject very much in the forefront of everyone's thinking even today, a quarter-century after the story was written.

Two of these tales are not really science fiction. One of them is a fantasy about a dragon, and the other is a "straight" story about my favorite sport, fencing. Both of them come directly from experiences in my younger years in South Philadelphia, that heartland of pop singers, steak sandwiches, and Rocky Balboa.

None of these tales has "come true" as yet, but that is not important. Each of them examines a reality of its own. Each of them places real people in strange and challenging situations. Each of them tests the human spirit in one way or another. Each of them presents a "world model" that forecasts a future that *might* come to pass.

Ben Bova
West Hartford, Connecticut

ESCAPE!

We tell ourselves a lot of lies about prisons. The biggest lie is calling it "the criminal justice system;" it is not a system, it has nothing to do with justice, and if there is anything criminal about it, it's the fact that jails tend to make their inmates lifelong antisocial animals.

I started my writing career on newspapers, and spent a lot of those early years covering the police beat in an upper-middle-class suburban area outside my native Philadelphia. As an investigative reporter (we didn't know that term back in the Fifties, we just called it legwork) I spent a summer probing into the problem of juvenile crime. The eventual result was Escape!, which was published originally as a short novel.

Two other factors went into writing this story; both involved the idea of a "perfect" jail. One was the notion that the lure of escape was the only thing that kept most inmates alive, especially the ones with long or indeterminate sentences. I read somewhere about a prison chaplain saying that if the inmates truly believed that they could never possibly escape from the jail they were in, they would go insane or commit suicide. The other factor was the kind of idea that only a science fiction writer would think of: suppose we made a jail that is as good as we can possibly imagine, a jail that actually works the way we good citizens say we want our jails to work, a jail that helps its inmates to become honest, upright, tax-paying citizens.

The result was the campus-like and absolutely escape-proof prison in Escape!, with its electronic sentries and all-seeing computer, SPECS. But to make the prison work the way I wanted it to, there had to be a human side to it. The machines can do only so much; the jail with its electronic marvels is merely a box in which to hold prisoners. To make the jail work in a way that would transform those prisoners into healthy, self-reliant, honest citizens required a human mind, a human soul, a human purpose. Thus Joe Tenny entered the equation, and became the main force in the resulting story.

Joe is modelled very closely on a man I knew and worked with for several years. The real "Joe Tenny" was a man of enormous talents and passions, a teacher, a scientist, a man who had worked himself too hard for his own good. He died much too early. The world is poorer for that. A pale shadow of him lives on in this story. That's not enough, but if this story shows you how we can use what's best in us to make the world better, then Joe's vital spark of life is not completely extinguished.

Escape!, incidentally, has generated more mail from readers than any other single story I have ever written. I credit "Joe Tenny's" indomitable spirit for that; he was the kind of man who made people feel good about themselves.

CHAPTER ONE

The door shut behind him.

Danny Romano stood in the middle of the small room, every nerve tight. He listened for the click of the lock. Nothing.

Quiet as a cat, he tiptoed back to the door and tried the knob. It turned. The door was unlocked.

Danny opened the door a crack and peeked out into the hallway. Empty. The guards who had brought him here were gone. No voices. No footsteps. Down at the far end of the hall, up near the ceiling, was some sort of TV camera. A little red light glowed next to its lens.

He shut the door and leaned against it.

"Don't lem 'em sucker you," he said to himself. "This is a jail."

Danny looked all around the room. There was only one bed. On its bare mattress was a pile of clothes, bed sheets, towels and stuff. A TV screen was set into the wall at the end of the bed. On the other side of the room was a desk, an empty bookcase, and two stiff-back wooden chairs. Somebody had painted the walls a soft blue.

"This can't be a cell . . . not for me, anyway. They made a mistake."

The room was about the size of the jail cells they always put four guys into. Or sometimes six.

And there was something else funny about it. *The smell, that's it!* This room smelled clean. There was even fresh air blowing in through the open window. And there were no bars on the window. Danny tried to remember how

many jail cells he had been in. Eight? Ten? They had all
stunk like rotting garbage.

He went to the clothes on the bed. Slacks, real slacks.
Sport shirts and turtlenecks. And colors! Blue, brown, tan.
Danny yanked off the gray coveralls he had been wearing,
and tried on a light blue turtleneck and dark brown slacks.
They even fit right. Nobody had ever been able to find him
a prison uniform small enough to fit his wiry frame before
this.

Then he crossed to the window and looked outside. He
was on the fifth or sixth floor, he guessed. The grounds
around the building were starting to turn green with the
first touch of early spring. There were still a few patches
of snow here and there, in the shadows cast by the other
buildings.

There were a dozen buildings, all big and square and
new-looking. Ten floors high, each of them, although
there were a couple of smaller buildings farther out. One
of them had a tall smokestack. The buildings were arranged around a big, open lawn that had cement paths
through it. A few young trees lined the walkways. They
were just beginning to bud.

"No fences," Danny said to himself.

None of the windows he could see had bars. Everyone
seemed to enter or leave the buildings freely. No guards
and no locks on the doors? Out past the farthest building
was an area of trees. Danny knew from his trip in here,
this morning, that beyond the woods was the highway that
led back to the city.

Back to Laurie.

Danny smiled. What were the words the judge had
used? *In . . . in-de-ter-minate sentence.* The lawyer had
said that it meant he was going to stay in jail for as long as
they wanted him to. A year, ten years, fifty years. . . .

"I'll be out of here tonight!" He laughed.

A knock on the door made Danny jump. *Somebody heard me!*

Another knock, louder this time. "Hey, you in there?" a man's voice called.

"Y . . . yeah."

The door popped open. "I'm supposed to talk with you and get you squared away. My name's Joe Tenny."

Joe was at least forty, Danny saw. He was stocky, tough-looking, but smiling. His face was broad; his dark hair combed straight back. He was a head taller than Danny and three times wider. The jacket of his suit looked tight across the middle. His tie was loosened, and his shirt collar unbuttoned.

A cop, Danny thought. *Or maybe a guard. But why ain't he wearing a uniform?*

Joe Tenny stuck out a heavy right hand. Danny didn't move.

"Listen, kid," Tenny said, "we're going to be stuck together for a long time. We might as well be friends."

"I got my own friends," said Danny. "On the outside."

Tenny's eyebrows went up while the corners of his mouth went down. His face seemed to say, *Who are you trying to kid, wise guy?*

Aloud, he said, "Okay, suit yourself. You can have it any way you like, hard or easy." He reached for one of the chairs and pulled it over near the bed.

"How long am I going to be here?"

"That depends on you. A couple of years, at least." Joe turned the chair around backwards and sat on it as if it were a saddle, leaning his stubby arms on the chair's back.

Danny swung at the pile of clothes and things on the bed, knocking most of them onto the floor. Then he plopped down on the mattress. The springs squeaked in complaint.

Joe looked hard at him, then let a smile crack his face.

"I know just what's going through your mind. You're thinking that two years here in the Center is going to kill you, so you're going to crash out the first chance you get. Well, for*get* it! The Center is escape-proof."

In spite of himself, Danny laughed.

"I know, I know. . . ." Tenny grinned back at him. "The Center looks more like a college campus than a jail. In fact, that's what most of the kids call it—the campus. But believe me, Alcatraz was easy compared to this place. We don't have many guards or fences, but we've got TV cameras, and laser alarms, and SPECS."

"Who's Specks?" Danny asked.

Joe called out, "SPECS, say hello."

The TV screen on the wall lit up. A flat, calm voice said, "GOOD MORNING DR. TENNY. GOOD MORNING MR. ROMANO. WELCOME TO THE JUVENILE HEALTH CENTER."

Danny felt totally confused. Somebody was talking through the TV set? The screen, though, showed the words he was hearing, spelled out a line at a time. But they moved too fast for Danny to really read them. And Specks, whoever he was, called Joe Tenny a doctor.

"Morning SPECS," Tenny said to the screen. "How's it going today?"

"ALL SYSTEMS ARE FUNCTIONING WELL, DR. TENNY. A LIGHT TUBE IN CORRIDOR SIX OF BUILDING NINE BURNED OUT DURING THE NIGHT. I HAVE REPORTED THIS TO THE MAINTENANCE CREW. THEY WILL REPLACE IT BEFORE LUNCH. THE MORNING CLASSES ARE IN PROGRESS. ATTENDANCE IS . . ."

"Enough, skip the details." Joe turned back to Danny. "If I let him, he'd give me a report on every stick and stone in the Center."

"Who is he?" Danny asked.

"Not a *he*, really. An *it*. A computer. Special Computer System. Take the 's-p-e' from 'special' and the 'c' and 's' from 'computer system' and put the letters together: SPECS. He runs most of the Center. Sees all and knows all. And he never sleeps."

"Big deal," said Danny, trying to make it sound tough.

Joe Tenny turned back to the TV screen, which was still glowing. "SPECS, give me Danny Romano's record, please."

The reply came without an instant's wait: "DANIEL FRANCIS ROMANO. AGE SIXTEEN. HEIGHT FIVE FEET TWO INCHES. WEIGHT ONE HUNDRED THIRTEEN POUNDS. SENTENCED TO INDETERMINATE SENTENCE IN THE JUVENILE HEALTH CENTER. FOUND GUILTY OF ATTEMPTED MURDER, RIOTING, LOOTING, ATTACKING A POLICE OFFICER WITH A DEADLY WEAPON, RESISTING ARREST. EARLIER CONVICTIONS INCLUDE PETTY THEFT, AUTOMOBILE THEFT, ASSAULT AND BATTERY, RESISTING ARREST, VANDALISM. SERVED SIX MONTHS IN STATE PRISON FOR BOYS. ESCAPED AND RECAPTURED . . ."

"That's enough," Joe said. "Bad scene, isn't it?"

"So?"

"So it's why you're here."

Danny asked, "What kind of place is this? How come I'm not in a regular jail?"

Joe thought a minute before answering. "This is a new place. This Center has been set up for kids like you. Kids who are going to kill somebody—or get themselves killed—unless we can change them. Our job is to help you to change. We think you can straighten out. There's no need for you to spend the rest of your life in trouble and in jail. But you've got to let us help you. And you've got to help yourself."

"How . . . how long will I have to stay here?"

Tenny's face turned grim. "Like I said, a couple of years, at least. But it really depends on you. You're going to stay as long as it takes. If you don't shape up, you stay. It's that simple."

CHAPTER TWO

Joe Tenny went right on talking. He used SPECS' TV screen to show Danny a map of the Center and the layouts of the different buildings. He pointed out the classrooms, the cafeteria, the gym and shops, and game rooms.

But Danny didn't see any of it, didn't hear a single word. All he could think of was: *as long as it takes. If you don't shape up, you stay.*

They were going to keep him here forever. Danny knew it. Tenny was a liar. They were all liars. Like that lousy social worker when he was a kid. She told him they were sending him to a special school. "It's for your own good, Daniel." Good, real good. Some school. No teacher, no books. Just guards who belted you when they felt like it, and guys who socked you when the guards weren't looking.

If you don't shape up, you stay. Shape up to what? Get a job? How? Where? Who would hire a punk sixteen-year-old who's already spent half his life in jails?

"We gave you a good room," Joe said, getting up suddenly from his chair. "Your building's right next-door to the cafeteria."

Danny snapped his attention back to the real world.

"Come on, it's just about lunchtime."

He followed Joe Tenny out into the hallway, to the elevator, and down to the ground floor of the building. Danny saw that somebody had scratched his initials on the metal inner door of the elevator, and somebody else had worked very hard to erase the scratches. They were barely visible.

They pushed through the glass doors and followed a

cement walkway across the piece of lawn that separated the two buildings. Danny shivered in the sudden chill of the outside air. Tenny walked briskly, like he was in a hurry.

Groups of boys—two, three, six, eight in a bunch—were walking across the campus grounds toward the cafeteria building. They were talking back and forth, joking, horsing around.

But Danny's mind was still racing. *I can't stay here. Can't leave Laurie alone on the outside. Some other guy will grab her. By the time I get out, she won't even remember me. Got to get out fast!*

Joe pushed open the glass doors of the cafeteria building. It was warm inside, and noisy. And it smelled of cooking.

"DR. TENNY," called a loudspeaker. Danny thought it sounded like SPECS' voice only much louder and with a bit of an echo to it. "DR. TENNY, PLEASE REPORT TO THE ADMINISTRATION BUILDING."

"Looks like I miss lunch," Joe said, glancing up at the loudspeaker. Danny saw that it was set into the panelled ceiling. There was a TV lens with its unblinking red eye next to it, watching them.

"Have a good feed, Danny. The rest of the day's yours. Move around, make some friends. SPECS will get you up at the right time tomorrow morning and tell you which classes to go to. See you!"

And with a wave of a heavy, thick-wristed hand, Joe headed back for the glass doors and outside.

Danny watched him go. Then a half-dozen boys pushed through the doors and walked in toward the cafeteria. They were laughing and wise-cracking among themselves. No one said hello or seemed to notice Danny at all.

Turning, Danny headed for the food. Around a corner of the hallway was a big, open, double doorway. Inside it was the cafeteria, noisy and busy with at least a hundred boys. They were standing in line, waving across the big room to friends, rushing toward tables with trays of steaming food, talking, laughing, eating. They moved as freely as they wanted and they all seemed to be talking as loudly as their lungs would let them.

The tables were small, four or six places each. In a few spots, boys had pushed together a couple of tables to make room for a bigger group.

Danny remembered the dining room in the State Prison. You marched in single file and ate at long, wooden tables that were so old the paint was gone. The wood itself was cracked and carved with the initials of fifty years' worth of boys.

This cafeteria was sparkling new. The walls, the tables, the floors all gleamed with fresh paint and plastic and metal. One whole wall was glass. Outside you could see a stretch of grass and a few young trees.

He took a place at the end of the food line. The boys moved along quickly, even though some of them were talking and kidding back and forth. Soon Danny was taking a tray and a wrapped package of spoon, knife, and fork. All plastic.

It surprised him to see that there were no people behind the food counter. Everything was automatic. Boys took a bowl of soup, or a sandwich, or a metal-foil dish that held an entire hot dinner in it. As soon as one piece was taken, another popped through a little door in the wall to replace it.

"You're new here, aren't you?"

Danny turned to see, in line behind him, a tall boy with sandy hair and a scattering of freckles across his snub nose.

"My name's Alan Peterson, No, don't tell me yours. Let me see if I can remember it. SPECS flashed pictures of

all the new guys on the news this morning. You're . . .
emm . . . Danny something-or-other. Right?''

''Danny Romano.''

Alan grinned. ''See, I got it. Almost.''

''Yeah.'' Danny reached for a sandwich and an apple.
The only drinks he could see were milk, either white or
chocolate. He took a chocolate,

Stepping away, Danny looked around for a table.

''Come on with me,'' Alan said cheerfully. ''I'll sit you
down with some of the guys. You ought to make friends.''

Alan steered him toward a six-place table. Three of the
seats were already filled. Danny stopped suddenly.

''I ain't sittin' there.''

''Why not?''

Danny jerked his head toward one of the boys at the
table. ''Cause I don't eat with niggers, that's why not.''

CHAPTER THREE

Alan looked at Danny in a funny way. Not sore, but
almost.

''Okay,'' he said softly. ''Find your own friends.''

He left Danny standing there with the tray in his hands
and went to the table. Another black came up at the same
time and sat beside Alan.

Danny found a small table that was empty and sat there
alone, with his back to the doors and the food line. He was
facing the glass wall and the outside.

He ate quickly, thinking, *Don't waste any time. Walk
around, see how big the place is, how hard it'll be to get out.*

He got up from the table and started to walk away. But
SPECS' voice came from an overhead loudspeaker:

"PLEASE TAKE YOUR TRAY TO THE DISPOSAL SLOT IF
YOU ARE FINISHED EATING. THANK YOU."

Danny looked up at the ceiling, then turned and saw
other boys bringing their trays to a slot in the wall, not far
from the table where he was. With a small shrug, he took
his tray to the slot.

He watches everything, Danny thought as he glanced up at
one of the TV cameras in the ceiling.

It was still chilly outside after lunch, even though the
sun was shining. Danny thought he had seen a jacket—a
windbreaker—among the clothes on his bed. But he didn't
bother going back to his room. Instead, he jammed his
fists in his slacks pockets, hunched his shoulders, and
headed toward the trees that were out at the edge of the
campus.

He didn't get far.

From behind him, a soft voice said, "Hear you don't
like eatin' with black men, skinny."

Danny turned around. Two blacks were standing there,
grinning at him. But there was no friendship in their
smiles. Danny thought they might be the two boys who
had been at the table Alan tried to steer him to.

For a moment they just stood there, looking each other
over. There were a couple of other boys around, white and
black, but they stayed a little distance away. Out of it.
Danny could feel himself tensing, his fists clenching hard
inside his pockets.

One of the blacks was Danny's own height, and not
much heavier. The other was tall and thin, built for
basketball. He had sleepy-looking eyes, and a bored, cool
look on his face.

"That true, skinny?" the tall one asked. "You don't
want to eat with us?"

Danny swore at him.

"My, my, such language," said the smaller of them. "Real rough one, this guy. Hard as nails."

"Yeah . . . fingernails."

They both laughed. Danny said nothing.

The tall black said slowly, "Listen baby. You got a problem. You're bein' put down in the schedule to fight Lacey here, first of the month."

Lacey nodded and grinned brightly. "So start workin' out in the gym, Whitey, or you won't last even half a round."

"Yeah." The tall one added, "And in case you don't know it, Lacey here's the lightweight champ o' this whole Center. And he ain't gonna be playing games with you in that ring. Dig?"

And they both walked away, as quickly and softly as they had come. Danny stood there alone, trembling with rage. He was so angry that his chest was starting to hurt.

The other boys who had been hanging around, started to drift back toward the buildings. But one of the white boys came up to Danny.

"My name's Ralph Malzone. I seen what them black bastards done to ya."

Ralph was a big redhead, huge and solid, like a pro-football player. His face was round and puffy, with tiny eyes squinting out, and little round ears plastered flat against his skull. He looked as if his skin was stretched as tight as it could go, another ounce would split it apart. But Ralph didn't look fat; he looked *hard*.

Danny looked up at him. "I couldn't even understand what they were saying, half the time."

"I heard 'em," Ralph answered. "You're new, huh? Well, there's a boxing match here every month. You been put down to fight Lacey. He's the lightweight champ. If you don't fight him, everybody'll think you're chicken."

Danny didn't answer. He just stood there, feeling cold whenever the wind gusted by.

"Lacey's fast. Hits hard for a little guy."

"I'm shaking," Danny said.

Ralph laughed. "Hey, you're okay. Listen, I'll help you out. In the gym. I know a lot about fighting."

"Why should you help me?"

Ralph's face started to look mean. "I don't like to see white guys gettin' picked on. And I want that Lacey creamed. He needs his head busted. Only, they won't let me fight him. I'm a heavyweight."

Grinning, Danny asked, "Why wait for the first of the month? Get him outside."

"Boy, wouldn't I like to!" Ralph said. "But it ain't as easy as it sounds. Too many TV cameras around. Step out of line and they catch you right away. . . . But you got the right idea. Boy, I'd *love* to mash that little crumb."

Nodding, Danny said, "Okay . . . uh, I'll see you in the gym sometime."

"Good," said Ralph. "I'll look for you."

CHAPTER FOUR

Ralph headed back for one of the classroom buildings. Danny started out again for the trees.

It was colder in the woods. The bare branches of the trees seemed to filter out almost all of the sun's warmth. The sky had turned a sort of milky-gray. The ground under Danny's sneakers was damp and slippery from melted snow and the remains of last year's fallen leaves.

Danny hated the cold, hated the woods, hated everything and everybody except the few blocks of city street where he had lived and the guys who had grown up on those streets with him. They were the only guys in the world you could trust. Can't trust grown-ups. Can't trust teachers or cops or lawyers or judges or jail guards. Can't trust Tenny. Can't even trust this new guy, Ralph. Just your own guys, the guys you really know. And Laurie. He had to get back to Laurie.

His feet were cold and wet and he could feel his chest getting tight, making it hard to breathe. Soon his chest would be too heavy to lift, and he'd have to stop walking and wait for his breathing to become normal again. But Danny kept going, puffing little breaths of steam from his mouth as he trudged through the woods.

And there it was!

The fence. A ten-foot-high wire fence. And on the other side of it, the highway. The outside world, with cars zipping by and big trailer trucks shifting gears with a grinding noise as they climbed the hill.

Danny stood at the edge of the trees, a dozen feet from the fence. Two hours down that highway was home. And Laurie.

He leaned his back against a tree, breathing hard, feeling the rough wood through his thin shirt. He listened to himself wheezing. *Like an old man,* he told himself angrily. *You sound like a stupid old man.*

When his breathing became normal again, Danny started walking along the fence. But he stayed in among the trees, so that he couldn't be seen too easily.

No guards. The fence was just a regular wire fence, the kind he'd been able to climb since he was in grade school. There wasn't even any barbed wire at the top. And nobody around to watch.

He could scramble over the fence and hitch a ride back to the city. He wasn't even wearing a prison uniform!

Danny laughed to himself. Why wait? He stepped out toward the fence.

"Hold it Danny! Hold it right there!"

CHAPTER FIVE

Danny spun around. Standing there among the trees was Joe Tenny, grinning broadly at him.

"Did you ever stop to think that the fence might be carrying ten thousand volts of electricity?" Joe asked.

Danny's mouth dropped open. Without thinking about it, he took a step back from the fence.

Joe walked past him and reached a hand out to the wire fence. "Relax, it's not 'hot.' We wouldn't want anybody to get hurt."

Danny felt his chest tighten up again. Suddenly it was so hard to breathe that he could hardly talk. "How . . . how'd you . . . know . . .?"

"I told you the Center was escape-proof. SPECS has been watching you every step of the way. You crossed at least eight different alarm lines. . . . No, you can't see them. But they're there. SPECS called me as soon as you started out through the woods. I hustled down here to stop you."

He's big but but he's old, Danny thought. *Getting fat. If I can knock him down and get across the fence . . .*

· "Okay, come on back now," Joe was saying.

Danny aimed a savage kick below Joe's belt. But it never landed. Instead he felt himself swept up, saw the highway and then the cloudy sky flash past his eyes, and then landed face-down on the damp grass. Hard.

"For*get* it, kid," Joe said from somewhere above him.

"You're too small and I'm too good a wrestler. I'm part Turk, you know,"

Danny tried to get up. He tried to get his knees under his body and push himself off the ground. But he couldn't breathe, couldn't move. Everything was black, smelled of wet leaves. He was choking. . . .

He opened his eyes and saw a green curtain in front of him. Blinking, Danny slowly realized that he was in a hospital bed. It was cranked up to a sitting position.

Joe Tenny was sitting beside the bed, his face very serious.

"You okay?" Joe asked.

Danny nodded. "Yeah . . . I think so . . ."

"You scared me! I thought I had really hurt you. The doctors say it's asthma. How long have you had it?"

"Had what?"

Joe pulled his chair up closer. "Asthma. How long have you had trouble breathing?"

Danny took a deep breath. His chest felt okay again. Better than okay. It had never felt this good.

"It comes and goes," he said. "Hits when I'm working hard . . . running . . . things like that."

"And not a sign of it showed up in your physical exams," Joe muttered. "How old were you when it first hit you?"

"I don't know. What difference does it make?"

"How old?" Joe repeated. His voice wasn't any louder, but it somehow seemed ten times stronger than before.

Danny turned his head away from Joe's intense stare. "Five, maybe six." Then he remembered. "It was the year my father died. I was five."

Joe grunted. "Okay. The doctors need to know."

"I thought you was a doctor," Danny said, turning back to him.

Tenny smiled. "I am, but not a medical doctor. I'm a

doctor of engineering. Been a teacher a good part of my life."

"Oh. . . ."

"You don't think much of teachers? Well, I don't blame you much."

Joe got up from his chair.

Danny looked around. The bed was screened off on three sides by the green curtain. The fourth side, the head of the bed, was against a wall.

"Where am I? How long I been here?" he asked.

"In the Center's hospital. You've been here about six hours. It's past dinnertime."

"I figured I'd be back home by now," Danny mumbled.

Joe looked down at him. "You've had a rough first day. But you've made it rough on yourself. Listen . . . there's a lot I could tell you about the Center. But I think it's better for you to find out things for yourself. All I want you to understand right now is one thing: around here, you'll get what you earn. Understand that? For the first time in your life, you're going to get *exactly* what you earn."

Danny frowned.

"It works both ways," Joe went on. "Make life rough for yourself and you'll earn trouble. Work hard, and you'll earn yourself an open door to the outside. You're the only one who can open that door. It's up to you."

"Sure."

"I mean it. I know you don't believe it, but you can trust me. You're going to learn that, in time, You don't trust anybody, that's one of the reasons why you're here . . . ."

Danny snapped, "I'm here because I nearly killed a fat-bellied cop in a riot that some niggers started!"

"*Wrong!* You're here because the staff of this Center decided there's a chance we might be able to help you. Otherwise you'd be in a *real* jail."

"What d'ya mean . . . ?"

Joe grabbed the chair again and sat on it. "Why do you think we call this the Juvenile *Health* Center? Because you're sick. All the kids here are sick, one way or another. You come from a sick city, a sick block. Maybe it's not all your fault that you're the way you are, but nobody's going to be able to make you well—nobody! Only you can do that. We're here to help, but we can't do much unless you work to help yourself."

Danny mumbled some street words.

"I understand that," Joe said, his eyes narrowing. "I'm part Sicilian, you know."

"You know everything, huh?"

"Wrong. But I know a lot more than you do. I even know more about Danny Romano than you do. I know there's enough in you to make a solid man. You've got to learn how to become a whole human being, though. My job is to help you do that."

CHAPTER SIX

It was lunchtime the next day before the doctors would let Danny go. He walked across the campus slowly. It was a warmer day, bright with sunshine, and Danny felt pretty good.

Then he remembered that he had failed to escape. He was trapped here at the Center.

"For a while," he told himself. "Not for long, just for a while. Until I figure out how to get around those alarms . . . whatever they are."

He had lunch alone in the crowded, noisy cafeteria. He sat at the smallest table he could find, in a corner by the glass wall. He saw Lacey walk by with a group of blacks, laughing and clowning around.

Danny finished eating quickly and decided to find the gym. He didn't have to look far. Just outside the cafeteria door was a big overhead sign with an arrow: ELEVATOR TO LIBRARY, POOL, GAME ROOMS, GYM.

He walked down the hall toward the elevator. Other boys were going the same way, some of them hurrying to get into the elevator before it filled up. Danny squeezed in just as the doors slid shut.

"FLOORS PLEASE." It was SPECS' voice.

"Gym," somebody said.

"Library."

"Pool."

"Hey Lou, you goin' swimmin' *again?*"

"It beats takin' a bath!"

Everybody in the elevator laughed.

The gym was on the top floor. The elevator door slid open and a burst of noise and smells and action hit Danny. A basketball game was in full swing. Boys shouting, ball pounding the floorboards. referee blasting on his whistle. Overhead, on a catwalk that went completely around the huge room, other boys were jogging and sprinting, their gray gym suits turning dark with sweat.

But at the far end of the gym was the thing that struck Danny the hardest. A boxing ring. And in it, Lacey was sparring with another black boy.

Danny stood by the elevator and watched, all the sights and sounds and odors of the gym fading away into nothing as he focused every nerve in his body on Lacey.

The guy was good. He moved around the ring like he was gliding on ice skates. His left snapped hard, jerking the other guy's head back when it landed. Then he winged a right across the other guy's guard and knocked him over backwards onto his back.

Turning, Lacey spotted Danny and waved. His black body was gleaming with sweat. His face was one enormous smile, made toothless by the rubber protector that filled his mouth.

"Hello, Danny."

Turning, he saw Alan Peterson standing beside him.

"Hi."

"Watching the champ? I hear you're scheduled to fight him the first of the month."

"Yeah." Danny kept his eyes on Lacey. A new sparring partner had come into the ring now. Lacey was jab-jab-jabbing him to death.

"Were you in the hospital yesterday?" Alan asked. "There's a story going around. . . ."

"Yeah, I was." Danny still watched Lacey.

"Are you sick? I mean, will you miss the fight? You can't fight anybody if you're sick."

"I ain't sick."

"But. . . ."

Lacey floored his new partner, this time with a left hook.

"I ain't sick!" Danny snapped. "I'll fight him the first of the month!"

"Okay, don't get sore," said Alan. "It's your funeral."

The loudspeaker suddenly cut through all the noise of the gym: "DANIEL FRANCIS ROMANO, PLEASE REPORT TO DR. TENNY'S OFFICE AT ONCE."

Danny felt almost relieved. He didn't want to hang around the gym any more, but he didn't want Lacey to see him back away. Now he had an excuse to go.

"I'll take you," Alan offered.

Danny said, "I can find it by myself."

CHAPTER SEVEN

He had to ask directions once he was outside on the campus. Finally, Danny found the building that the boys called "the front office." It was smaller than the other buildings, only three stories high. The sign over the main door said ADMINISTRATION. Danny wasn't quite sure he knew what it meant.

Inside the door was a sort of a counter, with a girl sitting at a telephone switchboard behind it. She was getting old, Danny saw. Way over thirty, at least. She was reading a paperback book and munching an apple.

"Where's Joe Tenny's office?" Danny asked her.

She swallowed a bite of apple. "*Dr*. Tenny's office is the first door on your left."

Danny went down the hallway that she had pointed to. The first door on the left was marked: DR. J. TENNY, DIRECTOR.

Instead of knocking, he walked back to the switchboard girl. She was bent over her book again, her back to Danny. He noticed for the first time that there was a clear plastic shield between the top of the counter and the ceiling. Like bulletproof glass. He tapped it.

The girl jumped, surprised, and nearly dropped the book out of her lap.

"Hey," Danny asked, "is Tenny the boss of this whole place?"

She looked very annoyed. "This Center was Dr. Tenny's idea. He fought to get it started and he fought to make it the way it is. Of course he runs it."

"Oh. . . . Uh, thanks."

Danny went back and knocked at Joe's door.

"Come in!"

Joe's office was smaller than Danny's room. It was crammed with papers. Papers covered his desk, the table behind the desk, and lapped over the edges of the bookshelves that filled one whole wall. In a far corner stood an easel with a half-finished painting propped up on it. Brushes and tubes of paint were scattered on the floor beside the easel.

Joe leaned back in his chair. He squinted through the harsh-smelling smoke from the stubby cigar that was clamped in his teeth.

"How're you feeling?"

"Okay."

"Sit down. The smoke bother you?"

"No, it's okay." Danny saw that there was only one other chair in the office, over by the half-open window.

Sitting in it, he asked, "Uh . . . did you tell any of the other guys about, eh, what happened yesterday?"

"About you trying to escape?" Joe shook his head. "No, that's no business of anybody else's. SPECS knows it, of course. But I've ordered SPECS to hold the information as private. Only the staff people who work on your case will be able to learn about it. None of the kids."

Danny nodded.

"Quite a few people saw me carrying you into the hospital, though."

"Yeah . . . I guess so."

Joe tapped the ash off his cigar into the wastebasket next to his desk. "Listen. You're going to start classes tomorrow. Most of the kids spend their mornings studying, and use the afternoons for different things. You're expected to work a couple of hours each afternoon. You can work in one of the shops, or join the repair gang, or something else. Everybody works at something to help keep the

Center shipshape. Otherwise the place would fall apart.''

Danny frowned. "You mean it's like a job?"

"Right," said Joe, with a grin. "Don't look so glum. It won't hurt you. You get credit for every hour you work, and you can buy things in the Center 's store. SPECS runs the store and keeps track of the credits. And it's only a couple hours a day. Then the rest of the day's all yours."

"A job," Danny muttered.

"You can learn a lot from some honest work. And you'll be helping to keep the Center looking neat. You might even get to like it."

"Don't bet on it."

Joe made a sour face. "Okay, I'm not here to argue with you. You have a visitor. She's in the next room."

"She? Laurie?"

Nodding, Joe said, "You can spend the rest of the afternoon with her. But she's got to leave at five."

Without another word, Danny hurried from Dr. Tenny's office and burst into the next room. Laurie was sitting on the edge of a big leather chair. She jumped up and ran into his arms.

After a few minutes, Danny pulled away from her and closed the door.

"How are you?" They both said it at the same time. They laughed.

Laurie was a little thinner than Danny remembered her. And sort of pale. She was a small girl, almost frail-looking, with hair and eyes as dark as Danny's own. Danny knew prettier girls, but no one like Laurie. Of all the people in the world, she was the only one that needed Danny. And the only one that he needed.

"You look good," she said.

"You look great."

"Are they treating you okay?"

He nodded. "Sure. Fine. This is more like a school than a jail. How about you? Everything okay?"

"Uh-huh."

They moved slowly to the couch, by the room's only window.

"How's Silvio and the other guys?" Danny asked as they sat down.

"They're all right. . . . Danny, are you really okay?"

Laughing, he said, "Sure. I told you. This ain't really a jail. I nearly broke out of here yesterday. Looks easy. Hardly any guards. I'll probably be out in a couple weeks. Soon's I figure out a couple things."

Laurie's eyes widened. She looked frightened. "Danny, don't do anything they can catch you on. If you get into more trouble. . . ."

"You feel like waitin' around for five years?" he snapped. "Or ten? Twenty? If I can break out, I'm goin' to do it. Reason the other guys don't try it is 'cause they're too soft. They got it too easy here, so they stay. Not me!"

"But they'll just hunt you down again and bring you back. Or maybe put you in a worse place. . . ."

"You *want* me to stay?"

"No. I mean. . . ."

"Listen, I got it figured," Danny said. "Soon's I get out, we grab a car and get up to Canada. Then they can't touch us."

Laurie just looked scared. "All the way to Canada?"

"Just the two of us. We can start all over again. I'll even get a job. . . ."

"Me, too," Laurie said. Then she started to say something else, stopped, and finally said, "Oh, Danny . . . I wanted to tell you. I got a job now. I'm helping my sister in the restaurant where she works. . . ."

"Waiting on tables?" Danny felt his face twist into a frown.

Laurie nodded. Her voice was very low. "And . . . cleaning up, helping in the kitchen."

"I don't want my girl doin' that kind of work!"

"Well, I need some money. . . ." She looked away from him, out toward the window. "I want to be able to live on my own. And the bus to come here costs money."

Danny's frown melted. But he didn't feel any better.

Laurie went on, "Dr. Tenny said I could come once a week, if I wanted to. And he said he thought you could do real good here. Maybe get out in two years."

"I'll be out in a couple weeks," said Danny.

"Please . . . don't do anything they'll catch you on."

"I'll be out in a couple of weeks," Danny repeated.

CHAPTER EIGHT

Laurie left at five. Danny went over to the cafeteria and picked at his dinner.

Ralph Malzone pulled up a chair and sat beside Danny. He looked much too big for the thin-legged plastic chair.

"Hey, I heard you was sick yesterday. Not going to back out of the fight with Lacey, are ya?"

Danny pushed his tray of food away. "No, I'll fight him."

"Good," said Ralph. He leaned across, took a slice of bread from Danny's tray, and started buttering it. "C'mon over to the gym tomorrow afternoon. I'll show you some tricks. Help make you the new lightweight champ."

Nodding, Danny said, "Sure."

Danny got up to leave. Ralph was still picking food from his tray, so Danny left it there with him.

When he got back to his room and shut the door, the lights turned on and the TV screen lit up.

"GOOD EVENING, MR. ROMANO," said SPECS. The screen spelled out the words.

"How'd you know I was in here?" Danny asked, stopping suddenly by the door and frowning at the screen.

"THERE IS A SENSING DEVICE IN THE DOORWAY. AND THE ROOM LIGHTS WENT ON. I HAVE A. . . ."

"But how'd you know it was me? Can you see me?"

"THERE ARE NO CAMERAS IN THE STUDENTS' ROOMS. I DID NOT KNOW FOR CERTAIN THAT IT WAS YOU. HOWEVER, THE CHANCES WERE BETTER THAN NINETY PERCENT THAT ONLY YOU WOULD ENTER YOUR OWN ROOM AT THIS TIME OF THE EVENING. I HAVE A MES. . . ."

"Well then, how'd you know I'm Danny Romano? I could of been anybody."

SPECS' voice did not change a bit, but somehow Danny felt that the computer was getting sore at him. "YOUR VOICE IS THE VOICE OF DANIEL FRANCIS ROMANO, AND NO ONE ELSE'S. I HAVE A MESSAGE. . . ."

"You know everybody's voice?"

"I AM PROGRAMMED TO RECOGNIZE THE SPEECH PATTERNS AND VOCAL TONES OF EVERYONE IN THE CENTER. I HAVE A MESSAGE FOR YOU FROM THE MEDICAL DEPARTMENT."

SPECS waited patiently for Danny to reply. Finally, Danny said, "Okay, what's the message?"

"YOU WILL FIND A BOTTLE OF PILLS ON THE TABLE BY YOUR BED. THEY ARE FOR ASTHMA. DIRECTIONS ARE WRITTEN ON THE LABEL. THEY READ AS FOLLOWS: 'TAKE ONE PILL BEFORE GOING TO BED AT NIGHT, AND A PILL WHENEVER NEEDED DURING THE DAY. KEEP THIS BOTTLE WITH YOU AT ALL TIMES. NOTIFY THE MEDICAL DEPARTMENT WHEN ONLY FIVE PILLS ARE LEFT.' "

"These pills'll make me breathe okay?"

"I DO NOT HAVE THAT INFORMATION. I CAN PUT YOU IN

CONTACT WITH THE MEDICAL DEPARTMENT. DR. MAKOWITZ IS ON DUTY AT THE MOMENT."

"Naw, that's okay."

Danny went to the bed and saw the bottle of pills on the bed table. They were white, plain-looking. He glanced up at the TV screen and saw that it had gone dead.

"Hey SPECS."

The screen glowed again. "YES, MR. ROMANO?"

"Uh . . . any other messages for me?" Suddenly Danny felt foolish, talking to a TV screen.

"NO OTHER MESSAGES. I HAVE YOUR SCHEDULE FOR TOMORROW'S CLASSES, BUT I AM PROGRAMMED TO GIVE THIS INFORMATION TO YOU TOMORROW MORNING, AFTER YOU AWAKEN."

"Can you give it to me now?"

"IF YOU ORDER THE INFORMATION, I AM PROGRAMMED TO ANSWER YOUR REQUEST."

"You mean if I tell you to do it, you'll do it?"

"YES."

"Suppose I tell you to turn off all the alarms in the Center?"

"I AM NOT PROGRAMMED TO ANSWER THAT REQUEST."

Danny plopped down on the bed, his mind running fast.

"Listen SPECS. Who can give you orders about the alarms? Who can make you turn 'em off?"

The answer came at once. "DR. TENNY, THE CAPTAIN OF THE GUARDS, THE HIGHEST MEMBER OF THE GUARDS WHO IS ON DUTY, THE CHIEF OF THE MAINTENANCE DEPARTMENT, THE HIGHEST RANKING MEMBER OF THE MAINTENANCE DEPARTMENT WHO IS ON DUTY."

Danny thought for a moment. "Suppose the guard captain told you right now to turn off all the alarms. Could you do that?"

"YES."

"Okay SPECS," Danny suddenly said loud and firm, "turn off all the alarms!"

"I AM NOT PROGRAMMED TO ANSWER THAT REQUEST."

"This is the captain of the guards. I order you to turn off all the alarms!"

Danny could have sworn that SPECS was ready to laugh at him. "YOU ARE NOT THE CAPTAIN OF THE GUARD FORCE. YOU ARE DANIEL FRANCIS ROMANO. YOUR VOICE INDEX SHOWS IT."

"Okay SPECS. You got me cold."

"I DO NOT UNDERSTAND THAT STATEMENT."

"You won't tell Tenny about this, will you?"

"THIS CONVERSATION IS RECORDED IN MY MEMORY BANK. IF DR. TENNY OR ANOTHER STAFF MEMBER ASKS TO VIEW IT, I AM PROGRAMMED TO ANSWER THAT REQUEST."

"But you won't tell 'em unless they ask?"

"CORRECT."

Danny grinned. *Tenny can't ask for something unless he knows it exists.*

"Okay. G'night SPECS."

"GOOD NIGHT, MR. ROMANO."

As Danny undressed, he wondered to himself, *Now, where can I get a tape recorder? And maybe I ought to get a gun, too . . . just in case.*

CHAPTER NINE

When Danny got to his first class the next morning, he thought he was in the wrong room.

It didn't look like a classroom. There were nine other boys already there, sitting around in chairs that were scattered across the floor. A man of about thirty or so was sitting among them, and they were talking back and forth.

"Come on in and take a seat," the teacher said. "My name is Cochran. Be with you in a minute."

Mr. Cochran looked trim and wiry. His hair was clipped very short, like a military crewcut. His back was rifle-straight. He looked to Danny more like a Marine in civilian clothes than a teacher.

Danny picked a seat toward the back of the room. On one side of him the wall was lined with windows. On the other was a row of bookshelves, like a library. There was a big TV screen at the front of the room.

Turning around in his chair, Danny saw that the back of the room was filled with a row of little booths. They looked about the size of telephone booths. Maybe a bit bigger. They were dark inside.

"Hello. You're Daniel Romano?" Mr. Cochran pulled up one of the empty chairs and sat next to Danny. The other boys were reading or writing, or pulling books from the shelves.

"This is a reading class," Cochran explained. "Different boys are working on different books. I'd like you to start out today on this one."

For the first time, Danny saw that the teacher had a book in his hands. The title was *Friends in the City*.

Danny took the book and thumbed through it. It was filled with pictures of smiling people—grocers, cops, firemen, housewives—living in a clean, bright city.

"You got to be kidding!" He handed the book back to Mr. Cochran.

The teacher grinned. "I know. It's kid stuff. If you think it's too easy for you we can go on to something better. But first you'll have to take a test to see if you're ready for harder work."

He walked Danny back to one of the booths. Opening the door, Mr. Cochran stepped inside and flicked on the lights. Danny saw that the booth had a little desk in it, and the desk was covered with dials and push-buttons. Just above the desk, on the wall of the booth, was a small TV screen.

Mr. Cochran fiddled with the dials and buttons for a few moments, then stepped outside and said to Danny, "Okay, it's all yours. Just sit right down and have fun. SPECS is going to give you a reading test."

With a shrug, Danny went into the booth and sat down. Mr. Cochran shut the door. The window on it was made of darkened glass, so that Danny could hardly see the classroom outside. The booth felt soundproofed, too. It had that quiet, cushion-like feeling to it.

The TV screen lit up. "GOOD MORNING," said SPECS' voice.

"Hi. You know who this is?"

"DANIEL FRANCIS ROMANO."

"Right again." *Cripes*, thought Danny, *ain't he ever wrong?* Then he got a sudden idea. "Hey SPECS, where can I get a tape recorder?"

"TAPE RECORDERS ARE USED IN THE LANGUAGE CLASSES."

"Can you take 'em back to your room? Are they small enough to carry?"

"YES TO BOTH QUESTIONS. AND NOW, ARE YOU READY TO RECEIVE STANDARD READING TEST NUMBER ONE?"

Smiling to himself, Danny said, "Sure, go ahead."

By the time the test was over, Danny was no longer smiling. He was sweating. SPECS flashed words on the TV screen. Danny had to decide if they were spelled right. He pushed one button if he thought the spelling was right, another button if he thought it was wrong.

After what seemed like an hour of spelling questions, SPECS began putting whole sentences on the screen. Danny had to tell him what was wrong, if anything, with each sentence.

Finally, SPECS put a little story on the screen. Then it disappeared and some questions about the story came on. Danny had to answer the questions.

When he was finished, Danny slumped back in the padded seat. His head hurt, he felt tired. And he knew he had done poorly.

The door to the booth opened and Mr. Cochran pushed in. Danny saw, past him, that the classroom was now empty.

"How'd it go?" The teacher leaned over and touched a few buttons on the desk top. Numbers sprang up on the screen.

"Not good, huh?" Danny said weakly.

Mr. Cochran looked down at him. "No, not so very good. But, frankly, you did better than I thought you would."

Danny sat up a little straighter.

"Look," Mr. Cochran said, "I know *Friends in the City* is a kind of dumb book. But why don't you just work your way through it? Read it in your room. You don't have to show up here in class every morning. SPECS can help you when you're stuck on a word. Then, when you think you've got it licked, come in and take the test again."

"How long will it take?"

Cochran waved a hand. "Depends on you. Three, four days, at most. You're smart enough to get the hang of it pretty fast, if you really want to."

Danny said nothing.

Mr. Cochran stepped out of the booth and Danny got up and went outside, too.

"Look," the teacher said, "reading is important. No matter what you want to do when you get out of the Center, you'll need to be able to read well. Unless you can read okay, Dr. Tenny won't let you leave here. So it's up to you."

"Okay," said Danny. "Give me the book. I'll learn it."

But as he walked down the hall to his next class, Danny told himself, *Let 'em think I'm trying to learn. Then they won't know I'm working on a break-out.*

CHAPTER TEN

Danny went to two more classes that morning: history and arithmetic. He fell asleep in the history class. No one bothered him until the teacher poked him on the shoulder, after the rest of the boys had left.

"I don't think you're ready for this class," the old man said. His thin face was white with the struggle to keep himself from getting angry.

The arithmetic class was taught by Joe Tenny. To his surprise, Danny found that he could do most of the problems that Tenny flashed on the TV screen.

"You've got a good head for numbers," Joe told him as the class ended and the boys were filing out for lunch.

"Yeah. Maybe I'll be a bookie when I get out."

Joe gave him that who-are-you-trying-to-kid look. "Well, you've got to plan on being *something*. We're not just going to let you go, with no plans and no job."

They left the classroom together and started down the hall for the outside doors.

"Uh . . . the history teacher told me not to come back to his class. I . . . uh, I fell asleep."

"That was smart," said Joe.

"Well, uh, look . . . can I take something else instead of history? Maybe learn Italian. . . . I already talk it a little. . . ."

"I know."

Danny felt his face go red. "Well, what I mean is, maybe I could learn to talk it right."

Joe looked slightly puzzled. "I don't understand why you'd want to study a foreign language. But if that's what you want to do, okay, we'll try it. Just don't fall asleep on the job."

Grinning, Danny promised, "I won't!"

After lunch, Danny went up to the gym. One of the older boys showed him where the lockers were. Danny changed into a sweat suit and went back onto the gym floor. He lifted weights for a while, then tried to jog around the track up on the catwalk. He had to stop halfway; it got too hard to breathe.

Got to get one of those pills.

He went back to his locker and took a pill. After a few minutes he was able to breathe easily again. He went back to the gym and found a row of punching bags lined up behind the ring. No one was using them. Lacey was nowhere in sight. Danny felt glad of that. Ralph Malzone came from around the corner of the ring, though.

"Hiya, Danny. Starting training for the fight? You only got two weeks."

Jabbing at a punching bag, Danny answered, "Yeah, I know."

Ralph looked bigger than ever in his gym suit. He towered over Danny. "C'mon back here, behind the bags. I'll show you a few things."

For the next half-hour, Ralph showed Danny how to use his elbows, his knees, and his head to batter and trip up his opponent.

"All strictly illegal," Ralph said, grinning broadly. "But you can get away with 'em if you're smart. Main thing, with Lacey, is keepin' him off balance. Trip him, step on his feet. Butt him with your head. Grab him and give him the elbow."

Danny nodded. Then suddenly he asked, "Hey Ralph . . . where can I get a gun?"

"What?"

"A gun. A zip'll do. Or at least a blade. . . ."

Ralph's smile vanished. His round, puffy face with its tiny eyes suddenly looked grim, suspicious.

"What do you want a piece for?"

"For getting out of here, what else?" Danny said.

Ralph thought it over in silence for a minute. Then he said, "Go take a shower, get dressed, and meet me in the metal shop. Two floors down from here."

"Okay."

Danny took his time. He wanted to be sure Ralph was in the shop when he got there.

The metal shop smelled of oil and hummed with the electrical throb of machines that cut or drilled or shaped pieces of steel and aluminum. Boys were making bookshelves, repairing desk chairs, building other things that Danny didn't recognize.

There was a pair of men in long, shapeless shop coats wandering slowly through the aisles between the benches, stopping here and there to talk with certain boys, showing them how to use a machine, what to do next. Back in the farthest corner, Ralph was tinkering with some long pieces of pipe.

Danny made his way back toward Ralph's bench. No one stopped him or bothered him.

"Hi."

Ralph looked coldly at him. "I just been wondering

about you. Asking about a gun. Somebody tell you to ask me?''

Danny shook his head. "What are you talking about?''

Ralph whispered, "I ain't told nobody about this. But I'm showing it to you. If you're a fink for Tenny . . . you ain't just going to see this, you're going to *feel* it.''

Keeping his eyes on the closest teacher, who was several benches away, Ralph bent down slightly and reached underneath his bench. He pulled and then brought his hand out far enough for Danny to see what was in it.

"Hey!'' Danny whispered.

It looked crude but deadly. The pistol grip was a sawed-off piece of pipe. The trigger was wired to a heavy spring. The barrel was another length of pipe.

"Shoots darts,'' Ralph whispered proudly. He took a pair of darts from his shirt pocket. They looked to Danny like big lumber nails that had been filed down to needle points.

"You made it all yourself?'' asked Danny.

Ralph nodded. He put the darts back in his pocket and tucked the gun inside his shirt. It made a heavy bulge in his clothing.

"Now I got to test it. There's a spot out in the woods I know. No TV eyes to watch you there. If it works, then tonight I go sailing out of here. Right through the front gate.''

Danny gave a low whistle. "That takes guts.''

"With this,'' Ralph said, tapping the gun, "I can do it. Now, you start walking out. I'll be right behind you. Don't go too fast. Take it easy, look like everything's cool. And remember, if you peep one word, I'll test this piece out on you.''

"Hey, I'm with you,'' Danny insisted.

They walked together toward the door, with Ralph slightly behind Danny so that no one could see the bulge in his shirt.

They threaded their way past the work benches, where the other boys were busy on their projects. The two teachers paid no attention to them at all. They got past the last bench and were crossing the final five feet of open floor space to the door.

The door swung shut.

All by itself. It shut with a slam. All the power machinery stopped. The room went dead silent. Danny stopped in his tracks, only two steps from the door. He could hear Ralph breathing just behind him.

"ONE OF THE BOYS AT THE DOOR IS CARRYING SEVERAL POUNDS OF METAL," said SPECS from a loudspeaker in the ceiling. "I HAVE NO RECORD OF PERMISSION BEING GIVEN TO CARRY THIS METAL AWAY FROM THE SHOP."

Danny turned and saw all the guys in the shop staring at him and Ralph. The two teachers were hurrying toward them. With a shrug of defeat, Ralph pulled the gun from his shirt and held it out at arm's length, by the barrel.

One of the teachers, his chunky face frowning, took the gun. "You ought to know better, Malzone."

Ralph made a face that was half smile, half frown.

"And what's your name?" the teacher asked Danny. "How do you fit into this? I haven't seen you in here before."

"He don't fit in," Ralph said, before Danny could answer. "He didn't know anything about it. I built it all myself. He didn't even know I had it on me."

The teacher shook his head. "I still want your name, son."

"Romano. Danny Romano."

The second teacher took the gun from the first one, looked it over, hefted it in his hand. "Not a bad job, Malzone. Heavier than it needs to be. Who were you going to shoot?"

"Whoever got between me and the outside."

The teacher said, "If you'd put this much effort into something useful, you could walk out the front gate, and do it without anyone trying to stop you."

"Yeah, sure."

"And, by the way, SPECS won't let anybody through the door if he's heavier than he was when he walked in. We're all standing on a scale, right now. It's built into the floor."

"Thanks for telling me," said Ralph.

"Okay, get out of here," the teacher said. "And don't either one of you come back until you've squared it with Dr. Tenny."

Ralph started for the door. It clicked open.

Danny followed him.

Out in the hall, Danny said, "Thanks for keeping me off the hook."

Ralph shrugged. "And I was afraid you was working for Tenny. With that lousy SPECS, he don't need no finks."

"What happens to you now?" Danny asked as they headed for the elevator.

"I'll get a lecture from Tenny, and for a couple months I'll have to take special classes instead of shop work."

"Is that all?"

Ralph stopped walking and looked at Danny. His eyes seemed filled with tears. "No it ain't all. I thought I'd be out of here tonight. Now I'm further behind the eight ball than ever. I don't know when I'll get out. Maybe never!"

CHAPTER ELEVEN

Danny worked hard for the next two weeks. He paid attention in classes. He passed his first reading test with SPECS, and Mr. Cochran let him pick out his own books. Danny started reading books about airplanes and rockets.

The arithmetic class with Joe Tenny was almost fun.

"You keep going this well," Tenny told him, "and I'll start showing you how to work with SPECS on really tough problems."

Danny smiled and nodded, and tried not to show how much he wanted to get SPECS to work for him.

Danny worked especially hard in the language class, so that the teacher would let him take one of the class's pocket tape recorders back to his room. For extra homework.

Sure.

The teacher—a careful, balding old man—said he'd let Danny have the tape recorder "in a little while."

Afternoons, Danny spent mostly in the gym. He took an asthma pill before every workout, but found that he needed another one after a few minutes of heavy work.

Ralph was still showing him dirty tricks, still telling him to "break Lacey's head open." Ralph even got into the ring and sparred with Danny.

And Danny took on a job. He joined the Campus Clean-up Crew. It was a pleasant outdoor job now that the weather had turned warm and the trees were in full leaf. Danny spent two hours each afternoon raking lawns, cutting grass, picking up any litter that the boys left around the campus. And he was also learning to spot the little black boxes lying nearly buried in the ground, the boxes that held the cameras and lasers and alarms for SPECS.

The day before his fight with Lacey, Danny's language teacher finally let him have a pocket tape recorder. But it was too late to try a breakout before the fight. Danny figured he would need at least a week to get the right words from Joe Tenny onto a tape. Then he'd have to juggle the words onto another tape until he had exactly the right order to give SPECS.

Danny wasn't looking forward to fighting Lacey. It would have been fine with him if he could have escaped the Center before the fight. But he wasn't going to back out of it.

Maybe Lacey'll help get me out of here, Danny thought, with a grim smile. *On a stretcher.*

CHAPTER TWELVE

The gym had been changed into an arena. All the regular equipment had been put away, the ring dragged out to the center of the gym, and surrounded by folding chairs. All the chairs were filled with teachers and boys who cheered and hollered for their favorite boxers. And they booed the poor ones without mercy.

Danny could hear the noise of the crowd from inside the locker room. Ralph had helped him find a pair of trunks that fit him. They were bright red, with a black stripe. *The color of blood,* Danny thought. One of the gym teachers wrapped tape around Danny's hands and helped him into the boxing gloves. Then they fit him with a head protector and mouthpiece.

There were no other boxers in the locker room. Danny's

fight was the last one of the evening. Lacey was getting ready in another locker room, on the other side of the building.

"Now remember," Ralph whispered to Danny when the teacher left them alone, "get in close, grab him, trip him up, push him off-balance. Then hit him with everything you got! Elbows, head, everything. You got a good punch, so use it."

Danny nodded.

The crowd roared and broke into applause. He could hear the bell at ringside ringing.

"Okay Romano," the teacher called from the doorway. "It's your turn."

The head protector felt heavy, and clumsy. *The mouthpiece tastes funny, like a new automobile tire might taste,* Danny thought.

As he entered the gym a big cheer went up. Danny started to smile, but then saw that the cheering was for Lacey, who was coming toward the ring from the other side of the gym.

As he walked toward the ring, boys hollered at him:

"You're goin' to get mashed, Romano!"

"Sock it to him, Danny!"

"Hey, skinny, you won't last one round!"

Dr. Tenny was standing at the ringside steps. His jacket was off. He was wearing a short-sleeved shirt with no tie.

"All set, Danny?"

"Yeah."

"I've checked with the medics. They're not too happy about you fighting."

"I'll be okay."

"Did you take a pill?" Joe asked.

Nodding, Danny said, "Two of 'em. Before I left my room."

"Good. If you need more, I've got some right here in my pocket."

"Thanks. I'll be okay."

Joe stepped aside and Danny climbed up into the ring, with Ralph right behind him. The crowd was cheering and booing at the same time. *Guess who the cheers are for!*

The referee was one of the gym teachers. He called the boys to the center of the ring and gave them a little talk:

"No hitting low, no holding and hitting, no dirty stuff. If I tell you to break it up, you stop fighting and step back. Just do what I tell you, and don't lose your tempers. Let's have a good, clean fight."

They went back to their corners. Danny stood there, alone now, and stared at Lacey. He seemed to be all muscle, all hard and strong.

The bell rang.

Danny couldn't do anything right. He charged out to the middle of the ring and got his head snapped back by Lacey's jab. He swung, missed. Lacey moved too fast! Danny tried to follow him, tried to get in close. But Lacey danced rings around him, flicking out jabs like a snake flicks out his tongue. Most of them hit. And hurt.

The crowd was yelling hard. The noise roared in Danny's ears, like the time he was at the seashore and a wave knocked him down and held him under the water.

Lacey slammed a hard right into Danny's middle. The air gasped out of Danny's lungs. He doubled over, tried to grab the black. His gloves reached Lacey's body, but then slipped away. Danny straightened up, turned to find Lacey, and got another stinging left in his face.

It was getting hard to breathe. *No, don't!* Danny told himself. *Don't get sick!* But his chest was starting to feel heavy. Another flurry of punches to his body made it feel even worse.

Danny finally grabbed Lacey and pulled himself so close that their heads rubbed together.

"You want to dance, baby?" Lacey laughed.

Then, suddenly, he blasted half a dozen punches into Danny's guts, broke away, and cracked a solid right to Danny's cheek. Danny felt his knees wobble.

The bell rang.

Ralph was angry. "You didn't do nothing I told you to! You got to get in close, hold him, butt him!"

Danny gasped, "You try it."

He sat on the stool, chest heaving. His face felt funny, like it was starting to swell. It stung.

The bell sounded for the second round, and it was more of the same. Lacey was all over the ring, grinning, laughing, popping Danny with lefts and rights. Danny felt as if he was wearing iron boots. He just couldn't keep up with Lacey. The crowd was roaring so loudly that it hurt his ears. He tasted blood in his mouth. And Lacey kept gliding in on him, peppering him with a flurry of punches, then slipping away before he could return a blow.

Danny's chest was getting bad now. He was puffing, gasping, unable to get air into his lungs.

It seemed as if an hour had gone by. Finally, Lacey backed into the ropes and Danny made a desperate grab for him. He locked his arms around Lacey, wheezing hard.

"Hey, you sick?" Lacey's voice, muffled behind the mouth protector, sounded in Danny's right ear. "You sound like a church organ."

He pushed Danny away, but instead of hitting him, just tapped his face with a light jab and danced off toward the center of the ring. The crowd booed.

"Finish him!"

"Knock him out, Lacey!"

The bell ended round two.

Joe Tenny was at his corner when Danny sagged tiredly on the stool.

"You'd better take another pill," he said.

Shaking his head, Danny gasped out, "Naw . . . I'll be . . . okay. . . . Only one . . . more round."

Tenny started to say something, then thought better of it. He went back down the stairs to his seat.

"You got to get him this round!" Ralph hollered in Danny's ear, over the noise of the crowd. "It's now or never! When th' bell rings, go out slow. He thinks he's got you beat. Soon's he's in reach, sock him with everything you've got!"

Danny nodded.

The bell rang. Danny pushed himself off the stool. He went slowly out to the middle of the ring, his hands held low. The referee was looking at him in a funny way. Lacey danced out, on his toes, still full of bounce and smiling.

Lacey got close enough and Danny fired his best punch, an uppercutting right, a pistol shot from the hip, hard as he could make it.

It caught Lacey somewhere on the jaw. He went down on the seat of his pants, looking very surprised.

The crowd leaped to its feet, screaming and cheering.

The referee was bending over Lacey, counting. But he got up quickly. His face looked grim, the smile was gone. The referee took a good look into Lacey's eyes, then turned toward Danny and motioned for him to start fighting again.

Danny managed to take two steps toward Lacey, and then the hurricane hit him. Lacey swarmed all over him, anger and pride mixed with his punches now. He wasn't smiling. He wasn't worried about whether Danny might be sick or not. He attacked like a horde of Vikings, battering Danny with a whirlwind of rights and lefts.

Danny felt himself smashed back into the ropes, his legs melting away under him. He leaned against the ropes, let them hold him up. He tried to keep his hands up, to ward off some of the punches. But he couldn't cover himself. Punches were landing like hail in a thunderstorm.

Through a haze of pain, Danny lunged at Lacey and wrapped his arms around the black waist. He leaned his face against Lacey's chest and hung on, his legs feeling like rubber bands.

The crowd was making so much noise he couldn't tell if Lacey was saying anything to him or not. He felt the referee pull them apart, saw his worried face staring at him.

Danny stepped past the referee and put up his gloved hands to fight. They each weighed a couple of tons. Lacey looked different now, not angry any longer. More like he was puzzled.

They came together again, and again Danny was buried under a rain of punches. Again he grabbed Lacey and held on.

"Go down, dummy!" Lacey yelled into his ear. "What's holding you up?"

Danny let go with his right arm and tried a few feeble swings, but Lacey easily blocked them. He felt somebody pulling them apart, stepping between them, pushing him away from Lacey. Through blurred eyes, Danny saw the referee raising Lacey's arm in the victory signal.

CHAPTER THIRTEEN

Somebody was helping him back to the stool in his corner. The crowd was still yelling. Danny sat down, his chest raw inside, his body filled with pain.

"The winner, in one minute and nine seconds of the third round . . . Lacey Arnold!"

Joe Tenny was bending through the ropes, his face close to Danny's. "You okay?"

Danny didn't answer.

Another man was beside Joe, frowning. Danny remembered that he was one of the doctors from the hospital.

"Get him back to the locker room," the doctor said, angry. "I'll have to give him a shot."

"Can you stand up?" Ralph's voice asked from somewhere to Danny's right. He realized then that he couldn't see out of his right eye. It was swollen shut.

"Yeah . . . I'm okay. . . ." Danny grabbed the ropes and tried to stand. His legs were very shaky. He felt other people's arms holding him, helping him to stand.

Lacey was in front of him. "Hey, Danny, you all right?"

"Sure," Danny said, through swollen lips.

Back in the locker room they sat him on a bench. The doctor stuck a needle into Danny's leg, and within a few seconds his chest started to feel better.

The doctor growled to Tenny, "You should never have let this boy exert himself like that. . . ."

Joe nodded, his face serious. "Maybe you're right."

"I'm okay," Danny insisted. His chest really felt pretty good now. But his face hurt like fire and he felt more tired than he ever had before in his life.

"This whole business of staging fights is wrong," the doctor said.

Joe said, "If they don't fight in the ring, they'll do it behind our backs. I'd rather have it done under our control. It's a good emotional outlet for everybody."

Danny turned to Ralph, who was sitting glumly on the bench beside him. "Guess I didn't do too good."

Ralph shrugged and tried to cheer up. "Yeah, he smacked you around pretty good. But that one sock you caught him with was a beauty! Did ya see th' look on his face when he hit the floor? I thought his eyes was going to pop out !"

Just then Lacey came by, a robe thrown over his shoulders and his gloves off.

"Good fight, Danny. Man, if the ref didn't stop it when he did, my arms was going to fall off. I hit you with everything! How come you didn't go down like you're supposed to?" He was grinning broadly.

"Too dumb," said Danny.

"Smart enough to deck me," Lacey shot back. "Got me sore there for half a minute. Well, anyway . . . good fight."

Lacey stuck out his right hand. The tape was still wrapped around it. Danny was surprised to see that his own gloves had been taken off by somebody. He looked at his hands for a moment, then grasped Lacey's. It was the first time he had ever shaken hands with a black.

CHAPTER FOURTEEN

To his surprise, Danny was something of a hero the next morning. He felt good enough to go to his reading class, even though his eye was still swollen, and really purple now. His arms and legs were stiff and sore. His ribs ached. But he went to class anyway.

"Here comes the punching bag," somebody said when he came into the classroom.

"Look at that shiner!"

"Tough luck, Danny. You showed a lot of guts."

"First time Lacey's ever been knocked down."

"Goin' to fight him again next month?"

Danny let himself sink into one of the chairs. "Not me. Next fight I have is goin' to be with somebody a lot easier than Lacey. Like maybe King Kong."

Mr. Cochran came in, looked a little surprised at seeing Danny there, and then put them all to work.

*   *

Laurie was shaken up when she visited that week and saw Danny's eye. But he laughed it off and made her feel better. By the time she came back, the following week, Danny's face was just about back to normal.

By that time, Danny had enough of Joe Tenny's voice on tape to do the job he wanted to. One afternoon he went back to the language classroom. It was empty.

The booths in the back of the room had big tape recorders in them. Danny worked for more than an hour, taking Tenny's words off his pocket recorder and getting them onto the big machine's tape in just the right way. Finally, he had it exactly as he wanted it to sound:

"SPECS," said Dr. Tenny's voice, "I want you to turn off all the alarm systems right now."

It didn't sound exactly right. Some of the words were louder than others. If you listened carefully, you could hear different background noises from one word to the next, because they had been recorded at different times. Danny hoped SPECS wouldn't notice.

He got his faked message onto the tape of his pocket recorder and erased the tape on the big machine. Then he headed back toward his room.

"Tonight," he told himself.

It was nearly midnight when he tried it.

"SPECS, you awake?"

The TV screen at the foot of his bed instantly glowed to life. "I DO NOT SLEEP, MR. ROMANO."

Danny laughed nervously. "Yeah, I know. I was only kidding."

"I AM NOT PROGRAMMED TO RECOGNIZE HUMOR, AL-THOUGH I UNDERSTAND THE BASIC THEORY INVOLVED IN IT. THERE ARE SEVERAL BOOKS IN MY MEMORY BANKS ON THE SUBJECT."

"Groovy. Look . . . Dr. Tenny wants to talk to you. Can you see him here in the room with me?"

"THERE IS NO TV CAMERA IN YOUR ROOM, SO I CANNOT SEE WHO IS THERE."

"Well, you know Dr. Tenny's in here, don't you?"

"MY SENSORS CANNOT TELL ME IF DR. TENNY IS WITH YOU OR IF YOU ARE ALONE."

"Okay, take my word for it. He's here and he wants to tell you something." Danny flicked the button of his pocket recorder.

Dr. Tenny's voice said, "SPECS, I want you to turn off all the alarm systems right now."

Danny found that he was holding his breath.

"ALL THE ALARM SYSTEMS ARE SHUT DOWN."

Without another word, Danny dropped the recorder onto his bed and rushed out of his room.

He made his way swiftly toward the fence. It was a warm night, and he knew every inch of the way, now that he had put in so many weeks on the clean-up crew. It was dark, cloudy, but Danny hurried through the trees and got to the fence in less than twenty minutes. He had taken an asthma pill just before calling SPECS, and had the bottle in his pants pocket.

He got to the fence and without waiting a moment he jumped up onto it and started climbing.

A strong hand grabbed at his belt and yanked him down to the ground.

Danny felt as if a shock of electricity had ripped through him. He landed hard on his feet and spun around. Joe Tenny was standing there.

"How . . . how'd you . . .?"

Joe's broad face was serious-looking. "You had me fooled. I thought you were really starting to work. But you still haven't got it straight, have you?"

"How'd you know? All the alarms are off!"

Shaking his head, Joe answered, "Didn't you ever stop to think that we'd have back-up alarms? When the main alarms go off, the back-ups come on. And SPECS automatically calls a half-dozen places, including .my office. I happened to be working late tonight, otherwise the guards would've come out after you."

"Back-up alarms," Danny muttered.

"Come on," said Joe, "let's get back to your room. Or are you going to try to jump me again?"

Shoulders sagging, chin on his chest, Danny went with Dr. Tenny. When they got back to his room, Danny trudged wearily to his bed and sat on it.

"So what's my punishment going to be?"

"Punishment?" Joe made a sour face. "You still don't understand how this place works."

Danny looked up at him.

"You're punishing yourself," Joe explained. "You've been here about a month and you've gone no place. You've just wasted your time. As far as I'm concerned, tomorrow's just like your first day here. You haven't learned a thing yet. All you've done is added several weeks to the time you'll be staying here."

"I'm never getting out," Danny muttered.

"Not at this rate."

"You'll never let me out. We're all in here to stay."

"Wrong! Ask Alan Peterson. He's leaving next week. And he was a lot tougher than you when he first came in here. Nearly knifed me his first week."

Danny said nothing.

"Okay," said Joe. "Think it over. . . . And you'd better give me the tape recorder."

It was still on the bed, where Danny had left it. He picked it up and tossed it to Joe.

CHAPTER FIFTEEN

Danny sat slumped on the bed for a long time after Joe left, staring at the black-and-white tiled floor.

A month wasted.

He looked up at the TV screen. "SPECS," he called.

The screen began to glow. "YES, MR. ROMANO."

"You didn't tell me about the back-up alarms," Danny said, with just the beginnings of a tremble in his voice.

"YOU DID NOT ASK ABOUT THE BACK-UP ALARMS."

"You let me walk out there and get caught like a baby."

"THE BACK-UP SYSTEMS GO ON AUTOMATICALLY WHEN THE MAIN ALARM SYSTEMS GO OFF. I HAVE NO CONTROL OVER THEM."

Danny got up and faced the screen. "You lied to me," he said, his voice rising. "You let me go out there and get caught again. You lied to me!"

"IT IS IMPOSSIBLE FOR ME TO TELL A LIE, IN THE SENSE. . . ."

"Liar!" Danny crossed the room in three quick steps and grabbed the desk chair.

"*Liar!*" he screamed, and threw the chair into the TV screen. It bounced off harmlessly.

Danny picked up the chair and smashed it across the screen. Again and again. The hard plastic of the screen didn't even scratch, but the chair broke up, legs splintering and falling, seat cracking apart, until all Danny had in his hands was the broken ends of the chair's back.

"I AM CALLING THE MEDICAL STAFF," said SPECS calmly. "YOU ARE BEHAVING IN AN HYSTERICAL MANNER."

"Dirty rotten liar!" Danny threw the broken pieces of the chair at the screen and cursed at SPECS.

Then he turned around, kicked the side of his desk, then knocked over his bookcase. The half-dozen books he had in it spilled out onto the floor. Danny reached down and took one, tore it to bits, and then ran to the door.

A couple of medics were hurrying up the hall toward his room. Danny ran the other way. But the door at the far end of the hall was closed and locked. SPECS had locked all the doors now.

"Come on son, calm down now," said one of the medics. They were both big and young, dressed in white suits. One of them carried a small black kit in his hand.

Danny swore at them and tried to leap past them. They grabbed him. He struggled as hard as he could. Then he felt a needle being jabbed into his arm. Danny cursed and hollered and tried to squirm away from them. But everything was starting to get fuzzy. Soon he slid into sleep.

He awoke in his own room. Early morning sunlight was coming through the window. The broken pieces of the chair were still scattered across the floor, mixed with the pages from the torn book. The bookcase was still face down. He was still in the same clothes he had been wearing the night before, except that his shoes had been taken off.

Danny sat up. His head felt a little whoozy. One of the doctors entered the room without knocking. He checked Danny over quickly and then said, "You'll be okay for classes this morning. Have a good breakfast first."

As the doctor left, the TV screen lit up. Joe Tenny's face appeared on it.

"Got it out of your system?"

Danny glared at him.

Joe grinned. "Okay, you had your little temper tantrum. You're going to have to fix the chair by yourself, in the wood shop. We'll give you a new book to replace the one you tore up, but you ought to do something to earn it. Maybe you can work Saturday morning in the laundry room."

Danny frowned, but he nodded slowly.

"Okay," said Joe. "See you in class."

CHAPTER SIXTEEN

It can't be escape-proof, Danny told himself. *There's got to be a way out.*

Yeah, he answered himself. *But you ain't goin' to find it in a day or two.*

Alan Peterson left the next week, but not before Danny asked him if he had ever tried to escape.

Alan smiled at the question. "Yes, I tried it a few times. Then I got smart. I'll walk out the front gate. Joe Tenny helped to get me a job outside. You can do the same thing, Danny. It's the only sure-fire way to escape."

The day Alan left, Danny asked Ralph Malzone about escaping.

Ralph said, "Sure, I tried it four—five times. No go. SPECS is too smart. Can't even carry a knife without SPECS knowing it."

Danny asked all the guys in his classes, everybody he knew. He even asked Lacey.

Lacey grinned at him. "Why would I want to get out? I got it good here. Better than back home. Sure, they'll throw me out someday. But not until I got a good job and a good place to live waitin' for me outside. And until then, man, I'm the champ around here."

Danny dropped his class in Italian. But his reading got better quickly. He found that he could follow the words printed on SPECS' TV screens easily now. And he was almost the best guy in the arithmetic class.

Joe Tenny told Danny he should take another class. Danny picked science. It wasn't really easy, but it was fun. They didn't just sit around and read, they did lab work.

One morning Danny cleared out the lab by mixing two chemicals that gave off bright yellow smoke. It smelled horrible. The teacher yelled for everybody to get out of the lab. All the kids boiled out of the building completely and ran onto the lawn.

The kids all laughed and pounded Danny's back. The teacher glowered at him. Danny tucked away in his mind the formula he had used to make the smoke. *Might come in handy some time,* he told himself.

The weeks slipped by quickly. Laurie came every week, sometimes twice a week. Joe gave permission for them to walk around on the "outside" lawn, on the other side of the administration building, where the bus pulled up. There was a fence between them and the highway. And SPECS' cameras watched them. Danny knew.

Danny played baseball most afternoons. Then the boys switched to football as the air grew cooler and the trees started to change color.

Thanksgiving weekend there were no classes at all, and the boys set up a whole schedule of football games.

The first snow came early in December. Before he really thought much about it, Danny found himself helping some of the guys to decorate a big Christmas tree in the cafeteria.

His own room had changed, over the months. The bookcase was nearly filled now. Many of the books were about airplanes and space flight. His desk was always covered with papers, most of them from his arithmetic class. He had "bought" pictures and other decorations for

his walls from the student-run store in the basement of the
cafeteria building.

Thumbtacked to the wall over Danny's desk was a
Polaroid picture of Laurie. She was wearing a yellow
dress, Danny's favorite, and standing in front of the restaurant where she worked. She was smiling into the camera,
but her eyes looked more worried than happy.

Danny worked at many different jobs. He helped the
cooks in the big, nearly all-automated kitchen behind the
cafeteria. He worked on the air-conditioning machines on
the roofs of buildings, and on the heaters in the basements.
He went back to working with the clean-up crew for a
while, getting a deep tan the hottest months of the summer.

All the time he was looking, learning, searching for the
weak link, the soft spot in the Center's escape-proof network of machines and alarms. *There's got to be something*,
he kept telling himself.

Danny even worked for a week in SPECS' own quarters;
a big, quiet, chilled-down room in the basement of the
administration building. The computer was made of row
after row of huge consoles, like oversized refrigerators:
big, square boxes of gleaming metal. Some of them had
windows on their fronts, and Danny could see reels of tape
spinning so fast that they became nothing but a blur.

If I could knock SPECS out altogether. . . . But how?

The answer came when the boys turned on the lights of
the Christmas tree in the cafeteria.

It was a big tree, scraping the ceiling. Joe Tenny had
brought in a station wagon full of lights for it. Danny and
the other boys spent a whole afternoon on ladders, string-
ing the lights across its broad branches. Then they plugged
in all the lines and turned on the lights.

The whole cafeteria went dark.

The boys started to groan, but the cafeteria lights went
on again in a moment. The tree stayed unlit, though.

SPECS' voice came through the loudspeakers in the ceiling: "YOU HAVE OVERLOADED THE ELECTRICAL LINES FOR THE CAFETERIA. YOU CANNOT PLUG THE TREE LIGHTS INTO THE CAFETERIA'S REGULAR ELECTRICAL LINES. PLEASE SET UP A SPECIAL LINE DIRECTLY FROM THE POWER STATION FOR THE TREE."

Some of the boys nodded as if they knew what SPECS was talking about. But Danny stood off by himself, staring at the unlit tree.

Electric power! That's the key to this whole place! If I can knock out all the electric power, everything shuts down. All the alarms, all the cameras, SPECS, everything!

CHAPTER SEVENTEEN

The Saturday before Christmas, Joe Tenny knocked on Danny's door. "You doing anything special tonight?" he asked.

Danny was sitting at his desk. He looked up from the book he was reading. It was a book about electrical power generators.

"No, nothing special," he answered.

Joe grinned. "Want a night outside? I've got a little party cooking over at my house. Thought you might like to join the fun."

"Outside? You mean out of the Center?"

With a nod, Joe said, "It might *look* like I spend all my time here, but I do have a home with a wife and kids."

"Sure, I'll come with you."

"Good. Pick you up around four-thirty. Don't eat too much lunch, you're going to get some home-cooking tonight. Greek style. I'm part Greek, you know."

Danny laughed.

* * *

Joe's house was a surprise to Danny. He had expected
something like a governor's mansion, like he'd seen on
TV. But as Joe drove his battered old Cadillac toward the
city, they zipped right through the fanciest suburbs, where
the biggest and plushest houses were. Finally, Joe pulled
into a driveway in one of the oldest sections of the suburbs,
practically in the city itself.

"Here we are."

It was already dark, and Danny couldn't see too much
of the house. It was big, but not fancy-looking. It needed a
paint job. There were four cars already parked on the street
in front of the house. Another car was pulled off to one
side of the driveway. The hood was off and there was no
motor inside it.

"My oldest son's big project," Joe said as they got out
of his car. "He's going to rebuild the engine. I've been
waiting since last spring for him to finish the job."

Inside, the party was already going on. In quick order,
Danny met Mrs. Tenny, Joe's two sons, a huge dog named
Monster, and six or seven guests. He lost count and couldn't
remember all the names. More people kept arriving every
few minutes.

Joe's older son, John, took Danny in tow. He was
Danny's age, maybe a year older. But he was a full head
taller than Danny, with shoulders twice his size. About
half the guests were teenagers, John's friends. John made
sure that Danny met them all, especially the girls. They
were pretty and friendly. Danny found himself wishing
that Laurie was with him . . . and then began to feel guilty
because he was enjoying himself without her.

There were more than twenty people at dinner. The regular dining room table couldn't hold them all, so Joe and his
sons brought in the kitchen table while Danny helped one

of the guests set up a card table. Everybody helped push all three tables into one long row, and then spread table-cloths over them.

They ate and laughed and talked for hours, grownups and kids together. Then they moved into the living room. Joe turned on some records and they danced.

Most of the adults quickly dropped out of the dancing but Joe and a few others kept going as long and as hard as the teenagers did. Then they switched to older, slower music, and some of the other grownups got up again.

Then somebody put on Greek music. Everyone joined hands in a long line that snaked through the living room, the front hall, the dining room and kitchen, and back into the living room. Danny couldn't get his feet to make the right steps. But he saw that hardly anybody else could, either. Everyone was laughing and stumbling along, with the reedy Greek music screeching in their ears. The man leading the line, though, was very good. He was short and plump, with a round face and a little black mustache. He went through the complex steps of the Greek dance without a hitch.

When they stopped dancing and collapsed into the living room chairs, the same man started doing magic tricks. His name was Homer, and he had Danny really puzzled. He pulled cigarettes out of the air, picked cards out of a deck from across the room, changed a handkerchief into a flower.

Everyone applauded him.

"Boy, he's great," Danny said to John, who was sitting next to him on the sofa. "Is he on TV?"

John laughed. "He's my high school principal. Magic's just his hobby."

Danny felt staggered. *A principal? Homer couldn't be. He was . . . well, he was too happy!*

After a while, Danny went over to where Homer was

sitting and they started talking. He even showed Danny a couple of card tricks,

"How's Joe treating you at the Center?" Homer asked.

"Huh? Oh . . . pretty good."

Homer smiled. "I don't see where he gets all his energy. He's at that Center almost twenty-four hours a day. You should have seen him when he was trying to get the Center started! He gave up his job at the State University and battled with the Governor and the State Legislature until I thought they were going to throw him out on his ear. He even went to Washington to get Congress to put up extra money to help with the Center."

Squirming unhappily, Danny said, "I didn't know that."

"It's true," Homer said. "The Center is Joe's baby. You boys are all his kids."

"Yeah. He's . . . he's okay," said Danny.

CHAPTER EIGHTEEN

The party went on well past midnight. As people began to leave, Joe came over to Danny and said quietly, "Think you can sleep with John without any problems?"

Danny blinked. "You mean sleep here tonight? Not go back to the Center?"

Nodding, Joe said, "Don't get any ideas. Monster's a watch dog, you know, and he sleeps right outside John's door every night. And I'm part Apache Indian. So you won't be able to sneak out."

In spite of himself, Danny smiled. "Okay, I'll behave myself. I won't even snore."

"Good. Maybe tomorrow we can drive over to your old neighborhood and see your girlfriend. . . ."

"Laurie!"

"Yes. I tried to get her to come here tonight, but I couldn't reach her on the phone."

Danny hardly slept at all. John's snoring and tossing in the bed helped to keep him awake, but mainly he was excited about going back to his turf, going back to see Laurie. Would she be surprised!

But Joe couldn't get her on the phone. Why not? Where was she? Had she moved out of her sister's apartment? Wasn't she working at the restaurant anymore? Danny thought back to Laurie's last visit to the Center. It had been about a week ago. She hadn't said anything about moving. Had she looked worried? Was something bothering her? Or some*body?*

They got up late the next morning. By the time Joe put Danny and Monster into his car and started for the city, it was a little past noon. They drove in silence through the quiet streets. Monster huddled on the back seat, his wet nose snuffling gently behind Danny's ear.

They got to the heart of the city and drove down narrow streets where the buildings cut off any hope of sunshine. Danny gave Joe directions for getting to his old neighborhood.

"Pull up over there," he said, pointing. "By the cigar store."

Nothing had changed much. As he got out of the car, Danny suddenly realized that it had been almost a year since he'd been around here.

Only a couple of young kids were in sight, sitting on the front steps of one of the houses halfway up the block. The street was just as dirty as ever, with old newspaper pages and other bits of trash laying crumpled against the buildings and in the gutters.

There were a few cars parked along the street. Danny

remembered the first time he had driven a car. He had stolen it right here, from in front of the cigar store.

The store was closed. The windows were too dirty to look through. *Funny,* Danny thought to himself, *I never thought about how crummy everything is.*

"Where is everybody?" Joe asked. He was still inside the car, one elbow resting on the door where the window had been rolled down. Monster's heavy gray head was sticking out the back window, tongue out, big teeth showing.

"Some of the guys might be up at the schoolyard. It's about two blocks from here, around the corner."

Joe said, "Okay. Hop in."

Danny slammed the door shut and Joe gunned the motor. "What's the matter?" Joe asked.

Danny shrugged. "I don't know . . . it looks kind of, well, different."

"The neighborhood hasn't changed, Danny. You have."

"What d'you mean?"

Joe swung the car around the corner and headed up the street. "A writer once said, 'You can't go home again.' After you've been away, when you come back home everything seems changed. But what's changed is *you.* You're different than you were when you left. You'll never be able to come back to this neighborhood, Danny. In time, I don't think you'll want to."

Danny stared at Joe. Silently, he thought, *He must be nutty! Not want to come back to my own turf? Crazy!*

They got to the schoolyard and, sure enough, there were a few kids there shooting a scruffed-up basketball at a bare metal hoop that was set into the blank stone wall of the school.

Joe stayed in the car with Monster. The kids didn't recognize Danny as he got out of the car. They stopped shooting the ball and stared at him as he walked up, watching him silently. Then:

"Hey . . . holy cripes, it's *Danny!*"

"Danny!"

He broke into a big grin as they ran toward him.

"Hi, Mario. Hello, Sal. Eddie. . . ."

"Danny! Geez . . . you look like a million bucks!"

"Where did you get them clothes?"

"Hey, you break loose? How'd you do it?"

Laughing, Danny put up his hands. "Hey guys, I can't talk to all of you at once. No, I didn't break out. I sort of got the weekend off. The guy in the Cadillac back there . . . he's from the Center."

"Wow! Lookit the dog!"

"Yeah," Danny said, still grinning. "His name's Monster."

"You got to believe it."

"So how're they treating ya?" Mario asked. "You look good. Getting fat, ain't you?"

"I been eatin' good," Danny said. "The Center's okay, I guess. Tough to get out of. I tried a couple shots at it. . . . They got a computer running everything. And special alarms, better than they got in banks. Trickier. Can't even sneeze without 'em knowin' about it."

They talked for a few minutes, then Danny said, "Hey, I'm goin' over to Laurie's sister's place. She still livin' in the same apartment?"

The boys' grins disappeared. They became serious. Finally Mario answered, "Uh, yeah, she still lives there. But . . . uh . . . Laurie moved out. 'Bout two weeks ago. She don't live around here no more."

Danny felt the same flash of fear and anger that he had known when Joe pulled him down from the fence.

"What? What d'you mean?"

Shrugging inside his jacket, Mario said, "She just moved out. Didn't tell nobody where. Maybe her sister knows. We don't."

Danny grabbed him. "What happened? Why'd she move?"

Mario tried to back away. "Hey, Danny, it ain't my fault! A couple guys tried to make time with her, but we bounced 'em off. We been watchin' her for you."

"Yeah, you been watchin' her so good you don't even know where she is." Danny let go of him.

He sprinted back to the car. Sliding into the front seat beside Joe he said, "Let's go over to Laurie's sister's place . . . back where we were a couple minutes ago."

"What's the matter?"

Danny told him as he started the car.

Laurie's sister had no time for Joe and Danny. She was trying to take care of three babies—the oldest was barely four—and do a day's cooking at the same time.

She was trying to pin a diaper on the youngest baby, who was doing his best to wriggle away from her. She had him lying on the kitchen table, within arm's reach of the stove.

"I told you," she said sharply, "that she's okay. She's working uptown now, and she's got her own apartment, with two other girls. She promised she'd visit you every week, just like she's been doing all year. So if she wants to tell you where she's living, let her do it. I'm not going to."

Danny left the apartment with his fists clenched.

Joe tried to cool him down: "Look, she's been coming to see you every week, hasn't she?"

Danny nodded. His chest was feeling tight again, and he was angry enough to pound his fists into the grimy walls of the apartment building's stairway. But he didn't do that. He just nodded.

They walked out to the car and got into it. Joe started the motor and headed back toward the Center.

"You know," he said, "I might have had something to do with this."

"You?"

Joe nodded. "Last month Laurie and I had a talk, before I called you to the visiting room. She wanted to know what I thought about her working in the restaurant. She knew you didn't like the idea.

"I told her there are lots of schools in town that'll train her to be a secretary. Or anything else she wants to be. I gave her the name of a couple of friends of mine who could help her to get a better job and pick out a good night school."

Danny couldn't answer. So it was Joe Tenny. All the time he was pretending to be Danny's friend, he was really trying to get Laurie away. *You can't trust anybody,* Danny shouted to himself silently. *Nobody! Especially not Joe Tenny!*

CHAPTER NINETEEN

Monday morning, at breakfast in the cafeteria, Danny looked for Ralph Malzone.

"Hey listen," he said, sitting beside Ralph at a small table. "We got to get out of here."

"Sure," said Ralph through a mouth full of cereal. "Build me some wings an' I'll fly out."

"I'm not kidding! Trouble is, guys have been trying to break out one at a time. What we got to do is get a bunch of guys to work together. That's the only way."

Ralph shook his head. "Been tried before. SPECS an' all those alarms and automatic locks and everything . . . you couldn't get out o' here with an army."

"Oh yeah? I know how to fix SPECS and everything else."

Ralph laughed.

"I ain't kidding!" Danny snapped. "You listen to me and we'll be out of here in a couple months. Maybe sooner."

Ralph put his spoon down. "How you goin' to do it?"

"That's my secret," said Danny. "You just do what I tell you, and you'll be out in time for the opening game of the baseball season. But we'll need five or six other guys. Can you get 'em?"

"I'll get 'em," said Ralph.

Christmas morning Danny spent in his room, talking to SPECS.

"Where's the electricity in the Center come from?" he asked.

SPECS' calm, unhurried voice answered: "THE CENTER HAS ITS OWN POWER STATION, LOCATED IN BUILDING SEVENTEEN."

"Where's that?"

The TV screen showed a map of the Center. There was a red circle around building seventeen. Danny saw it was one of the smaller buildings, near the administration building. It was the only building on the campus with a smokestack.

"Suppose something happened to the power station, where would the electricity come from then?"

"THERE IS AN EMERGENCY POWER SYSTEM, ALSO LOCATED IN BUILDING SEVENTEEN."

"And suppose something happened to the emergency system, so it didn't work either?"

"ALL ELECTRICAL POWER IN THE CENTER WOULD BE SHUT OFF."

Danny thought a moment, then said, "If all the electrical power was shut off, what systems would stop?"

SPECS' calm, unhurried voice answered, "THE CEN-
TRAL HEATING AND AIR-CONDITIONING SYSTEMS, ALL ALARM
SYSTEMS, THE SPECIAL COMPUTER SYSTEM. . . ."

"Wait a minute. What about the phones?"

"THE TELEPHONE SYSTEM IS POWERED SEPARATELY, FROM
OUTSIDE THE CENTER."

"Show me how it works."

A drawing appeared on the TV screen, showing how the
telephone system was linked by a cable to the main power
line of the telephone company. Danny saw that the power
line ran underground along the highway, and the cable
connecting into the Center came to the administration building through a tunnel. *Cut that one cable, and all the
phones are dead.*

It was well after lunchtime when Danny finally said,
"Thanks SPECS. That's all I want to know. For now."

The TV screen went dark. Danny sat at his desk, not
hungry, too excited to eat, thinking about how to knock
out the power station, the emergency system, and the
phone line.

The screen glowed again. "MR. ROMANO."

"What?"

"YOU HAVE A VISITOR. MISS MURILLO."

Danny shot out of his chair and to the door without
stopping to get his coat.

He sprinted across the campus to the administration
building, through the wintry windy day. There were lots of
visitors today: parents mostly, grownups trying to look
happy when they were really miserable that their kids had
to spend Christmas in the Center.

But Danny didn't see it that way. He saw adults faking
it, laughing too loud, bringing presents to their kids that
they never got when the kids had been at home. Danny
wondered what his father would have been like, if he

would have lived. His mother was still alive, probably, wherever she was.

He found Laurie in one of the small visitors' rooms. She was wearing a new dress, a dark green one. And her hair was different. It was all swept back and smoothly arranged.

He blinked at her. "Hey, you look different . . . like, all grown up."

"Do you like the way I look?" Laurie was smiling and trying her hardest to look as pretty as she could.

Danny said slowly, "Yeah . . . I guess so, I . . . never saw you looking so . . . well, so fancy."

She stepped up to him and kissed him. "Thank you. And Merry Christmas."

"Merry . . . Hey! I almost forgot! What's all this about you moving to someplace uptown? What's goin' on?"

Holding his hand, Laurie brought Danny to the sofa by the tiny room's only window. They sat down.

"I've got a new job and a new apartment," she said happily. "I'm sharing the place with two other girls. We all work in the same building. I'm a clerk in an insurance company. They're teaching me the job as I go along. It pays a lot better. And I'm going to school at night to learn how to be a secretary."

Danny frowned. "But why? What for?"

"For me," Laurie said. "Danny, try to understand. I love you, honey, I really do. But I can't just sit in my sister's place and work in the restaurant for years and years."

"It won't be years. . . ."

"Shush," she said, putting a finger to his lips. "Listen for a minute. Dr. Tenny told me that he's trying to make you into the best person you can be. That's what the Center's for. Well, I'm trying to make myself the best person I can be."

"I don't like it."

"Don't you see? When you get out, Danny, I want to be something more than a skinny kid with a dirty apron. I want to be a *person*, somebody who can do things. Somebody who can help you, not drag you down."

Danny remembered something. "You been going out with other guys."

She nodded. "Only on double dates, or with a gang of people. Nothing serious, honest, Danny."

"I don't believe you."

Laurie's eyes widened. "Danny, honest . . ."

"I been sittin' here and you've been goin' out with other guys. Movin' uptown, getting big ideas. Joe Tenny's put you up to this! He's tryin' to get you away from me!"

"Danny, that's crazy. . . ."

"Oh yeah? Well, you'll see how crazy it is!"

He got up and stormed to the door.

"Wait," Laurie called. "I got you a Christmas present. . . ."

"Give it to your new boyfriend!" Danny slammed the door shut behind him.

CHAPTER TWENTY

There were no classes between Christmas and New Year's. Danny spent every morning in his room, studying the layout of the power station, learning every inch of the building.

"Hey SPECS, it looks like most of the time the power station runs itself."

"THE POWER STATION RUNS AUTOMATICALLY. I WATCH IT AND CONTROL IT."

"Don't they have a guard or somebody in there?"

"A GUARD STAYS INSIDE THE STATION AT NIGHT."

"Are the doors locked at night?"

"YES."

"What about the day time?"

"A MEMBER OF THE MAINTENANCE CREW IS ON DUTY AT THE POWER STATION AT ALL TIMES DURING THE WORKING DAY. HE HAS NOTHING TO DO, HOWEVER, SINCE I AM IN FULL CONTROL."

Danny laughed. "You mean he goofs off?"

"I DO NOT UNDERSTAND YOUR WORDS."

"He don't stay on the job. He goes to sleep or takes a walk outside or something like that."

"HE OFTEN LEAVES THE STATION FOR HALF AN HOUR OR SO. BUT HE ALWAYS LEAVES A STUDENT AT THE STATION, SO THAT SOMEONE IS PRESENT AT ALL TIMES."

"A student . . . one of us kids?"

"YES."

On New Year's Day, Danny invited Ralph up to his room, and asked him to bring the five boys he could trust.

They were an odd-looking gang. Ralph introduced them as they came in and sat on Danny's bed and chairs.

Hambone was even bigger than Ralph, but where Ralph looked mean, Hambone looked brainless. He wore a silly grin all the time. *Like a happy gorilla,* Danny thought.

"He don't look it," Ralph said, "but old Hambone is a fighter when he gets mad. Took a squad of cops to bring him down."

Hambone nodded happily. "I broke an arm on one of 'em." His voice sounded as if his nose was stopped up, like a prize-fighter's voice after he's been hit too many times.

The next boy was Noisy, who got his name because he hardly ever talked. He was about Danny's own size. He just nodded when Ralph introduced him. But he watched everything, listened to every word that was said. And his

eyes burned with a fierce glow that made Danny wonder
what he'd done to get into the Center.

Vic and Coop were two ordinary-looking guys. Midget
was the last of the gang. He was a kid of fifteen who
looked like he was only twelve. He was smaller and
skinnier than even Danny. *He's the guy who goes into the
tunnel to cut the phone line,* Danny decided.

"Okay," Danny said to them. "Now we all want to get
out of this dump. And we're going to do it. My way. I
know how to get out."

They all looked at each other, nodding and grinning.

"How?" Ralph asked. He had taken the chair by the
desk.

Danny, standing by the window, answered, "That's
my business. I got the plan right here in my head, and I
ain't tellin' *nobody.* You don't like it that way, then you
can get up and leave. Right now."

Nobody moved.

"Okay. Now . . . it's goin' to take hard work, and
some time. But we'll bust this place wide open."

"What d'you want us to do?"

Danny said, "I got jobs for all of you. They might look
stupid right now, but they're goin' to help us break out."

"What kind of jobs?" Ralph asked.

"I want you and Hambone to get on the clean-up crew,"
said Danny.

"Hey, that's work!" Hambone said.

Nodding, Danny went on, "I told you it's going to be
work. Hard work, too. But it's the only way to get out of
here."

"What're we supposed to be doin'?" Ralph asked.
"Besides talking to th' birds and flowers, that is."

"Just hang loose and don't act suspicious." Danny
turned to Noisy. "Think you can get yourself into the

photography class? We're going to need a camera and some film.''

Noisy nodded.

"Good," said Danny. "Midget, I want you to get an afternoon job in the administration building. Any kind of job, as long as it's in that building.''

"Can do," Midget answered.

Turning to Vic and Coop, Danny said, "You two guys got to get yourselves into the maintenance crew. Try to get jobs that involve big machinery, like the heaters. Okay?''

Vic shrugged. "I don't know nothing about machinery.''

"Then learn!" Danny snapped.

Ralph gave Danny a hard look. "And what're you goin' to be doin?''

"Me?" Danny smiled. "I'm gettin' myself a job with SPECS. He's got all the brains around here. He's got to tell me a few more things before we can blow this dump.''

CHAPTER TWENTY-ONE

They all met again in the cafeteria two days later. Each boy reported that he had gotten the job Danny wanted him to take.

"Good," Danny said as he hunched over the dinner dishes. He kept his voice low enough so that the others could just about hear it over the racket made by the rest of the crowd.

"Now listen. This is the last time we meet all together like this. From now on, I'll see each one of you alone, or maybe two of you together, at the most. Stay cool, work your jobs like you really mean it. In a month or so, we'll be out of here.''

When he got back to his room, there was an envelope on the floor just inside his door. Danny leaned down and picked it up, then shut the door as he looked it over. It was from outside. His name and the Center's address were neatly typed on the envelope.

The return address, in the upper left corner of the envelope, was from some insurance company. Then he spotted the hand-typed initials, LM, alongside the printing. It was from Laurie!

Danny ripped the envelope open as he went to his desk and flicked on the lamp. He had trouble pulling the letter out of the envelope.

Dear Danny:

I'm sorry about the blow-up on Christmas Day. I still have your present. I will give it to you when I visit you again. I won't be visiting again for a month or so. I think it might be better if we both sort of think things over before we see each other again.

I still love you, Danny. And I miss you a lot. I know it is very hard for you inside the Center. But we both have a lot of growing up to do before we can be happy together.

Love,
Laurie

Danny read the letter twice, then crumpled it in his fist and threw it in the wastebasket. For the first time in weeks, he had to take an asthma pill before he could get to sleep that night.

The weeks crawled by slowly.

Danny got his job at the computer center, down in the basement of the administration building. He often saw Midget there. Midget was working somewhere upstairs.

SPECS' home was a relaxing place to work in. It was quiet. For some reason, everybody tended to talk softly. SPECS himself made the most noise—a steady hum of electrical power. When he was working at some special problem, SPECS made a singsong noise while he flashed hundreds of little lights on the front control panel of his main unit.

Danny's job was to help the adults who programmed SPECS and feed him new information. He carried heavy reels of magnetic tape down the corridors between SPECS' big, boxlike consoles. There was a store room for the tapes that weren't being used, back behind the main computer room.

"These tapes carry SPECS' memory on them," said one of the computer programmers to Danny. "They're like a library . . . except that SPECS is the only one who can read them."

After a few weeks, Danny got to know most of the people who ran the computer. More important, they got to know him. They told him what to do when they needed him. The rest of the time they ignored him.

Which suited Danny fine. He found a few little corners of the big computer room where he could talk to SPECS, ask questions. If anyone saw him sitting at one of the tiny desks, talking to the TV screen on it, they would smile and say:

"Good kid, learning how to work with the machine."

One of the first things Danny learned from SPECS was that every conversation he had with the machine was stored on tape.

"Has anybody checked these tapes?"

"I HAVE NO RECORD OF THAT."

Danny spent a week quietly gathering the right tapes and erasing all his talks with SPECS. Now no one could ever find out what he had said to the computer. Then he got to work on his escape plan. He had a pocket-sized camera now, which Noisy had taken from the photography class.

"What's the layout of the power station?" Danny asked quietly. And when SPECS showed the right diagram on the TV screen, *click!* Danny got it on film.

"How does the power generator work?" *Click.*

"When the generator breaks down, what goes wrong with it most often?" *Click.*

"How's the emergency generator hooked into the Center's main power line?" *Click.*

Danny would keep the photographs and study them in his room for hours each night. And, of course, he erased all traces of his questions and their answers from SPECS' memory tapes.

The winter snows came and buried the Center in white. Ralph and Hambone, faces red from the wind, noses sniffling, wailed loudly to Danny about all the snow-shoveling that the clean-up crew was doing.

"I told you it'd be hard work," Danny said, trying hard not to laugh. If he got them angry, they could crack him like a teacup.

Danny started Vic and Coop, on the maintenance crew, checking into the electrical power lines in each building. He had to make sure he understood all about the Center's electrical system.

Vic said, "I ain't seen no other emergency generators any place. There's just the one at the main power station. None of the other buildings even has a flashlight battery laying around, far as I can tell."

Danny stopped Midget one afternoon in the hallway of the administration building.

"How's it going?"

"Okay. Got the phone line figured out. Any time you want to pull the cable, I'm all set."

"Good. Now, think you can find out when the maintenance man leaves the power station alone?"

Midget said, "He don't. There's always a kid in there."

"I know. That's what I mean. Try and find out when the kid's in there by himself. And who the kid is. Maybe we can get him on our side."

Nodding, Midget said, "Groovy. I'll get the word to you."

CHAPTER TWENTY-TWO

The snow melted a little, then more fell. Late in February, during a slushy cold rainstorm, Laurie visited the Center.

Danny ran through the driving rain toward the administration building, hunched over, hands in pockets, feet getting soaked in puddles.

She picked some day to come, he said to himself. *She's gettin' to be nothing but trouble. Why'd she come today?* And then he heard himself saying, *Maybe she's come to say goodbye . . . that she don't want me any more.*

By the time he got to the visitor's room, Danny felt cold, wet, angry, and—even though he didn't want to admit it— more than a little scared. He stopped at the water fountain outside the door and took an asthma pill. Then he went in.

Laurie was standing by the window, looking out at the rain. Danny saw that she was prettier than ever. Not so worried-looking any more. Dressed better, too.

She turned as he softly shut the door.

"Oh, Danny . . . you're soaking wet. I'm sorry, it's my fault."

He grinned at her. "It's okay. It'll dry."

They stood at opposite ends of the little room, about five paces apart. Then suddenly Danny crossed over toward her, and she was in his arms again.

"Hey," he said, smiling at her, "you even smell good."

"You look fine," Laurie said. "Wet . . . but fine."

They sat on the sofa and talked for a long time.

Finally Laurie said, "Dr. Tenny told me you're doing very well. You're working hard and doing good in class. He thinks you're on the right road."

Danny laughed. "Good, let him think that."

For the first time, the old worried look crept back into Laurie's face. "What do you mean?"

"You'll see. Maybe you better start lookin' at travel ads. See where you want to go in Canada. Or maybe Mexico."

"Danny, you're not . . ."

He silenced her with an upraised hand. "Don't worry about it. This time it'll work."

Laurie shook her head. "Danny, forget about it. You can't escape. . . ."

"I can and I will!" he snapped.

"Well, then, forget about me," Laurie snapped back.

"What?"

"Danny, I'm just getting to the point where I can live without looking over my shoulder to see who's following me. I've spent all my life with you and the other kids, dodging the cops, fighting in gangs. For the first time in my life, I'm out of that! I'm living like a free human being. I like it! Can't you understand? I don't want to go back to living scared every minute. . . ."

"You mean if I. . . ."

She grasped his hands and looked straight into his eyes. "I mean I want you to walk out of this place a free man. Not only free, but a *man*. Not a kid who doesn't care what he does. Not a convict who has to run every day and hide every night. I'll wait for you for a hundred years, Danny, if I have to. But only if you'll promise me that we can both be free when you get out."

Danny pulled his hands away. "I'm not waiting any

hundred years! Not even one year. I'm busting out of here, and then I'm coming to get you. And you'd better be there when I come for you!''

She shook her head. "I won't go back to living that way, Danny.''

"Oh no? We'll find out. And soon, too.''

"I'd better go now,'' Laurie got up from the sofa.

"If you blab any of this to Tenny. . . .''

She glared at him. "I won't. Not because I'm afraid of you. I won't say a word to anybody because I want *you* to decide. You've got to figure it out straight in your own mind. You've got a chance to make something good out of your life. If you try to break out of the Center, you'll just be running away from that chance. You'll be telling me that you're afraid of trying to stand on your own feet. That you want to be caught again and kept in jail.''

"Afraid?'' Danny felt his temper boil.

"That's right,'' Laurie said. "If you try to break out of here, you and me are finished.''

She walked to the door and left. Danny stood in the middle of the room, fists clenched at his sides, trembling with anger, chest hurting.

CHAPTER TWENTY-THREE

That night, after dinner, Danny and the other boys met in the gym. They took a basketball and shot baskets for a while, then sat together on one of the benches. The gym was only half full, and not as noisy as usual.

"Okay,'' Danny said. "I got enough scoop on how the generator works and how to blow it. We're going to turn off all the electricity in the Center and walk out of here while everybody else is runnin' around in the dark."

Their faces showed what he wanted to see; They liked the idea.

"I thought it was something like that."

"It'll be a blast."

Noisy asked, "What about the emergency generator?"

"Got it all worked out," Danny said. "Been getting all the info I need from SPECS."

"When do we go?"

"Tomorrow night," said Danny.

Hambone whistled softly. "You sure ain't fooling around."

"What time?"

"Six o'clock. Almost everybody'll be in the cafeteria for dinner. All the lights go, all the phones go, everybody goes crazy, and we split."

"Great!" said Midget. "The maintenance man at the power station goes to the cafeteria at six. That's when he leaves a kid in there alone for about fifteen minutes."

"I know, you told me," Danny said. "That's why I picked that time. Who's the kid tomorrow? Can we talk him into going with us or do we have to lump him?"

Midget answered, "It's Lacey. I don't think he'll go along with us."

"Lacey!"

Ralph laughed, low and mean. "Good old Lacey, huh? That's cool. I been wantin' to split that black big-mouth's head ever since he became lightweight champ. Hambone and me are going to have real fun takin' care of *him*."

Hambone nodded and giggled.

Danny didn't answer Ralph. But somehow he felt unhappy that it was going to be Lacey.

He hardly slept at all that night. And the next morning he just sat in class, paying no attention to anything around him. Danny's mind was a jumble of thoughts, pictures, voices. He kept trying to think about the escape plan, what he had to do to knock out the generator, every detail.

But he kept seeing Laurie, kept hearing her say, "Then you can forget about me."

He tried to get her out of his head, but instead he saw Lacey grinning at him, boxing gloves weaving in front of his face. He remembered their fight. He tried to make himself hate Lacey. It didn't work. Lacey fought clean and hard. Danny couldn't hate him.

"Hey, this isn't the history class, you know."

Danny snapped his attention to the classroom. Joe Tenny was standing over him, grinning. The other guys had left. The class was over.

"I . . . uh, I was thinkin' about . . . things."

"Sure you were." Joe laughed. "With your eyes closed."

"I wasn't asleep." Danny got up from his chair.

Joe nodded. "Okay, you were wide awake. Look, why don't you just grab a quick sandwich in the cafeteria and meet me in my office in about fifteen minutes. Got something I want to show you."

Every nerve in Danny's body tightened. His chest started to feel heavy, raw, *He knows about it!*

When he opened the door to Dr. Tenny's office, Joe was standing in front of his easel, slapping paint on a canvas with a small curved knife.

"Hi . . . Sit down a minute."

In one hand, Joe held a paint-dabbed piece of cardboard. He would dip the edge of the knife into a blob of color, and then smear the color across the canvas. Danny watched him.

Finally Joe stepped back, cocked his head to one side and squinted at the canvas, then tossed the cardboard and knife to the floor at the base of the easel.

"What do you think?" he asked.

Danny stared hard at the painting. It looked like some of the dark blobs were going to be boats. There were the beginnings of mountains and clouds in the background.

"Okay, don't answer," Joe said. "I'm just starting it. Wait'll you see the finished product!"

He yanked open his top desk drawer and pulled out a stubby cigar.

"Some days it just gets to be too much," he said. "Then I've got to slap paint around or go nuts."

Danny, sitting in the chair, said nothing.

Joe puffed the cigar to life. "I've been having a little discussion with a few members of the Governor's council.... About how much money the Center's going to need next year. I'm in no mood to work anymore today."

Danny shrugged.

"You like airplanes, don't you? Ever been up in one?"

"No. . . ."

"Okay, come on. Friend of mine just bought a new plane for himself. Said I could play with it this afternoon. Want to come?"

With a deep breath of relief, Danny said, "Sure!"

They drove to the airfield in Joe's car. There were still banks of snow along the highway, brown and rotting. The sky was clear, though, and the sun was shining.

The plane sparkled in the sunlight. Painted red and white, it had one engine, a low wing, and a cabin that seated four. It was parked beside a hangar in a small airfield that was used only for private planes.

Joe squeezed into the pilot's seat, and Danny crawled up after him and sat at his right. The control panel in front of him was covered with dials and instruments. A little half-wheel poked out of the panel, and there were two big pedals on the floor.

Joe showed Danny everything: the instruments, the controls, the throttle and fuel mixture sticks that were down on the floor between their two seats, the radio.

"Just like in the books," Danny said.

Joe nodded happily. "Let's see how she runs."

Within minutes they were speeding down the runway, the engine roaring in Danny's ears, the propeller an almost-invisible blur in front of him. Danny gripped the safety belt that was tightly latched across his lap.

Joe pulled back slightly on the wheel and the plane lifted its nose. Danny felt a split second when his stomach seemed to drop inside him. The ground tilted and dropped away. They were off!

Danny watched the airfield get smaller and farther behind them. Joe banked the plane over on its right wing tip, so Danny felt as if he were hanging by his seat belt, with nothing between him and the ground far below except the window he was looking through.

Then they climbed even higher. The plane bounced and shuddered through a big puffy cloud, and broke free again above the clouds.

Danny could feel himself grinning so hard that it almost hurt. "This is the greatest!"

Joe nodded. "She's a good ship. Nice and stable. Handles easy."

They flew for a few moments in silence, except for the droning engine. Danny looked down at the white-covered ground, sprinkled with the shadows of clouds. He looked across at the clouds themselves, floating peacefully. Then he looked up at the impossibly clear blue sky.

"Want to try her?" Joe shouted over the engine's noise.

"Huh?"

Joe took his hands off the wheel. "Take over. It's not hard. Just keep her nose pointed on the horizon."

Danny grabbed the wheel. Instantly the plane bucked upward, like a horse that didn't like its newest rider.

"Steady! Easy!" Joe shouted. "Just relax. Get her nose down a bit. That's it. . . ."

Danny slowly brought the plane under control. Under *his* control!

"Hey, I'm flying her!"

"You sure are," said Joe, with a huge grin.

Joe showed Danny how to turn the wheel and push the pedals at the same time, so that the plane would turn and bank smoothly. He explained how to work the throttle and fuel mixture controls, how to watch the instruments.

"This is fun!" Danny yelled.

They tried a few shallow dives and turns. Nothing very daring, nothing very fast.

Finally Joe said, "Look down there."

Danny followed where Joe's finger pointed. Far below them was a group of buildings clustered together, near the main highway. It took Danny a moment to realize that it was the Center.

"Looks different from up here," Danny said. "So small. . . ."

Then his eye caught another set of buildings, far from the highway, tucked away in the hills. These were gray and massive buildings. A high stone wall stood around them. They looked like something straight out of the Middle Ages.

"State prison," Joe said.

Danny said nothing.

"It's a big world," Joe said. "You've just got to start looking at it from the right point of view. Lots of the world is pretty crummy, I know. But take a look around you now. Looks kind of pretty, doesn't it?"

Danny nodded. It was a big world, from up here. Hills stretching off to the horizon; towns nestled among them; roads and rivers winding along.

"People make their own worlds, Danny. You're going to make a world for yourself, a world that you'll live in for the rest of your life. You can make it big and clean . . . or as small and dirty as it's been so far. It's up to you to choose.''

They flew back to the airfield, and Joe landed the plane. Then they drove back to the Center. Danny was silent, thinking, all the way back.

CHAPTER TWENTY-FOUR

It was a few minutes before six when Danny and Joe returned to the Center.

Danny went straight to the cafeteria. He could hear his own pulse pounding in his ears. His knees felt wobbly, and he knew his hands were shaking. His chest was starting to feel heavy. He fished in his pockets for the pills. *Forgot them! Left them in my room.*

Ralph and Hambone were finishing up an early dinner. Noisy was loafing by the water cooler. Vic and Coop were sitting off in a far corner.

Danny turned around and walked outside. In a few minutes the five others joined him.

"Where's Midget?" he asked. His chest was hurting now.

"He's at the administration building, just like you told him. When the lights go out, he'll go in the tunnel and cut the phone line."

"What're we waitin' for?" Ralph said. "Let's go!"

They walked through the darkness toward the power station. As they got close enough to see the building, the maintenance man who had been on duty there came out of the door and walked past them, heading for the cafeteria. Ralph began to jog and was soon far ahead of them.

"Come on!" he said. They started running for the power station.

Danny trotted behind the others. He couldn't run, couldn't catch his breath. His mind was spinning: Laurie, Joe, Lacey, Ralph . . . flying over the Center, looking at the world beyond its fences . . . Lacey punching him . . . Laurie's face when she told him to forget about her. . . .

And then he was inside the power station. It was like stepping into another world. The place was hot. It smelled of oil. The huge generator machinery, crammed up to the ceiling, seemed to bulge out the walls. The metal floorplates throbbed with the rumbling beat of power, and almost beyond the range of human hearing was the high-pitched whine of something spinning fast, fast.

Nobody could hear Danny wheezing as he stood just inside the doorway. Nobody watched him struggling his hardest, just to breathe.

The light in the generator room was bright and glaring. Lacey stood up on a steel catwalk that threaded between two big bulky piles of machinery, about twenty feet above the floor.

"Hiya guys!" Lacey called out above the whining hum of the generator. "What d'you want?"

"Come on down," Ralph said. He walked over to a tool bench near the door and picked up a heavy wrench. Hambone giggled.

Danny stared at the generator. He had only seen pictures of it before, drawings and diagrams on SPECS' TV screens. Now it looked huge, almost alive. And he had to kill it, make it silent and dead.

But before that, Ralph and Hambone were going to kill Lacey.

Lacey clattered down the steel steps to the floor. "What's going on, man? What you doing here?"

"Grab him," Ralph snapped.

Hambone wrapped his beefy arms around Lacey's slim body, pinning his arms to his sides.

"Hey . . . what you. . . ."

Ralph started toward Lacey, raising the heavy wrench in his big hand. The others stood frozen by the door.

Danny shouted, "Stop it!"

Ralph spun around to face Danny. Suddenly Danny could breathe, his chest was okay. Even the shakes were gone.

"It's no good," he said to Ralph. "Stop it. Forget the whole thing."

"What're you pulling?" Ralph's face was red with anger.

"I'm saving us all from a lot of trouble," Danny said. "Forget the whole deal. Breaking out of here is stupid. They'll just catch us again."

Ralph started to move toward Danny, his knuckles white on the wrench handle. "Listen kid . . . we're getting out. Now! And you're going to. . . ."

Danny slid over to the tool bench and reached for another wrench. "Forget it, Ralph. I'm the only one who knows how to knock out the generator. And I ain't going to do it. I changed my mind. The deal's off."

They stood glaring at each other, both armed with heavy metal wrenches. Then suddenly Hambone yowled with pain.

Lacey was loose and streaking up the steel steps to the catwalk. Hambone was hopping on one foot. "He kicked me!"

"Stop him!" Ralph screamed, pointing at Lacey.

Vic and Coop started for the stairway. Danny knew exactly where Lacey was heading. There was an emergency phone on the other side of the generator. He dashed toward the stairway, too, past Ralph, who seemed too stunned to move.

Danny barged into Vic and Coop at the foot of the steps, knocked them off balance, and got onto the stairs ahead of them. He raced to the top, two steps at a time. Then he stopped and turned to the rest of them.

"Before you can get to him you got to go through me!"

Danny shouted, holding the wrench up like a battle weapon. *If I can hold 'em off long enough for Lacey to make a call. . . .*

With a roar of rage, Ralph pushed past Vic and Coop and boiled up the stairs. Hambone came up right behind him. Danny swung his wrench at Ralph, then felt an explosion of pain in his side.

He began to crumple. The wrench slipped from Danny's fingers as another blow knocked him to his knees. He looked up and saw Ralph's furious face. Beside it was Hambone's, no longer grinning. The wrench in Ralph's hand looked twenty feet long. Danny tried to raise his arms to cover his face, to protect himself. The wrench came blurring down on him. Danny saw sparks shower everywhere.

Somewhere, far off, he could hear people yelling, screaming. But all he could see was bursts of light going off inside his head; all he could feel was pain.

CHAPTER TWENTY-FIVE

Danny awoke in the hospital. He blinked his eyes at the green curtain around his bed. His head felt heavy, like it was carrying pounds and pounds of cement on it. He reached up to touch it. It was covered with bandages.

Then he realized that he could only move one arm. The other was wrapped in a heavy, stiff cast.

The curtain opened and Joe Tenny stepped in, grinning at him.

"Feel better?"

Danny tried to answer, but found that his mouth was too swollen and painful.

"I don't mean your body," Joe said, pulling up a chair and straddling it cowboy-fashion. "I mean your conscience . . . your mind."

Danny shrugged. His side twinged.

"You made the right choice. It cost you a couple of teeth and a few broken bones, but that can all be fixed. You'll be out and around in a week or two."

"You . . ." It hurt, but he had to say it. "You knew."

Joe gave him that who-are-you-trying-to-kid look. "We knew that you were going to try a break. But we didn't know where or when. You covered up your tracks pretty darned well. If you hadn't been so smart, we could have saved you the beating you took."

"I . . . the asthma . . . it went away."

Nodding, Joe said, "The doctor told me it would, sooner or later. You didn't have anything wrong with your lungs. In your case, asthma was just a crutch . . . a little excuse you made up in the back of your mind. Whenever the going got tough, you started to wheeze. Then you could flake out, or at least have an excuse for not doing well."

Danny closed his eyes.

"But when the chips were down," Joe went on, "you ditched the excuse. No more asthma. You stood on your own feet and did what you had to do."

"How's Lacey?" Danny asked.

"When we got there, after Lacey called us, he was trying to pry Hambone and Ralph off of you. They never laid a finger on him . . . thanks to you."

"We would've never made it," Danny mumbled.

"That's right. Even if you got out of the Center, we'd have tracked you down. But it was important for you to try to escape."

"What?"

Joe pulled his chair closer. "Look, what's the one thing

that's kept you going ever since you first came here? The idea of escaping. Don't you think I knew that? Every prisoner wants to escape. I was a prisoner-of-war once. I tried to escape fourteen times.''

"Then, why. . . .''

"We *used* the idea of escaping to help you to grow up,'' Joe said. "Why do you think I told you the Center was escape-proof? To make sure you'd try to prove I was wrong! All the teaching and lecturing in the world couldn't have done as much as that one idea of escaping. Look what you did: you learned to read and study, you learned how to work SPECS, you learned how to plan ahead, to be patient, to control your temper, you even learned to work with other people. All because you were trying to escape.''

"But it didn't work. . . .''

"Sure! It didn't work because you finally learned the most important thing of all. You learned that the only way to escape jail—all jails—for keeps is to *earn* your way out.''

Danny let his head sink back on the pillow.

"And you played fair by Lacey. I think you learned something there, too.''

Looking up at the ceiling, Danny asked, "What happened to the other guys?''

"Vic and Coop are in their rooms. They'll stay in for a week or so, and then we'll let them start classes again. I'll have to start paying as much attention to them as I did to you. I don't think they've learned as much as you have . . . not yet. Same for Midget and Noisy, except that one of the other staff members is in charge of their cases.

"Ralph and Hambone are here in the hospital, upstairs. They've got emotional problems that're too deep to let them walk around the campus. I'm afraid they're going to stay inside for a long while.''

Danny took a deep breath. His side hurt, but his chest felt fine and clear.

"Look," Joe said. "When you get out of the hospital, it'll be almost exactly one year since you first came to the Center. I think you've learned a lot in your first year. The hard way. But you've finally learned it."

Danny nodded.

"Now, if you're ready for it I can start *really* teaching you. In another year or so, maybe we can let you out of here—on probation. I can see to it that you get into a real school. You can wind up studying engineering, if you want. Learn to build airplanes . . . and fly 'em."

In spite of the pain, Danny smiled. "I'd like that."

"Good. And it'll be a lot cheaper for the taxpayers to send you to school and get you into a decent career, than to keep you in jails the rest of your life."

Joe got up from the chair.

Danny found himself stretching out his right hand toward him. The teacher looked at it, then smiled in a way Danny had never seen him do before. He took Danny's hand firmly in his own.

"Thanks. I've been waiting a year for this."

"Thank you, Joe."

Joe let go of Danny's hand and started to turn away. Then he stopped and said:

"Oh yeah . . . Laurie's on her way here. She wants to see you. Says she's still got to give you your Christmas present."

"Great!" said Danny.

Joe pulled a cigar from his shirt pocket. "You two have a bright future ahead of you. And I can tell about the future. I'm part gypsy, you know."

A SLIGHT MISCALCULATION

It is not often that a writer has the pleasure of seeing one of his short stories dramatized. A Slight Miscalculation *was so honored by the Penn State Readers' Theater as one of the highlights of Paracon VI, the 1983 convention of the Penn State science fiction fans. It was great fun to see the characters of the story come to life, and even though most of the audience already knew the story, the final punch line achieved the desired gasp of surprise and laughter.*

This story originated over a bowl of Mulligatawny soup in an Indian restaurant in mid-town Manhattan. Judy-Lynn Benjamin (she had not yet married Lester Del Rey), was then the managing editor of Galaxy *magazine. She and I threw a few ideas back and forth and came up with "the ultimate California earthquake story." Unfortunately, the top editor at* Galaxy, *whose tenure was brief but not brief enough, failed to see the humor in the piece and asked me what scientific foundation I had for the story's premise. I sent the manuscript to Ed Ferman at* The Magazine of Fantasy and Science Fiction. *He brought it with no questions asked, proving that he has not only a delicately-tuned sense of humor, but a high standard of literary values, as well. Or so it seems to me.*

Nathan French was a pure mathematician. He worked for a

103

research laboratory perched on a California hill that overlooked the Pacific surf, but his office had no windows. When his laboratory earned its income by doing research on nuclear bombs, Nathan doodled out equations for placing men on the moon with a minimum expenditure of rocket fuel. When his lab landed a fat contract for developing a lunar-flight profile, Nathan began worrying about air pollution.

Nathan didn't look much like a mathematician. He was tall and gangly, liked to play handball, spoke with a slight lisp when he got excited and had a face that definitely reminded you of a horse. Which helped him to remain pure in things other than mathematics. The only possible clue to his work was that, lately, he had started to squint a lot. But he didn't look the slightest bit nervous or highstrung, and he still often smiled his great big toothy, horsey smile.

When the lab landed its first contract (from the State of California), to study air pollution, Nathan's pure thoughts turned—naturally—elsewhere.

"I think it might be possible to work out a method of predicting earthquakes," Nathan told the laboratory chief, kindly old Dr. Moneygrinder.

Moneygrinder peered at Nathan over his half-lensed bifocals. "Okay, Nathan my boy," he said heartily. "Go ahead and try it. You know I'm always interested in furthering man's understanding of his universe."

When Nathan left the chief's sumptuous office, Moneygrinder hauled his paunchy little body out of its plush desk chair and went to the window. *His* office had windows on two walls: one set overlooked the beautiful Pacific; the other looked down on the parking lot, so the chief could check on who got to work at what time.

And behind that parking lot, which was half-filled with aging cars (business had been deteriorating for several years), back among the eucalyptus trees and paint-freshened grass, was a remarkably straight little ridge of ground, no more than four feet high. It ran like an elongated step behind the whole length of the laboratory and out past the abandoned pink stucco church on the crest of the hill. A little ridge of grass-covered earth that was called the San Andreas Fault.

Moneygrinder often stared at the Fault from his window, rehearsing in his mind exactly what to do when the ground started to tremble. He wasn't afraid, merely careful. Once a tremor had hit in the middle of a staff meeting. Moneygrinder was out the window, across the parking lot, and on the far side of the Fault (the eastern, or "safe" side), before men half his age had gotten out of their chairs. The staff talked for months about the astonishing agility of the fat little waddler.

A year, almost to the day, later the parking lot was slightly fuller and a few of the cars were new. The pollution business was starting to pick up, since the disastrous smog in San Clemente. And the laboratory had also managed to land a few quiet little Air Force contracts—for six times the amount of money it got from the pollution work.

Moneygrinder was leaning back in the plush desk-chair, trying to look both interested and noncommittal at the same time, which was difficult to do, because he never could follow Nathan when the mathematician was trying to explain his work.

"Then it's a thimple matter of transposing the progression," Nathan was lisping, talking too fast because he was excited as he scribbled equations on the fuchsia-colored chalkboard with nerve-ripping squeaks of the yellow chalk.

"You thee?" Nathan said at last, standing beside the chalkboard. It was totally covered with his barely legible numbers and symbols. A pall of yellow chalk dust hovered about him.

"Um . . ." said Moneygrinder. "Your conclusion, then . . ."

"It's perfectly clear," Nathan said. "If you have any reasonable data base at all, you can not only predict when an earthquake will hit and where, but you can altho predict its intensity."

Moneygrinder's eyes narrowed. "You're sure?"

"I've gone over it with the CalTech geophysicists. They agree with the theory."

"H'mm." Moneygrinder tapped his desktop with his pudgy fingers. "I know this is a little outside your area of interest, Nathan, but . . . ah, can you really predict actual earthquakes? Or is this all theoretical?"

"Sure you can predict earthquakes," Nathan said, grinning like Francis, the movie star. "Like next Thursday's."

"Next Thursday's?"

"Yeth. There's going to be a major earthquake next Thursday."

"Where?"

"Right here. Along the Fault."

"Ulp."

Nathan tossed his stubby piece of chalk into the air nonchalantly, but missed the catch and it fell to the carpeted floor.

Moneygrinder, slightly paler than the chalk, asked, "A major quake, you say?"

"Uh-huh."

"Did . . . did the CalTech people make this prediction?"

"No, I did. They don't agree. They claim I've got an inverted gamma factor in the fourteenth set of equations. I've got the computer checking it right now."

Some of the color returned to Moneygrinder's flabby cheeks. "Oh . . . oh, I see. Well, let me know what the computer says."

"Sure."

The next morning, as Moneygrinder stood behind the gauzy drapes of his office window, watching the cars pull in, his phone rang. His secretary had put in a long night, he knew, and she wasn't in yet. Pouting, Moneygrinder went over to the desk and answered the phone himself.

It was Nathan. "The computer still agrees with the CalTech boys. But I think the programming's slightly off. Can't really trust computers, they're only as good as the people who feed them, you know."

"I see," Moneygrinder answered. "Well, keep checking on it."

He chuckled as he hung up. "Good old Nathan. Great at theory, but hopeless in the real world."

Still, when his secretary finally showed up and brought him his morning coffee and pill and nibble on the ear, he said thoughtfully:

"Maybe I ought to talk with those bankers in New York, after all."

"But you said that you wouldn't need their money now that business is picking up," she purred.

He nodded, bulbously. "Yes, but still . . . arrange a meeting with them for next Thursday. I'll leave Wednesday afternoon. Stay the weekend in New York."

She stared at him. "But you said we'd . . . ."

"Now, now . . . business comes first. You take the Friday night jet and meet me at the hotel."

Smiling, she answered, "Yes, Cuddles."

Matt Climber had just come back from a Pentagon lunch when Nathan's phone call reached him.

Climber had worked for Nathan several years ago. He had started as a computer programmer, assistant to Nathan. In two years he had become a section head, and Nathan's direct supervisor. (On paper only. Nobody bossed Nathan, he worked independently.) When it became obvious to Moneygrinder that Climber was heading his way, the lab chief helped his young assistant to a government job in Washington. Good experience for an up-and-coming executive.

"Hiya Nathan, how's the pencil-pushing game?" Climber shouted into the phone as he glanced at his calendar-appointment pad. There were three interagency conferences and two staff meetings going this afternoon.

"Hold it now, slow down," Climber said, sounding friendly but looking grim. "You know people can't understand you when you talk too fast."

Thirty minutes later, Climber was leaning back in his chair, feet on the desk, tie loosened, shirt collar open, and the first two meetings on his afternoon's list crossed off.

"Now let me get this straight, Nathan," he said into the phone. "You're predicting a major quake along the San Andreas Fault next Thursday afternoon at two-thirty Pacific Standard Time. But the CalTech people and your own computer don't agree with you."

Another ten minutes later, Climber said, "Okay, okay . . . sure, I remember how we'd screw up the programming once in a while. But you made mistakes too. Okay, look—tell you what, Nathan. Keep checking. If you find out definitely that the computer's wrong and you're right, call me right away. I'll get the President himself, if we have to. Okay? Fine. Keep in touch."

He slammed the phone back onto its cradle and his feet on the floor, all in one weary motion.

Old Nathan's really gone 'round the bend, Climber told himself. *Next Thursday, Hah! Next Thursday. H'mmm . . .*

He leafed through the calendar pages. Sure enough, he had a meeting with the Boeing people in Seattle next Thursday.

If there is *a major 'quake, the whole damned West*

*Coast might slide into the Pacific. Naw . . . don't be silly.
Nathan's cracking up, that's all. Still . . . how far north
does the Fault go?* .

He leaned across the desk and tapped the intercom
button.

"Yes, Mr. Climber?" came his secretary's voice.

"That conference with Boeing on the hypersonic ramjet
transport next Thursday," Climber began, then hesitated a
moment. But, with absolute finality, he snapped, "Cancel
it."

Nathan French was not a drinking man, but by Tuesday
of the following week he went straight from the laboratory
to a friendly little bar that hung from a rocky ledge over
the surging ocean.

It was a strangely quiet Tuesday afternoon, so Nathan
had the undivided attention of both the worried-looking
bartender and the freshly-painted whore, who worked the
early shift in a low-cut, black cocktail dress and overpowering perfume.

"Cheez, I never seen business so lousy as yesterday and
today," the bartender mumbled. He was sort of fidgeting
around behind the bar, with nothing to do. The only dirty
glass in the place was Nathan's, and he was holding on to
it because he liked to chew the ice cubes.

"Yeah," said the girl. "At this rate, I'll be a virgin
again by the end of the week."

Nathan didn't reply. His mouth was full of ice cubes,
which he crunched in absent-minded cacophony. He was
still trying to figure out why he and the computer didn't
agree about the fourteenth set of equations. Everything
else checked out perfectly: time, place, force level on the
Richter scale. But the vector, the directional value—
somebody was still misreading his programming instructions.
That was the only possible answer.

"The stock market's dropped through the floor," the bartender said darkly. "My broker says Boeing's gonna lay off half their people. That ramjet transport they was gonna build is getting scratched. And the lab up the hill is getting bought out by some East Coast banks." He shook his head.

The girl, sitting beside Nathan with her elbows on the bar and her styrofoam bra sharply profiled, smiled at him and said, "Hey, how about it, big guy? Just so I don't forget how to, huh?"

With a final crunch on the last ice cube, Nathan said, "Uh, excuse me. I've got to check that computer program."

By Thursday morning, Nathan was truly upset. Not only was the computer still insisting that he was wrong about equation fourteen, but none of the programmers had shown up for work. Obviously, one of them—maybe all of them—had sabotaged his program. But why?

He stalked up and down the hallways of the lab searching for a programmer, somebody, anybody—but the lab was virtually empty. Only a handful of people had come in, and after an hour or so of wide-eyed whispering among themselves in the cafeteria over coffee, they started to sidle out to the parking lot and get into their cars and drive away.

Nathan happened to be walking down a corridor when one of the research physicists—a new man, from a department Nathan never dealt with—bumped into him.

"Oh, excuse me," the physicist said hastily, and started to head for the door down at the end of the hall.

"Wait a minute," Nathan said, grabbing him by the arm. "Can you program the computer?"

"Uh, no, I can't."

"Where is everybody today?" Nathan wondered aloud, still holding the man's arm. "Is it a national holiday?"

"Man, haven't you heard?" the physicist asked, goggle-eyed. "There's going to be an earthquake this afternoon. The whole damned state of California is going to slide into the sea!"

"Oh, that."

Pulling his arm free, the physicist scuttled down the hall. As he got to the door he shouted over his shoulder, "Get out while you can! East of the Fault! The roads are jamming up fast!"

Nathan frowned. "There's still an hour or so," he said to himself. "And I still think the computer's wrong. I wonder what the tidal effects on the Pacific Ocean would be if the whole state collapsed into the ocean?"

Nathan didn't really notice that he was talking to himself. There was no one else to talk to.

Except the computer.

He was sitting in the computer room, still poring over the stubborn equations, when the rumbling started. At first it was barely audible, like very distant thunder. Then the room began to shake and the rumbling grew louder.

Nathan glanced at his wristwatch: two-thirty-two.

"I knew it!" he said gleefully to the computer. "You see? And I'll bet all the rest of it is right, too. Including equation fourteen."

Going down the hallway was like walking through the passageway of a storm-tossed ship. The floor and walls were swaying violently. Nathan kept his feet, despite some awkward lurches here and there.

It didn't occur to him that he might die until he got outside. The sky was dark, the ground heaving, the roaring deafened him. A violent gale was blowing dust everywhere, adding its shrieking fury to the earth's tortured groaning.

Nathan couldn't see five feet ahead of him. With the wind tearing at him and the dust stinging his eyes, he couldn't tell which way to go. He knew the other side of the Fault meant safety, but where was it?

Then there was a biblical crack of lightning and the ultimate grinding, screaming, ear-shattering roar. A tremendous shock wave knocked Nathan to the ground and he blacked out. His last thought was, "I was right and the computer was wrong."

When he woke up, the sun was shining feebly through a gray overcast. The wind had died away. Everything was strangely quiet.

Nathan climbed stiffly to his feet and looked around. The lab building was still there. He was standing in the middle of the parking lot; the only car in sight was his own, caked with dust.

Beyond the parking lot, where the eucalyptus trees used to be, was the edge of a cliff, where still-steaming rocks and raw earth tumbled down to a foaming sea.

Nathan staggered to the cliff's edge and looked out across the water, eastward. Somehow he knew that the nearest land was Europe.

"Son of a bitch," he said with unaccustomed vehemence. "The computer was right after all."

VINCE'S DRAGON

One of the little burdens I bear as gracefully as I can manage is the fact that of the six Hugo Awards decorating my office, none of them are for writing. My work as an editor, first at Analog *and then at* Omni, *has greatly overshadowed my work as a writer. Like Orson Welles, who has always maintained that he is an amateur actor and a professional director, I have always considered editing a temporary part of my life. Writing* is *my life.*

I was very flattered, then, to have one of the writers I "discovered" while editing Analog *ask me to contribute an original story to an anthology he was creating. It was a pleasure to publish Orson Scott Card's first short stories and novelets in* Analog. *But when he asked me to contribute to his planned anthology about dragons I was nonplussed. Dragons? In science fiction? No matter what my dear friend Anne McCaffrey may say, dragons are the stuff of fantasy, not science fiction. They are aerodynamically impossible and biochemically illogical. A giant flying reptilian that breathes flame? Not science fiction of the kind I write! No sir!*

On the other hand, there is more to the world than hard-and-fast literary categories, and I got this niggling idea of how a dragon might be useful to certain kinds of people I used to know when I was growing up in the narrow streets of South Philadelphia. Writers are always told to write about what they know, so I invented the world's first—and probably last—Mafia dragon.

The thing that worried Vince about the dragon, of course, was that he was scared that it was out to capture his soul.

Vince was a typical young Family man. He had dropped out of South Philadelphia High School to start his career with the Family. He boosted cars, pilfered suits from local stores, even spent grueling and terrifying hours learning how to drive a big trailer rig so he could help out on hijackings.

But they wouldn't let him in on the big stuff.

"You can run numbers for me, kid," said Louie Bananas, the one-armed policy king of South Philly.

"I wanna do somethin' big," Vince said, with ill-disguised impatience. "I wanna make somethin' outta myself."

Louie shook his bald, bullet-shaped head. "I dunno, kid. You don't look like you got th' guts."

"Try me! Lemme in on th' sharks."

So Louie let Vince follow Big Balls Falcone, the loan sharks' enforcer, for one day. After watching Big Balls systematically break a guy's fingers, one by one, because he was ten days late with his payment, Vince agreed that loan sharking was not the business for him.

Armed robbery? Vince had never held a gun, much less fired one. Besides, armed robbery was for the heads and zanies, the stupids and desperate ones. *Organized* crime didn't go in for armed robbery. There was no need to. And a guy could get hurt.

After months of wheedling and groveling around Louie Bananas' favorite restaurant, Vince finally got the break he wanted.

"Okay, kid, okay," Louie said one evening as Vince

stood in a corner of the restaurant watching him devour linguine with clams (white sauce). "I got an openin' for you. Come here."

Vince could scarcely believe his ears.

"What is it, *Padrone*? What? I'll do anything!"

Burping politely into his checkered napkin, Louie leaned back in his chair and grabbed a handful of Vince's curly dark hair, pulling Vince's ear close to his mouth.

Vince, who had an unfortunate allergy to garlic, fought hard to suppress a sneeze as he listened to Louie whisper, "You know that ol' B&O warehouse down aroun' Front an' Washington?"

"Yeah." Vince nodded as vigorously as he could, considering his hair was still in Louie's iron grip.

"Torch it."

"Burn it down?" Vince squeaked.

"Not so loud, *chidrool*!"

"Burn it down?" Vince whispered.

"Yeah."

"But that's arson."

Louie laughed. "It's a growth industry nowadays. Good opportunity for a kid who ain't afraid t' play with fire."

Vince sneezed.

It wasn't so much of a trick to burn down the rickety old warehouse, Vince knew. The place was ripe for the torch. But to burn it down without getting caught, that was different.

The Fire Department and Police and, worst of all, the insurance companies all had special arson squads who would be sniffing over the charred remains of the warehouse even before the smoke had cleared.

Vince didn't know anything at all about arson. But, desperate for his big chance, he was willing to learn.

He tried to get in touch with Johnnie the Torch, the

leading local expert. But Johnnie was too busy to see him, and besides Johnnie worked for a rival Family, 'way up in Manayunk. Two other guys that Vince knew, who had something of a reputation in the field, had mysteriously disappeared within the past two nights.

Vince didn't think the library would have any books on the subject that would help him. Besides, he didn't read too good.

So, feeling very shaky about the whole business, very late the next night he drove a stolen station wagon filled with jerry cans of gasoline and big drums of industrial paint thinner out to Front Street.

He pushed his way through the loosely-nailed boards that covered the old warehouse's main entrance, feeling little and scared in the darkness. The warehouse was empty and dusty, but as far as the insurance company knew, Louie's fruit and vegetable firm had stocked the place up to the ceiling just a week ago.

Vince felt his hands shaking. *If I don't do a good job, Louie'll send Big Balls Falcone after me.*

Then he heard a snuffling sound.

He froze, trying to make himself invisible in the shadows.

Somebody was breathing. And it wasn't Vince.

Kee-rist, they didn't tell me there was a night watchman here!

"I am not a night watchman."

Vince nearly jumped out of his jockey shorts.

"And I'm not a policeman, either, so relax."

"Who . . ." His voice cracked. He swallowed and said again, deeper, "Who are you?"

"I am trying to get some sleep, but this place is getting to be a regular Stonehenge. People coming and going all the time!"

A bum, Vince thought. *A bum who's using this warehouse to flop . . .*

"And I am not a bum!" the voice said, sternly.

"I didn't say you was!" Vince answered. Then he shuddered, because he realized he had only thought it.

A glow appeared, across the vast darkness of the empty warehouse. Vince stared at it, then realized it was an eye. A single glowing, baleful eye with a slit of a pupil, just like a cat's. But this eye was the size of a bowling ball!

"Wh . . . wha . . ."

Another eye opened beside it. In the light from their twin smolderings, Vince could just make out a scaley head with a huge jaw full of fangs.

He did what any man would do. He fainted.

When he opened his eyes he wanted to faint again. In the eerie moonlight that was now filtering through the old warehouse's broken windowpanes, he saw a dragon standing over him.

It had a long, sinuous body covered with glittering green and bluish scales, four big paws with talons on them the size of lumberjacks' saws. Its tail coiled around and around, the end twitching slightly all the way over on the other side of the warehouse.

And right over him, grinning down toothily at him, was this huge fanged head with the giant glowing cat's eyes.

"You're cute," the dragon said.

"Huh?"

"Not at all like those other bozoes Louie sent over here the past couple of nights. They were older. Fat, blubbery men."

"Other guys . . . ?"

The dragon flicked a forked tongue out between its glistening white fangs. "Do you think you're the first arsonist Louie's sent here? I mean, they've been clumping around here for the past several nights."

Still flat on his back, Vince asked, "Wh . . . wh . . . what happened to them?"

The dragon hunkered down on its belly and seemed, incredibly, to *smile* at him. "Oh, don't worry about them. They won't bother us." The tongue flicked out again and brushed Vince's face. "Yes, you are *cute*!"

Little by little, Vince's scant supply of courage returned to him. He kept speaking with the dragon, still not believing this was really happening, and slowly got up to a sitting position.

"I can read your mind," the dragon was saying. "So you might as well forget about trying to run away."

"I . . . uh, I'm supposed to torch this place," Vince confessed.

"I know," said the dragon. Somehow, it sounded like a female dragon.

"Yes, you're right," she admitted. "I am a female dragon. As a matter of fact, all the dragons that you humans have ever had trouble with have been females."

"You mean like St. George?" Vince blurted.

"That pansy! Him and his silly armor. Aunt Ssrishha could have broiled him alive inside that pressure cooker he was wearing. As it was, she got to laughing so hard at him that her flame went out."

"And he killed her."

"He did not!" She sounded really incensed, and a little wisp of smoke trickled out of her left nostril. "Aunt Ssrishha just made herself invisible and flew away. She was laughing so hard she got the hiccups."

"But the legend . . ."

"A human legend. More like a human public relations story. Kill a dragon! The human who can kill a dragon hasn't been born yet!"

"Hey, don't get sore. I didn't do nuthin."

"No. Of course not." Her voice softened. "You're cute, Vince."

His mind was racing. Either he was crazy or he was talking with a real, fire-breathing dragon.

"Uh . . . what's your name?"

"Ssrzzha," she said."I'm from the Polish branch of the dragon family."

"Shh . . . Zz . . ." Vince tried to pronounce.

"You may call me 'Sizzle,' " the dragon said, grandly.

"Sizzle. Hey, that's a cute name."

"I knew you'd like it."

If I'm crazy, they'll come and wake me up sooner or later, Vince thought, and decided to at least keep the conversation going.

"You say all the dragons my people have ever fought were broads . . . I mean, females?"

"That's right, Vince. So you can see how silly it is, all those human lies about our eating young virgins."

"Uh, yeah. I guess so."

"And the bigger lies they tell about slaying dragons. Utter falsehoods."

"Really?"

"Have you ever seen a stuffed dragon in a museum? Or dragon bones? Or a dragon's head mounted on a wall?"

"Well . . . I don't go to museums much."

"Whereas *I* could show you some very fascinating exhibits in certain caves, if you want to see bones and heads and . . ."

"Ah, no, thanks. I don't think I really wanna see that," Vince said hurriedly.

"No, you probably wouldn't."

"Where's all the male dragons? They must be *really* big."

Sizzle huffed haughtily and a double set of smoke-rings wafted past Vince's ear.

"The males of our species are tiny! Hardly bigger than you are. They all live out on some islands in the Indian Ocean. We have to fly there every hundred years or so for mating, or else our race would die out."

"Every hundred years! You only get laid once a century?"

"Sex is not much fun for us, I'm afraid. Not as much as it is for you, but then you're descended from monkeys, of course. Disgusting little things. Always chattering and making messes."

"Uh, look . . . Sizzle. This's been fun an' it was great meetin' you an' all, but it's gettin' late and I gotta go now, and besides . . ."

"But aren't you forgetting why you came here?"

Truth to tell, Vince had forgotten. But now he recalled, "I'm supposed t' torch this warehouse."

"That's right. And from what I can see bubbling inside your cute little head, if you don't burn this place down tonight, Louie's going to be very upset with you."

"Yeah, well, that's my problem, right? I mean, you wanna stay here an' get back t' sleep, right? I don't wanna bother you like them other guys did, ya know? I mean, like, I can come back when you go off to th' Indian Ocean or somethin' . . ."

"Don't be silly, Vince," Sizzle said, lifting herself ponderously to her four paws. "I can sleep anywhere. And I'm not due for another mating for several decades, thank the gods. As for those other fellows . . . well, they annoyed me. But you're cute!"

Vince slowly got to his feet, surprised that his quaking knees held him upright. But Sizzle coiled her long, glittering body around him, and with a grin that looked like a forest made of sharp butcher knives, she said:

"I'm getting kind of tired of this old place, anyway. What do you say we belt it out?"

"Huh?"

"I can do a much better job of torching this firetrap than you can, Vince cutie," said Sizzle. "And *I* won't leave any telltale gasoline fumes behind me."

"But . . ."

"You'll be completely in the clear. Anytime the police come near, I can always make myself invisible."

"Invisible?"

"Sure. See?" And Sizzle disappeared.

"Hey, where are ya?"

"Right here, Vince." The dragon reappeared in all its glittering hugeness.

Vince stared, his mind churning underneath his curly dark hair.

Sizzle smiled at him. "What do you say, cutie? A life of crime together? You and I could do wonderful things together, Vince. I could get you to the top of the Family in no time."

A terrible thought oozed up to the surface of Vince's slowly-simmering mind. "Uh, wait a minute. This is like I seen on TV, ain't it? You help me, but you want me to sell my soul to you, right?"

"Your *soul*? What would I do with your soul?"

"You're workin' for th' devil, an' you gimme three wishes or somethin' but in return I gotta let you take my soul down t' hell when I die."

Sizzle shook her ponderous head and managed to look slightly affronted. "Vince—I admit that dragons and humans haven't been the best of friends over the millennia, but we do *not* work for the devil. I'm not even sure that he exists. I've never seen a devil, have you?"

"No, but . . ."

"And I'm not after your soul, silly boy."

"You don' want me t' sign nuthin?"

"Of course not."

"An' you'll help me torch this dump for free?"

"More than that, Vince. I'll help you climb right up to the top of the Family. We'll be partners in crime! It'll be the most fun I've had since Aunt Hsspss started the Chicago Fire."

"Hey, I just wanna torch this one warehouse!"

"Yes, of course."

"No Chicago Fires or nuthin like that."

"I promise."

It took several minutes for Vince to finally make up his mind and say, "Okay, let's do it."

Sizzle cocked her head slightly to one side. "Shouldn't you get out of the warehouse first, Vince?"

"Huh? Oh yeah, sure."

"And maybe drive back to your house, or—better yet—over to that restaurant where your friends are."

"Whaddaya mean? We gotta torch this place first."

"I'll take care of that, Vince dearie. But wouldn't it look better if you had plenty of witnesses around to tell the police they were with you when the warehouse went up?"

"Yeah . . ." he said, feeling a little suspicious.

"All right, then," said Sizzle. "You just get your cute little body over to the restaurant and once you're safely there I'll light this place up like an Inquisition pyre."

"How'll you know . . . ?"

"When you get to the restaurant? I'm telepathic, Vince."

"But how'll I know . . ."

"When this claptrap gets belted out? Don't worry, you'll see the flames in the sky!" Sizzle sounded genuinely excited by the prospect.

Vince couldn't think of any other objections. Slowly, reluctantly, he headed for the warehouse door. He had to step over one of Sizzle's saber-long talons on the way.

At the doorway, he turned and asked plaintively, "You sure you ain't after my soul?"

Sizzle smiled at him. "I'm not after your soul, Vince. You can depend on that."

The warehouse fire was the most spectacular anyone had seen in a long time, and the police were totally stymied about its cause. They questioned Vince at length, especially since he had forgotten to get rid of the gasoline and paint thinner in the back of the stolen station wagon. But they couldn't pin a thing on him, not even car theft, once Louie had Big Balls Falcone explain the situation to the unhappy wagon's owner.

Vince's position in the Family started to rise. Spectacularly.

Arson became his specialty. Louie gave him tougher and tougher assignments and Vince would wander off a night later and the job would be done. Perfectly.

He met Sizzle regularly, sometimes in abandoned buildings, sometimes in empty lots. The dragon remained invisible then, of course, and the occasional passerby got the impression that a young, sharply-dressed man was standing in the middle of a weed-choked, bottle-strewn empty lot, talking to thin air.

More than once they could have heard him asking, "You really ain't interested in my soul?"

But only Vince could hear Sizzle's amused reply, "No, Vince. I have no use for souls, yours or anyone else's."

As the months went by, Vince's rapid rise to Family stardom naturally attracted some antagonism from other young men attempting to get ahead in the organization. Antagonism sometimes led to animosity, threats, even attempts at violence.

But strangely, wonderously, anyone who got angry at Vince disappeared. Without a trace, except once when a single charred shoe of Fats Lombardi was found in the middle of Tasker Street, between Twelfth and Thirteenth.

Louie and the other elders of the Family nodded knowingly. Vince was not only ambitious and talented. He was smart. No bodies could be laid at his doorstep.

From arson, Vince branched into loan-sharking, which was still the heart of the Family's operation. But he didn't need Big Balls Falcone to terrify his customers into paying on time. Customers who didn't pay found their cars turned into smoking wrecks. Right before their eyes, an automobile parked at the curb would burst into flame.

"Gee, too bad," Vince would say. "Next time it might be your house," he'd hint darkly, seeming to wink at somebody who wasn't there. At least, somebody no one else could see. Somebody very tall, from the angle of his head when he winked.

The day came when Big Balls Falcone himself, understandably put out by the decline in his business, let it be known that he was coming after Vince. Big Balls disappeared in a cloud of smoke, literally.

The years rolled by. Vince became quite prosperous. He was no longer the skinny, scared kid he had been when he had first met Sizzle. Now he dressed conservatively, with a carefully-tailored vest buttoned neatly over his growing paunch, and lunched on steak and lobster tails with bankers and brokers.

Although he moved out of the old neighborhood row house into a palatial ranch-style single near Cherry Hill, over in Jersey, Vince still came back to the Epiphany Church every Sunday morning for Mass. He sponsored the church's Little League baseball team and donated a free Toyota every year for the church's annual raffle.

He looked upon these charities, he often told his colleagues, as a form of insurance. He would lift his eyes at such moments. Those around him thought he was looking toward heaven. But Vince was really searching for Sizzle, who was usually not far away.

"Really Vince," the dragon told him, chuckling, "you still don't trust me. After all these years. I don't want your soul. Honestly I don't."

Vince still attended church and poured money into charities.

Finally Louie himself, old and frail, bequeathed the Family fortunes to Vince and then died peacefully in his sleep, unassisted by members of his own or any other Family. Somewhat of a rarity in Family annals.

Vince was now *Capo* of the Family. He was not yet forty, sleek, hair still dark, heavier than he wanted to be, but in possession of his own personal tailor, his own barber, and more women than he had ever dreamed of having.

His ascension to *Capo* was challenged, of course, by some of Louie's other lieutenants. But after the first few of them disappeared without a trace, the others quickly made their peace with Vince.

He never married. But he enjoyed life to the full.

"You're getting awfully overweight, Vince," Sizzle warned him one night, as they strolled together along the dark and empty waterfront where they had first met. "Shouldn't you be worrying about the possibility of a heart attack?"

"Naw," said Vince. "I don't get heart attacks, I give 'em!" He laughed uproariously at his own joke.

"You're getting older, Vince. You're not as cute as you once were, you know."

"I don't hafta be *cute*, Sizzle. I got the power now. I can look and act any way I wanna act. Who's gonna get in my way?"

Sizzle nodded, a bit ruefully. But Vince paid no attention to her mood.

"I can do anything I want!" he shouted to the watching heavens. "I got th' power and the rest of those dummies are scared to death of me. Scared to death!" He laughed and laughed.

"But Vince," Sizzle said, "I helped you to get that power."

"Sure, sure. But I got it now, an' I don't really need your help anymore. I can get anybody in th' Family to do whatever I want!"

Dragons don't cry, of course, but the expression on Sizzle's face would have melted the heart of anyone who saw it.

"Listen," Vince went on, in a slightly less bombastic tone, "I know you done a lot to help me, an' I ain't gonna forget that. You'll still be part of my organization, Sizzle old girl. Don't worry about that."

But the months spun along and lengthened into years, and Vince saw Sizzle less and less. He didn't need to. And secretly, down inside him, he was glad that he didn't have to.

I don't need her no more, and I never signed nuthin about givin' away my soul or nuthin. I'm free and clear!

Dragons, of course, are telepathic.

Vince's big mistake came when he noticed that a gorgeous young redhead he was interested in seemed to have eyes only for a certain slick-looking young punk. Vince thought about the problem mightily, and then decided to solve two problems with one stroke.

He called the young punk to his presence, at the very same restaurant where Louie had given Vince his first big break.

The punk looked scared. He had heard that Vince was after the redhead.

"Listen kid," Vince said gruffly, laying a heavily be-ringed hand on the kid's thin shoulder. "You know the old clothing factory up on Twenty-Eighth and Arch?"

"Y . . . yessir," said the punk, in a whisper that Vince could barely hear.

"It's a very flammable building, dontcha think?"

The punk blinked, gulped, then nodded. "Yeah. It is. But . . ."

"But what?"

His voice trembling, the kid said, "I heard that two-three different guys tried beltin' out that place. An' they . . . they never came back!"

"The place is still standin', ain't it?" Vince asked severely.

"Yeah."

"Well, by tomorrow morning, either *it* ain't standin' or *you* ain't standin'. *Capisce*?"

The kid nodded and fairly raced out of the restaurant. Vince grinned. One way or the other, he had solved a problem, he thought.

The old factory burned cheerfully for a day and a half before the Fire Department could get the blaze under control. Vince laughed and phoned his insurance broker.

But that night, as he stepped from his limousine onto the driveway of his Cherry Hill home, he saw long coils of glittering scales wrapped halfway around the house.

Looking up, he saw Sizzle smiling at him.

"Hello Vince. Long time no see."

"Oh, hi Sizzle ol' girl. What's new?" With his left hand, Vince impatiently waved his driver off. The man backed the limousine down the driveway and headed for the garage back in the city, goggle-eyed that The Boss was talking to himself.

"That was a real cute fellow you sent to knock off the factory two nights ago," Sizzle said, her voice almost purring.

"Him? He's a punk."

"I thought he was really cute."

"So you were there, huh? I figured you was, after those other guys never came back."

"Oh Vince, you're not cute anymore. You're just soft and fat and ugly."

"You ain't gonna win no beauty contests yourself, Sizzle."

He started for the front door, but Sizzle planted a huge taloned paw in his path. Vince had just enough time to look up, see the expression on her face, and scream.

Sizzle's forked tongue licked her lips as the smoke cleared.

"Delicious," she said. "Just the right amount of fat on him. And the poor boy thought I was after his *soul*!"

THE LAST DECISION

One of the things that makes science fiction such a vital and vivid field is the synergy that manifests itself among the writers. Whereas in most other areas of contemporary letters the writers appear to feel themselves in competition with each other (for headlines, if nothing else) the writers of science fiction have long seen themselves as members of a big family. They share ideas, they often work together, and they help each other whenever they can.

A large part of this synergy stems from the old, original Milford Science Fiction Writers Conference, which used to be held annually in Milford, Pa. Everlasting thanks are due to Damon Knight, the late James Blish, and Judith Merrill, who first organized the conferences. For eight days out of each June, a small and dedicated group of professional writers—about evenly mixed between old hands and newcomers—ate, slept, breathed, and talked about writing. Lifelong friendships began at Milford, together with the synergy that makes two such friends more effective working together than the simple one-plus-one equation would lead you to think.

I met Gordon R. Dickson at the first Milford I attended, back in the early Sixties, and we have been firm friends ever since. We collaborated on a children's fantasy, Gremlins, Go Home!, some years later, and even though

*Gordy lives in Minneapolis and I in New England, it's a
rare six months when we do not see each other.*

*The Last Decision is an example of the synergy between
writers. Gordy wrote a marvelous story, Call Him Lord,
which stuck in my mind for years. In particular, I was
haunted by the character of the Emperor of the Hundred
Worlds, as powerful a characterization as I have found
anywhere, even though he is actually a minor player in
Gordy's story. I wanted to see more of the Emperor, and
finally asked Gordy if he would allow me to "use" the
character in a story of my own. He graciously gave his
permission, and the result is The Last Decision.*

I

The Emperor of the Hundred Worlds stood at the head of
the conference chamber, tall, gray, grim-faced. Although
there were forty other men and women seated in the
chamber, the Emperor knew he was alone.

"Then it is certain?" he asked, his voice grave but
strong despite the news they had given him. "Earth's Sun
will explode?"

The scientists had come from all ends of the Empire to
reveal their findings to the Emperor. They shifted uneasily
in their sculptured couches under his steady gaze. A few of
them, the oldest and best-trusted, were actually on the
Imperial Planet itself, only an ocean away from the palace.
Most of the others had been brought to the Imperial Solar
System from their homeworlds, and were housed on the
three other planets of the system.

Although the holographic projections made them look as
solid and real as the Emperor himself, there was always a

slight lag in their responses to him. The delay was an indication of their rank within the scientific order, and they had even arranged their seating in the conference chamber the same way: the farther away from the Emperor, the lower in the hierarchy.

Some things cannot be conquered, the Emperor thought to himself as one of the men in the third rank of couches, a roundish, bald, slightly pompous little man, got to his feet. *Time still reigns supreme. Distance we can conquer, but not time. Not death.*

"Properly speaking, Sire, the Sun will not explode. It will not become a nova. Its mass is too low for that. But the eruptions that it will suffer will be of sufficient severity to heat Earth's atmosphere to incandescence. It will destroy all life on the surface. And, of course, the oceans will be drastically damaged; the food chain of the oceans will be totally disrupted."

Goodbye to Earth, then, thought the Emperor.

But aloud he asked, "The power satellites, and the shielding we have provided the planet—they will not protect it?"

The scientist stood dumb, patiently waiting for his Emperor's response to span the light-minutes between them. *How drab he looks*, the Emperor noted. *And how soft.* He pulled his own white robe closer around his iron-hard body. He was older than most of them in the conference chamber, but they were accustomed to sitting at desks and lecturing to students. He was accustomed to standing before multitudes and commanding.

"The shielding," the bald man said at last, "will not be sufficient. There is nothing we can do. Sometime over the next three to five hundred years, the Sun will erupt and destroy all life on Earth and the inner planets of its system. The data are conclusive."

The Emperor inclined his head to the man, curtly, a

gesture that meant both "thank you" and "be seated."
The scientist waited mutely for the gesture to reach him.

The data are conclusive. The integrator woven into the
molecules of his cerebral cortex linked the Emperor's mind
with the continent-spanning computer complex that was
the Imperial memory.

Within milliseconds he reviewed the equations and found
no flaw in them. Even as he did so, the other hemisphere
of his brain was picturing Earth's daystar seething, writh-
ing in a fury of pent-up nuclear agony, then erupting into
giant flares. The Sun calmed afterward and smiled benignly
once again on a blackened, barren, smoking rock called
Earth.

A younger man was on his feet, back in the last row of
couches. The Emperor realized that he had already asked
for permission to speak. Now they both waited for the
photons to complete the journey between them. From his
position in the chamber and the distance between them, he
was either an upstart or a very junior researcher.

"Sire," he said at last, his face suddenly flushed in
embarrassed self-consciousness or, perhaps, the heat of
conviction, "the data may be conclusive, true enough.
But it is *not* true that we must accept this catastrophe with
folded hands."

The Emperor began to say, "Explain yourself," but
the intense young man never hesitated to wait for an
Imperial response. He was taking no chances of being
commanded into silence before he had finished.

"Earth's Sun will erupt only if we do nothing to prevent
it. A colleague of mine believes that we have the means to
prevent the eruptions. I would like to present her ideas on
the subject. She could not attend this meeting herself."
The young man's face grew taut, angry. "Her application
to attend was rejected by the Coordinating Committee."

The Emperor smiled inwardly as the young man's words

reached the other scientists around him. He could see a shock wave of disbelief and indignation spread through the assembly. The hoary old men in the front row, who chose the members of the Coordinating Committee, went stiff with anger.

Even Prince Javas, the Emperor's last remaining son, roused from his idle daydreaming where he sat at the Emperor's side and seemed to take an interest in the meeting for the first time.

"You may present yout colleague's proposal," the Emperor said. *That is what an Emperor is for*, he said silently, looking at his youngest son, seeking some understanding on his handsome untroubled face. *To be magnanimous in the face of disaster*.

The young man took a fingertip-sized cube from his sleeve pocket and inserted it into the computer input slot in the arm of his couch. The scientists in the front ranks of the chamber glowered and muttered to each other.

The Emperor stood lean and straight, waiting for the information to reach him. When it did, he saw in his mind a young darkhaired woman whose face would have been seductive if she were not so intensely serious about her subject. She was speaking, trying to keep her voice dispassionate, but almost literally quivering with excitement. Equations appeared, charts, graphs, lists of materials and costs; yet her intent, dark-eyed face dominated it all.

Beyond her, the Emperor saw a vague, star-shimmering image of vast ships ferrying megatons of equipment and thousands upon thousands of technical specialists from all parts of the Hundred Worlds toward Earth and its troubled Sun.

Then, as the equations faded and the starry picture went dim and even the woman's face began to pale, the Emperor saw the Earth, green and safe, smelt the grass and heard birds singing, saw the Sun shining gently over a range of softly rolling, ancient wooded hills.

He closed his eyes. *You go too far, woman*. But how was she to know that his eldest son had died in hills exactly like these, killed on Earth, killed *by* Earth, so many years ago?

II

He sat now. The Emperor of the Hundred Worlds spent little time on his feet anymore. *One by one the vanities are surrendered*. He sat in a powered chair that held him in a soft yet firm embrace. It was mobile and almost alive: part personal vehicle, part medical monitor, part communications system that could link him with any place in the Empire.

His son stood. Prince Javas stood by the marble balustrade that girdled the high terrace where his father had received him. He wore the gray-blue uniform of a fleet commander, although he had never bothered to accept command of even one ship. His wife, the Princess Rihana, stood at her husband's side.

They were a well-matched pair, physically. Gold and fire. The Prince had his father's lean sinewy grace, golden hair and star-flecked eyes. Rihana was fiery, with the beauty and ruthlessness of a tigress in her face. Her hair was a cascade of molten copper tumbling past her shoulders, her gown a metallic glitter.

"It was a wasted trip," Javas said to his father, with his usual sardonic smile. "Earth is . . . well," he shrugged, "nothing but Earth. It hasn't changed in the slightest."

"Ten wasted years," Rihana said.

The Emperor looked past them, beyond the terrace to

the lovingly landscaped forest that his engineers coulc never make quite the right shade of terrestrial green.

"Not entirely wasted, daughter-in-law," he said at last. "You only aged eighteen months . . ."

"We are ten years out of date with the affairs of the Empire," she answered. The smoldering expression on her face made it clear that she believed her father-in-law deliberately plotted to keep her as far from the throne as possible.

"You can easily catch up," the Emperor said, ignoring her anger. "In the meantime, you have kept your youthful appearance."

"I shall always keep it! *You* are the one who denies himself rejuvenation treatments, not me."

"And so will Javas, when he becomes Emperor."

"Will he?" Her eyes were suddenly mocking.

"He will," said the Emperor, with the weight of a hundred worlds behind his voice.

Rihana looked away from him. "Well even so, I shan't. I see no reason why I should age and wither when even the foulest shopkeeper can live for centuries."

"Your husband will age."

She said nothing. *And as he ages*, the Emperor knew, *you will find younger lovers. But of course, you have already done that, haven't you?* He turned toward his son, who was still standing by the balustrade.

"Kyle Arman is dead," Javas blurted.

For a moment, the Emperor failed to comprehend. "Dead?" he asked, his voice sounding old and weak even to himself.

Javas nodded. "In his sleep. A heart seizure."

"But he is too young . . ."

"He was your age, Father."

"And he refused rejuvenation treatments," Rihana said, sounding positively happy. "As if he were royalty! The pretentious fool. A servant . . . a menial . . ."

"He was a friend of this House," the Emperor said.

"He killed my brother," said Javas.

"Your brother failed the test. He was a coward. Unfit to rule." *But Kyle passed you*, the Emperor thought. *You were found fit to rule . . . or was Kyle still ashamed of what he had done to my firstborn?*

"And you accepted his story." For once, Javas' bemused smile was gone. There was iron in his voice. "The word of a backwoods Earthman."

"A pretentious fool," Rihana gloated.

"A proud and faithful man," the Emperor corrected. "A man who put honor and duty above personal safety or comfort."

His eyes locked with Javas'. After a long moment in silence, the Prince shrugged and turned away.

"Regardless," Rihana said, "we surveyed the situation on Earth, as you requested us to."

Commanded, the Emperor thought. *Not requested.*

"The people there are all primitives. Hardly a city on the entire planet! It's all trees and huge oceans."

"I know. I have been there."

Javas said, "There are only a few millions living on Earth. They can be evacuated easily and resettled on a few of the frontier planets. After all, they *are* primitives."

"Those 'primitives' are the baseline for our race. They are the pool of original genetic material, against which our scientists constantly measure the rest of humanity throughout the Hundred Worlds."

Rihana said, "Well, they're going to have to find another primitive world to live on."

"Unless we prevent their Sun from exploding."

Javas looked amused, "You're not seriously considering that?"

"I am . . . considering it. Perhaps not very seriously."

"It makes no difference," Rihana said. "The plan to

save the Sun—to save your precious Earth—will take hundreds of years to implement. You will be dead long before the first steps can be brought to a conclusion. The next Emperor can cancel the entire plan the day he takes the throne."

The Emperor turned his chair slightly to face his son, but Javas looked away, out toward the darkening forest.

"I know," the Emperor whispered, more to himself than to her. "I know that full well."

III

He could not sleep. The Emperor lay on the wide expanse of warmth, floating a single molecular layer above the gently soothing waters. Always before, when sleep would not come readily, a woman had solved the problem for him. But lately not even lovemaking helped.

The body grows weary but the mind refuses sleep. Is this what old age brings?

Now he lay alone, the ceiling of his tower bedroom depolarized so that he could see the blazing glory of the Imperial Planet's night sky.

Not the pale tranquil sky of Earth, with its bloated Moon smiling inanely at you, he thought. This was truly an Imperial sky, brazen with blue giant stars that studded the heavens like brilliant sapphires. No moon rode that sky; none was needed. There was never true darkness on the Imperial Planet.

And yet Earth's sky seemed so much friendlier. You could pick out old companions there: the two Bears, the Lion, the Twins, the Hunter, the Winged Horse.

Already I think of Earth in the past tense. Like Kyle. Like my son.

He thought of the Earth's warming Sun. How could it turn traitor? How could it . . . begin to die? In his mind's eye he hovered above the Sun, bathed in its fiery glow, watching its bubbling seething surface. He plunged deeper into the roiling plasma, saw filaments and streamers arching a thousand Earthspans into space, heard the pulsing throb of the star's energy, the roar of its power, blinding bright, overpowering, ceaseless merciless heat, throbbing, roaring, pounding . . .

He was gasping for breath and the pounding he heard was his own heartbeat throbbing in his ears. Soaked with sweat, he tried to sit up. The bed enfolded him protectively, supporting his body.

"Hear me," he commanded the computer. His voice cracked.

"Sire?" answered a softly female voice in his mind.

He forced himself to relax. Forced the pain from his body. The dryness in his throat eased. His breathing slowed. The pounding of his heart diminished.

"Get me the woman scientist who reported at the conference on the Sun's explosion, ten years ago. She was not present at the conference; her report was presented by a colleague."

The computer needed more than a second to reply, "Sire, there were four such reports by female scientists at that conference."

"This was the only one to deal with a plan to save the Earth's Sun."

IV

Medical monitors were implanted in his body now. Although the Imperial physicians insisted that it was impossible, the Emperor could feel the microscopic implants on the wall of his heart, in his aorta, alongside his carotid artery. The Imperial psychotechs called it a psychosomatic reaction. But since his mind was linked to the computers that handled all the information on the planet, the Emperor knew what his monitors were reporting before the doctors did.

They had reduced the gravity in his working and living sections of the palace to one-third normal, and forbade him from leaving these areas, except for the rare occasions of state when he was needed in the Great Assembly Hall or another public area. He acquiesced in this: the lighter gravity felt better and allowed him to be on his feet once again, free of the power chair's clutches.

This day he was walking slowly, calmly, through a green forest of Earth. He strolled along a parklike path, admiring the lofty maples and birches, listening to the birds and small forest animals' songs of life. He inhaled scents of pine and grass and sweet clean air. He felt the warm sun on his face and the faintest cool breeze. For a moment he considered how the trees would look in their autumnal reds and golds. But he shook his head.

No. There is enough autumn in my life. I'd rather be in springtime.

In the rooms next to the corridor he walked through, tense knots of technicians worked at the holographic systems that produced the illusion of the forest, while other groups of white-suited meditechs studied the readouts from the Emperor's implants.

Two men joined the Emperor on the forest path: Academician Bomeer, head of the Imperial Academy of Sciences, and Supreme Commander Fain, chief of staff of the Imperial Military Forces. Both were old friends and advisors, close enough to the Emperor to be housed within the palace itself when they were allowed to visit their master.

Bomeer looked young, almost sprightly, in a stylish robe of green and tan. He was slightly built, had a lean, almost ascetic face that was spoiled by a large mop of unruly brown hair.

Commander Fain was iron gray, square-faced, a perfect picture of a military leader. His black and silver uniform fit his muscular frame like a second skin. His gray eyes seemed eternally troubled.

The Emperor greeted them and allowed Bomeer to spend a few minutes admiring the forest simulation. The scientist called out the correct names for each type of tree they walked past and identified several species of birds and squirrel. Finally the Emperor asked him about the young woman who had arrived on the Imperial Planet the previous month.

"I have discussed her plan thoroughly with her," Bomeer said, his face going serious. "I must say that she is dedicated, energetic, close to brilliant. But rather naive and overly sanguine about her own ideas."

"Could her plan work?" asked the Emperor.

"Could it work?" the scientist echoed. He had tenaciously held onto his post at the top of the scientific hierarchy for nearly a century. His body had been rejuvenated more than once, the Emperor knew. But not his mind.

"Sire, there is no way to tell if it could work! Such an operation has never been done before. There are no valid data. Mathematics, yes. But even so, there is no more than theory. And the costs! The time it would take! The technical manpower! Staggering.''

The Emperor stopped walking. Fifty meters away, behind the hologram screens, a dozen meditechs suddenly hunched over their readout screens intently.

But the Emperor had stopped merely to repeat to Bomeer, ''Could her plan work?''

Bomeer ran a hand through his boyish mop, glanced at Commander Fain for support and found none, then faced his Emperor again. ''I . . . there is no firm answer, Sire. Statistically, I would say that the chances are vanishingly small.''

''Statistics!'' The Emperor made a disgusted gesture. ''A refuge for scoundrels and sociotechs. Is there anything scientifically impossible in what she proposes?''

''Nnn . . . not *theoretically* impossible, Sire,'' Bomeer said slowly. ''But in the practical world of reality . it . . . it's the *magnitude* of the project. The costs. Why, it would take half of Commander Fain's fleet to transport the equipment and material.''

Fain seized his opportunity to speak. ''And the Imperial Fleet, Sire, is spread much too thin for safety as it is.''

''We are at peace, Commander,'' said the Emperor.

''For how long, Sire? The frontier worlds grow more restless every day. And the aliens beyond our borders . . .''

''Are weaker than we are. I have reviewed the intelligence assessments, Commander.''

''Sire, the relevant factor in those reports is that the aliens are growing stronger and we are not.''

With a nod, the Emperor resumed walking. The scientist and the commander followed him, arguing their points unceasingly.

Finally they reached the end of the long corridor, where the holographic simulation showed them Earth's Sun setting beyond the edge of an ocean, turning the restless sea into an impossible glitter of opalescence.

"Your recommendations, then, gentlemen?" he asked wearily. Even in the one-third gravity his legs felt tired, his back ached.

Bomeer spoke first, his voice hard and sure. "This naive dream of saving the Earth's Sun is doomed to fail. The plan must be rejected."

Fain added, "The Fleet can detach enough squadrons from its noncombat units to initiate the evacuation of Earth whenever you order it, Sire."

"Evacuate them to an unsettled planet?" the Emperor asked.

"Or resettle them on the existing frontier worlds. The Earth residents are rather frontier-like themselves; they have purposely been kept primitive. They would get along well with some of the frontier populations. They might even serve to calm down some of the unrest on the frontier worlds."

The Emperor looked at Fain and almost smiled. "Or they might fan that unrest into outright rebellion. They are a cantankerous lot, you know."

"We can deal with rebellion," said Fain.

"Can you?" the Emperor asked. "You can kill people, of course. You can level cities and even render whole planets uninhabitable. But does that end it? Or do the neighboring worlds become fearful and turn against us?"

Fain stood as unmoved as a statue. His lips barely parted as he asked, "Sire, if I may speak frankly?"

"Certainly, Commander."

Like a soldier standing at attention as he delivers an unpleasant report to his superior officer, Fain drew himself up and monotoned, "Sire, the main reason for unrest among the frontier worlds is the lack of Imperial firmness in dealing with them. In my opinion, a strong hand is desperately needed. The neighboring worlds will respect their Emperor if—and only if—he acts decisively. The people value strength, Sire, not meekness."

The Emperor reached out and put a hand on the Commander's shoulder. Fain was still iron-hard under his uniform.

"You have sworn an oath to protect and defend this Realm," the Emperor said. "If necessary, to die for it."

"And to protect and defend you, Sire." The man stood straighter and firmer than the trees around them.

"But this Empire, my dear Commander, is more than blood and steel. It is more than any one man. It is an *idea*."

Fain looked back at him steadily, but with no real understanding in his eyes. Bomeer stood uncertainly off to one side.

Impatiently, the Emperor turned his face toward the ceiling hologram and called, "Map!"

Instantly the forest scene disappeared and they were in limitless space. Stars glowed around them, overhead, on all sides, underfoot. The pale gleam of the galaxy's spiral arms wafted off and away into unutterable distance.

Bomeer's knees buckled. Even the Commander's rigid self-discipline was shaken.

The Emperor smiled. He was accustomed to walking godlike on the face of the Deep.

"This is the Empire, gentlemen," he lectured in the darkness. "A handful of stars, a pitiful scattering of worlds set apart by distances that take years to traverse. All populated by human beings, the descendants of Earth."

He could hear Bomeer breathing heavily. Fain was a ramrod outline against the glow of the Milky Way, but his hands were outstretched, as if seeking balance.

"What links these scattered dust motes? What preserves their ancient heritage, guards their civilization, protects their hard-won knowledge and arts and sciences? The Empire, gentlemen. We are the mind of the Hundred Worlds, their memory, the yardstick against which they can measure their own humanity. We are their friend, their father, their teacher and helper.''

The Emperor searched the black starry void for the tiny yellowish speck of Earth's Sun, while saying:

''But if the Hundred Worlds decide that the Empire is no longer their friend, if they want to leave their father, if they feel that their teacher and helper has become an oppressor . . . what then happens to the human race? It will shatter into a hundred fragments, and all the civilization that we have built and nurtured and protected over all these centuries will be destroyed.''

Bomeer's whispered voice floated through the darkness, ''They would never . . .''

''Yes. They would never turn against the Empire because they know that they have more to gain by remaining with us than by leaving us.''

''But the frontier worlds,'' Fain said.

''The frontier worlds are restless, as frontier communities always are. If we use military might to force them to bow to our will, then other worlds will begin to wonder where their own best interests lie.''

''But they could never hope to fight against the Empire!''

The Emperor snapped his fingers and instantly the three of them were standing again in the forest at sunset.

''They could never hope to *win* against the Empire,'' the Emperor corrected. ''But they could destroy the Empire and themselves. I have played out the scenarios with the computers. Widespread rebellion *is* possible, once the majority of the Hundred Worlds becomes convinced that the Empire is interfering with their freedoms.''

''But the rebels could never win,'' the Commander said. ''I have run the same wargames myself, many times.''

"Civil war," said the Emperor. "Who wins a civil war? And once we begin to slaughter ourselves, what will your aliens do, my dear Fain? Eh?"

His two advisors fell silent. The forest simulation was now deep in twilight shadow. The three men began to walk back along the path, which was softly illuminated by bioluminescent flowers.

Bomeer clasped his hands behind his back as he walked. "Now that I have seen some of your other problems, Sire, I must take a stronger stand and insist—yes, Sire, *insist*— that this young woman's plan to save the Earth is even more foolhardy than I had at first thought it to be. The cost is too high, and the chance of success is much too slim. The frontier worlds would react violently against such an extravagance. And," with a nod to Fain, "it would hamstring the Fleet."

For several moments the Emperor walked down the simulated forest path without saying a word. Then, slowly, "I suppose you are right. It is an old man's sentimental dream."

"I'm afraid that's the truth of it, Sire," said Fain.

Bomeer nodded sagaciously.

"I will tell her. She will be disappointed. Bitterly."

Bomeer gasped. "She's here?"

The Emperor said, "Yes, I had her brought here to the palace. She has crossed the Empire, given up more than two years of her life to make the trip, lost a dozen years of her career over this wild scheme of hers . . just to hear that I will refuse her."

"In the palace?" Fain echoed. "Sire, you're not going to see her in person? The security . . ."

"Yes, in person. I owe her that much." The Emperor could see the shock on their faces. Bomeer, who had never stood in the same building with the Emperor until he had become Chairman of the Academy, was trying to suppress his fury with poor success. Fain, sworn to guard the Emperor as well as the Empire, looked worried.

"But Sire," the Commander said, "no one has personally seen the Emperor, privately, outside of his family and closest advisors," Bomeer bristled visibly, "in years . . . decades!"

The Emperor nodded but insisted, "She is going to see me. I owe her that much. An ancient ruler on Earth once said, 'When you are going to kill a man, it costs nothing to be polite about it.' She is not a man, of course, but I fear that our decision will kill her soul."

They looked unconvinced.

Very well then, the Emperor said to them silently. *Put it down as the whim of an old man . . . a man who is feeling all his years . . . a man who will never recapture his youth.*

V

She is only a child.

The Emperor studied Adela de Montgarde as the young astrophysicist made her way through the guards and secretaries and halls and antechambers toward his own private chambers. He had prepared to meet her in his reception room, changed his mind and moved the meeting to his office, then changed it again and now waited for her in his study. She knew nothing of his indecision; she merely followed the directions given her by the computer-informed staff of the palace.

The study was a warm old room, lined with shelves of private tapes that the Emperor had collected over the years. A stone fireplace big enough to walk into spanned one wall; its flames soaked the Emperor in lifegiving warmth. The opposite wall was a single broad window that looked out on the real forest beyond the palace walls. The window could also serve as a hologram frame; the Emperor could have any scene he wanted projected from it.

Best to have reality this evening, he told himself. *There is too little reality in my life these days.* So he eased back in his powerchair and watched his approaching visitor on the viewscreen above the fireplace of the richly carpeted, comfortably panelled old room.

He had carefully absorbed all the computer's information about Adela de Montgarde: born of a noble family on Gris, a frontier world whose settlers were slowly, painfully transforming from a ball of rock into a viable habitat for human life. He knew her face, her life history, her scientific accomplishments and rank. But now, as he watched her approaching on the viewscreen built into the stone fireplace, he realized how little knowledge had accompanied the computer's detailed information.

The door to the study swung open automatically, and she stood uncertainly, framed in the doorway.

The Emperor swivelled his powerchair around to face her. The viewscreen immediately faded and became indistinguishable from the other stones.

"Come in, come in, Dr. Montgarde."

She was tiny, the smallest woman the Emperor remembered seeing. Her face was almost elfin, with large curious eyes that looked as if they had known laughter. She wore a metallic tunic buttoned to the throat, and a brief skirt. Her figure was childlike.

The Emperor smiled to himself. *She certainly won't tempt me with her body.*

As she stepped hesitantly into the study, her eyes darting all around the room, he said:

"I am sure that my aides have filled your head with all

sorts of nonsense about protocol—when to stand, when to bow, what forms of address to use. Forget all of it. This is an informal meeting, common politeness will suffice. If you need a form of address for me, call me Sire. I shall call you Adela, if you don't mind.''

With a slow nod of her head she answered, ''Thank you, Sire. That will be fine.'' Her voice was so soft that he could barely hear it. He thought he detected a slight waver in it.

She's not going to make this easy for me, he said to himself. Then he noticed the stone that she wore on a slim silver chain about her neck.

''Agate,'' he said.

She fingered the stone reflexively. ''Yes . . . it's from my homeworld . . . Gris. Our planet is rich in minerals.''

''And poor in cultivable land.''

''Yes. But we are converting more land every year.''

''Please sit down,'' the Emperor said. ''I'm afraid it's been so long since my old legs have tried to stand in a full gravity that I'm forced to remain in this power chair . . . or lower the gravitational field in this room. But the computer files said that you are not accustomed to low g fields.''

She glanced around the warm, richly furnished room.

''Any seat you like. My chair rides like a magic carpet.''

Adela picked the biggest couch in the room and tucked herself into a corner of it. The Emperor glided his chair over to her.

''It's very kind of you to keep the gravity up for me,'' she said.

He shrugged. ''It costs nothing to be polite. . . . But tell me, of all the minerals that Gris is famous for, why did you choose to wear agate?''

She blushed.

The Emperor laughed. ''Come, come, my dear. There's

nothing to be ashamed of. It's well known that agate is a magical stone that protects the wearer from scorpions and snakes. An ancient superstition, of course, but it could possibly be significant, eh?''

''No . . . it's not that!''

''Then what is it?''

''It . . . agate also makes the wearer . . . eloquent in speech.''

''And a favorite of princes,'' added the Emperor.

Her blush had gone. She sat straighter and almost smiled. ''And it gives one victory over her enemies.''

''You perceive me as your enemy?''

''Oh no!'' She reached out toward him, her small, childlike hand almost touching his.

''Who then?''

''The hierarchy . . . the old men who pretend to be young and refuse to admit any new ideas into the scientific community.''

''I am an old man,'' the Emperor said.

''Yes . . .'' She stared frankly at his aged face. ''I was surprised when I saw you a few moments ago. I have seen holographic pictures, of course . . . but you . . . you've *aged*.''

''Indeed.''

''Why can't you be rejuvenated? It seems like a useless old superstition to keep the Emperor from using modern biomedical techniques.''

''No, no, my child. It is a very wise tradition. You complain of the inflexible old men at the top of the scientific hierarchy. Suppose you had an inflexible old man in the Emperor's throne? A man who would live not merely six or seven score of years, but many centuries? What would happen to the Empire then?''

''Ohh. I see.'' And there was real understanding and sympathy in her eyes.

"So the king must die, to make room for new blood, new ideas, new vigor."

"It's sad," she said. "You are known everywhere as a good Emperor. The people love you."

He felt his eyebrows rise. "Even on the frontier worlds?"

"Yes. They know that Fain and his troops would be standing on our necks if it weren't for the Emperor. We are not without our sources of information."

He smiled. "Interesting."

"But that is not why you called me here to see you," Adela said.

She grows bolder. "True. You want to save Earth's Sun. Bomeer and all my advisors tell me that it is either impossible or foolish. I fear that they have powerful arguments on their side."

"Perhaps," she said. "But I have the facts."

"I have seen your presentation. I understand the scientific basis of your plan."

"We can do it!" Adela said, her hands suddenly animated. "We can! The critical mass is really miniscule compared to . . ."

"Megatons are miniscule?"

"Compared to the effect it will produce. Yes."

And then she was on her feet, pacing the room, ticking off points on her fingers, lecturing, pleading, cajoling. The Emperor's powerchair nodded back and forth, following her intense, wiry form as she paced.

"Of course it will take vast resources! And time—more than a century before we know to a first-order approximation that the initial steps are working. I'll have to give myself up to cryosleep for decades at a time. But we *have* the resources! And we have the time . . . just barely. We can do it, if we want to."

The Emperor said, "How can you expect me to divert half the resources of the Empire to save Earth's Sun?"

"Because Earth is *important*," she argued back, a tiny fighter standing alone in the middle of the Emperor's study. "It's the baseline for all the other worlds of the Empire. On Gris we send biogenetic teams to Earth every five years to check our own mutation rate. The cost is enormous for us, but we do it. We have to."

"We can move Earth's population to another G-type star. There are plenty of them."

"It won't be the same."

"Adela, my dear, believe me, I would like to help. I know how important Earth is. But we simply cannot afford to try your scheme now. Perhaps in another hundred years or so . . ."

"That will be too late."

"But new scientific advances . . ."

"Under Bomeer and his ilk? Hah!"

The Emperor wanted to frown at her, but somehow his face would not compose itself properly. "You are a fierce, uncompromising woman," he said.

She came to him and dropped to her knees at his feet. "No, Sire. I'm not. I'm foolish and vain and utterly self-centered. I want to save Earth because I know I can do it. I can't stand the thought of living the rest of my life knowing that I could have done it, but never having had the chance to try."

Now we're getting at the truth, the Emperor thought.

"And someday, maybe a million years from now, maybe a billion . . . Gris' sun will become unstable. I want to be able to save Gris, too. And any other world whose star threatens it. I want all the Empire to know that Adela de Montgarde discovered the way to do it!"

The Emperor felt his breath rush out of him.

"Sire," she went on, "I'm sorry if I'm speaking impolitely or stupidly. It's just that I know we can do this thing, do it successfully, and you're the only one who can make it happen.''

But he was barely listening. "Come with me," he said, reaching out to grasp her slim wrists and raising her to her feet. "It's time for the evening meal. I want you to meet my son.''

VI

Javas put on his usual amused smile when the Emperor introduced Adela. *Will nothing ever reach under his everlasting facade of polite boredom?* Rihana, at least, was properly furious. He could see the anger in her face: A virtual barbarian from some frontier planet. Daughter of a petty noble. Practically a commoner. Dining with them!

"Such a young child to have such grandiose schemes," the Princess said when she realized who Adela was.

"Surely," said the Emperor, "you had grandiose schemes of your own when you were young, Rihana. Of course, they involved lineages and marriages rather than astrophysics, didn't they?"

None of them smiled.

The Emperor had ordered dinner out on the terrace, under the glowing night sky of the Imperial Planet. Rihana, who was responsible for household affairs, always had sumptuous meals spread for them: the best meats and fowl and fruits of a dozen prime worlds. Adela looked bewildered by the array placed in front of her by the human servants. Such riches were obviously new to her. The Emperor ate sparingly and watched them all.

Inevitably the conversation returned to Adela's plan to save Earth's Sun. And Adela, subdued and timid at first, slowly turned tigress once again. She met Rihana's scorn with coldly furious logic. She countered Javas' skepticism with:

"Of course, since it will take more than a century before the outcome of the project is proven, you will probably be the Emperor who is remembered by all the human race as the one who saved the Earth."

Javas' eyes widened slightly. *It hit home*, the Emperor noticed. *For once something affected the boy. This girl should be kept at the palace.*

But Rihana snapped, "Why should the Crown Prince care about saving Earth? His brother was murdered by an Earthman."

The Emperor felt his blood turn to ice.

Adela looked panic-stricken. She turned to the Emperor, wide-eyed, open-mouthed.

"My eldest son died on Earth. My second son was killed putting down a rebellion on a frontier world, many years ago. My third son died of a viral infection that *some* tell me," he stared at Rihana, "was assassination. Death is a constant companion in every royal house."

"Three sons . . ." Adela seemed ready to burst into tears.

"I have not punished Earth, nor that frontier world, nor sought to find a possible assassin," the Emperor went on, icily. "My only hope is that my last remaining son will make a good Emperor, despite his . . . handicaps."

Javas turned very deliberately in his chair to stare out at the dark forest. He seemed bored by the antagonism between his wife and his father. Rihana glowered like molten steel.

The dinner ended in dismal, bitter silence. The Emperor sent them all away to their rooms while he remained on the terrace and stared hard at the stars strewn across the sky so thickly that there could be no darkness.

He closed his eyes and summoned a computer-assisted image of Earth's Sun. He saw it coalesce from a hazy cloud of cold gas and dust, saw it turn into a star and spawn planets. Saw it beaming out energy that allowed life to grow and flourish on one of those planets. And then saw it age, blemish, erupt, swell, and finally collapse into a dark cinder.

Just as I will, thought the Emperor. *The Sun and I have both reached the age where a bit of rejuvenation is needed. Otherwise . . . death.*

He opened his eyes and looked down at his veined, fleshless, knobby hands. *How different from hers! How young and vital she is.*

With a touch on one of the control studs set into the arm of his powerchair, he headed for his bedroom.

I cannot be rejuvenated. It is wrong even to desire it. But the Sun? Would it be wrong to try? Is it proper for puny men to tamper with the destinies of the stars themselves?

Once in his tower-top bedroom he called for her. Adela came to him quickly, without delay or question. She wore a simple knee-length gown tied loosely at the waist. It hung limply over her boyish figure.

"You sent for me, Sire." It was not a question but a statement. The Emperor knew her meaning: *I will do what you ask, but in return I expect you to give me what I desire.*

He was already reclining in the soft embrace of his bed. The texture of the monolayer surface felt soft and protective. The warmth of the water beneath it eased his tired body.

"Come here, child. Come and talk to me. I hardly ever sleep anymore; it gives my doctors something to worry about. Come and sit beside me and tell me all about yourself . . . the parts of your life story that are not on file in the computers."

She sat on the edge of the huge bed, and its nearly-living surface barely dimpled under her spare body.

"What would you like to know?" she asked.

"I have never had a daughter," the Emperor said. "What was your childhood like? How did you become the woman you are?"

She began to tell him. Living underground in the mining settlements on Gris. Seeing sunlight only when the planet was far enough from its too-bright star to let humans walk the surface safely. Playing in the tunnels. Sent by her parents to other worlds for schooling. The realization that her beauty was not physical. The few lovers she had known. The astronomer who had championed her cause to the Emperor at that meeting nearly fifteen years ago. Their brief marriage. Its breakup when he realized that being married to her kept him from advancing in the hierarchy.

"You have known pain too," the Emperor said.

"It's not an Imperial prerogative," she answered softly. "Everyone who lives knows pain."

By now the sky was milky white with the approach of dawn. The Emperor smiled at her.

"Before breakfast everyone in the palace will know that you spent the night with me. I'm afraid I have ruined your reputation."

She smiled back. "Or perhaps *made* my reputation."

He reached out and took her by the shoulders. Holding her at arm's length, he searched her face with a long, sad, almost fatherly look.

"It would not be a kindness to grant your request. If I allow you to pursue this dream of yours, have you any idea of the enemies it would make for you? Your life would be so cruel, so filled with envy and hatred."

"I know that," Adela said evenly. "I've known that from the beginning."

"And you are not afraid?"

"Of course I'm afraid! But I won't turn away from what I must do. Not because of fear. Not because of envy or hatred or any other reason."

"Not even for love?"

He felt her body stiffen. "No," she said. "Not even for love."

The Emperor let his hands drop away from her and called out to the computer, "Connect me with Prince Javas, Acadamician Bomeer, and Commander Fain."

"At once, Sire."

Their holographic images quickly appeared on separate segments of the farthest wall of the bedroom. Bomeer, halfway across the planet in late afternoon, was at his ornate desk. Fain appeared to be on the bridge of a warship, in orbit around the planet. Javas, of course, was still in bed. It was not Rihana who lay next to him.

The Emperor's first impulse was disapproval, but then he wondered where Rihana was sleeping.

"I am sorry to intrude on you so abruptly," he said to all three of the men, while they were still staring at the slight young woman sitting on the bed with their Emperor. "I have made my decision on the question of trying to save the Earth's Sun."

Bomeer folded his hands on the desktop. Fain, on his feet, shifted uneasily. Javas arched an eyebrow and looked more curious than anything else.

"I have listened to all your arguments and find that there is much merit in them. I have also listened carefully to Dr. Montgarde's arguments, and find much merit in them, as well."

Adela sat rigidly beside him. The expression on her face was frozen: she feared nothing and expected nothing. She neither hoped nor despaired. She waited.

"We will move the Imperial throne and all its trappings to Earth's only Moon," said the Emperor.

They gasped. All of them.

"Since this project to save the Sun will take many human generations, we will want the seat of the Empire close enough to the project so that the Emperor may take a direct view of the progress."

"But you can't move the entire Capital!" Fain protested. "And to Earth! It's a backwater . . ."

"Commander Fain," the Emperor said sternly. "Yesterday you were prepared to move Earth's millions. I ask now that the Fleet move the Court's thousands. And Earth will no longer be a backwater once the Empire is centered once again at the original home of the human race."

Bomeer sputtered, "But . . . but what if her plan fails? The sun will explode . . . and . . . and . . ."

"That is a decision to be made in the future."

He glanced at Adela. Her expression had not changed, but she was breathing rapidly now. The excitement had hit her body, it hadn't yet penetrated her emotional defenses.

"Father," Javas said, "may I point out that it takes *five years* in realtime to reach the Earth from here? The Empire cannot be governed without an Emperor for five years."

"Quite true, my son. You will go to Earth before me. Once there, you will become acting Emperor while I make the trip."

Javas' mouth dropped open. "The acting Emperor? For five years?"

"With luck," the Emperor said, grinning slightly, "old age will catch up with me before I reach Earth, and you will be the fullfledged Emperor for the rest of your life."

"But I don't want . . ."

"I know, Javas. But you will be Emperor some day. It is a responsibility you cannot avoid. Five years of training will stand you in good stead."

The Prince sat up straighter in his bed, his face serious, his eyes meeting his father's steadily.

"And son," the Emperor went on, "to be an Emperor—even for five years—you must be master of your own house."

Javas nodded. "I know, Father. I understand. And I will be."

"Good."

Then the Prince's impish smile flitted across his face once again. "But tell me . . . suppose, while you are in transit toward Earth, I decide to move the Imperial Capital elsewhere? What then?"

His father smiled back at him. "I believe I will just have to trust you not to do that."

"You would trust me?" Javas asked.

"I always have."

Javas' smile took on a new pleasure. "Thank you, Father. I will be waiting for you on Earth's Moon. And for the lovely Dr. Montgarde, as well."

Bomeer was still livid. "All this uprooting of everything . . . the costs . . . the manpower . . . over an unproven theory!"

"Why is the theory unproven, my friend?" the Emperor asked.

Bomeer's mouth opened and closed like a fish's, but no words came out.

"It is unproven," said the Emperor, "because our scientists have never gone so far before. In fact, the sciences of the Hundred Worlds have not made much progress at all in several generations. Isn't that true, Bomeer?"

"We . . . Sire, we have reached a natural plateau in our understanding of the physical universe. It has happened before. Our era is one of consolidation and practical application of already-acquired knowledge, not new basic breakthroughs."

"Well, this project will force some new thinking and new breakthroughs, I warrant. Certainly we will be forced to recruit new scientists and engineers by the shipload. Perhaps that will be impetus enough to start the climb upward again, eh, Bomeer? I never did like plateaus."

The academician lapsed into silence.

"And I see you, Fain," the Emperor said, "trying to calculate in your head how much of your Fleet strength is going to be wasted on this old man's dream."

"Sire, I had no . . ."

The Emperor waved him into silence. "No matter. Moving the Capital won't put much of a strain on the Fleet, will it?"

"No Sire. But this project to save Earth . . ."

"We will have to construct new ships for that, Fain. And we will have to turn to the frontier worlds for those ships." He glanced at Adela. "I believe that the frontier worlds will gladly join the effort to save Earth's Sun. And their treasuries will be enriched by our purchase of thousands of new ships."

"While the Imperial treasury is depleted."

"It's a rich Empire, Fain. It's time we shared some of our wealth with the frontier worlds. A large shipbuilding program will do more to reconcile them with the Empire than anything else we can imagine."

"Sire," said Fain bluntly, "I still think it's madness."

"Yes. I know. Perhaps it is. I only hope that I live long enough to find out, one way or the other."

"Sire," Adela said breathlessly, "you will be reuniting all the worlds of the Empire into a closely knit human community such as we haven't seen in centuries!"

"Perhaps. It would be pleasant to believe so. But for the moment, all I have done is to implement a decision to *try* to save Earth's Sun. It may succeed; it may fail. But we are sons and daughters of planet Earth, and we will not allow our original homeworld to be destroyed without struggling to our uttermost to save it."

He looked at their faces again. They were all waiting for him to continue. *You grow pompous, old man.*

"Very well. You each have several lifetimes of work to accomplish. Get busy, all of you."

Bomeer's and Fain's images winked off immediately. Javas' remained.

"Yes, my son? What is it?"

Javas' ever-present smile was gone. He looked serious, even troubled. "Father . . . I am not going to bring Rihana with me to Earth. She wouldn't want to come, I know—at least, not until all the comforts of the court were established there for her."

The Emperor nodded.

"If I'm to be master of my own house," Javas went on, "it's time we ended this farce of a marriage."

"Very well, son. That is your decision to make. But, for what it's worth, I agree with you."

"Thank you, Father." Javas' image disappeared.

For a long moment the Emperor sat gazing thoughtfully at the wall where the holographic images had appeared.

"I believe that I will send you to Earth on Javas' ship. I think he likes you, and it is important that the two of you get along well together."

Adela looked almost shocked. "What do you mean by 'get along well together'?"

The Emperor grinned at her. "That's for the two of you to decide."

"You're scandalous!" she said, but she was smiling too.

He shrugged. "Call it part of the price of victory. You'll like Javas; he's a good man. And I doubt that he's ever met a woman quite like you."

"I don't know what to say . . ."

"You'll need Javas' protection and support, you know. You have defeated all my closest advisors, and that means that they will become your enemies. Powerful enemies. That is also part of the price of your triumph."

"Triumph? I don't feel very triumphant."

"I know," the Emperor said. "Perhaps that's what triumph really is: Not so much glorying in the defeat of your enemies as weariness that they couldn't see what seemed so obvious to you."

Abruptly, Adela moved to him and put her lips to his cheek. "Thank you, Sire."

"Why, thank you, child."

For a moment she stood there, holding his old hands in her tiny young ones.

Then, "I . . . have lots of work to do."

"Of course. We will probably never see each other again. Go and do your work. Do it well."

"I will," she said. "And you?"

He leaned back into the bed. "I've finished my work. I believe that now I can go to sleep, at last." And with a smile he closed his eyes.

MEN OF GOOD WILL

As Rudyard Kipling once pointed out:
   "There are nine and sixty ways of constructing tribal lays,
   "And—every—single—one—of—them—is—right!"
Some science fiction stories begin with the dream of a wonderful invention, or the nightmare of a dreadful discovery. Some start with a vision of a particular person, a magnificent hero such as Muad'Dib or an ordinary person thrust into extraordinary events such as Montag, the Fireman. Other stories begin with the bare bones of a situation, an idea, even a joke, such as A Slight Miscalculation. . . .
   Or the present offering, Men of Good Will.

"I had no idea," said the UN representative as they stepped through the airlock-hatch, "that the United States lunar base was so big, and so thoroughly well equipped."

"It's a big operation, all right," Colonel Patton answered, grinning slightly. His professional satisfaction showed even behind the faceplate of his pressure-suit.

The pressure in the airlock equalibrated, and they squirmed out of their aluminized protective suits. Patton was big, scraping the maximum limit for space-vehicle passengers;

Torgeson, the UN man, was slight, thin-haired, bespecta-cled and somehow bland-looking.

They stepped out of the airlock, into the corridor that ran the length of the huge plastic dome that housed Headquarters, U.S. Moonbase.

"What's behind all the doors?" Torgeson asked. His English had a slight Scandinavian twang to it. Patton found it a little irritating.

"On the right," the colonel answered, businesslike, "are officers' quarters, galley, officers' mess, various laboratories and the headquarters staff offices. On the left are the computers."

Torgeson blinked. "You mean that half this building is taken up by computers? But why in the world . . . that is, why do you need so many? Isn't it frightfully expensive to boost them up here? I know it cost thousands of dollars for my own flight to the moon. The computers must be—"

"Frightfully expensive," Patton agreed, with feeling. "But we need them. Believe me, we need them."

They walked the rest of the way down the long corridor in silence. Patton's office was at the very end of it. The colonel opened the door and ushered in the UN representative.

"A sizeable office," Torgeson said. "And a window!"

"One of the privileges of rank," Patton answered, smiling tightly. "That white antenna-mast off on the horizon belongs to the Russian base."

"Ah, yes. Of course. I shall be visiting them tomorrow."

Colonel Patton nodded and gestured Torgeson to a chair as he walked behind his metal desk and sat down.

"Now then," said the colonel. "You are the first man allowed to set foot in this moonbase who is not a security-cleared, triple-checked, native-born, government-employed American. God knows how you got the Pentagon to okay your trip. But—now that you're here, what do you want?"

Torgeson took off his rimless glasses and fiddled with

them. "I suppose the simplest answer would be the best. The United Nations must—absolutely must—find out how and why you and the Russians have been able to live peacefully here on the moon."

Patton's mouth opened, but no words came out. He closed it with a click.

"Americans and Russians," the UN man went on, "have fired at each other from orbiting satellite vehicles. They have exchanged shots at both the North and South Poles. Career diplomats have scuffled like prizefighters in the halls of the United Nations building . . ."

"I didn't know that."

"Oh, yes. We have kept it quiet, of course. But the tensions are becoming unbearable. Everywhere on Earth the two sides are armed to the teeth and on the verge of disaster. Even in space they fight. And yet, here on the moon, you and the Russians live side by side in peace. We must know how you do it!"

Patton grinned. "You came on a very appropriate day, in that case. Well, let's see now . . . how to present the picture. You know that the environment here is extremely hostile: airless, low gravity . . ."

"The environment here on the moon," Torgeson objected, "is no more hostile than that of orbiting satellites. In fact, you have some gravity, solid ground, large buildings— many advantages that artificial satellites lack. Yet there has been fighting aboard the satellites—and not on the moon. Please don't waste my time with platitudes. This trip is costing the UN too much money. Tell me the truth."

Patton nodded. "I was going to. I've checked the information sent up by Earthbase: you've been cleared by the White House, the AEC, NASA and even the Pentagon."

"So?"

"Okay. The plain truth of the matter is . . ." A soft

chime from a small clock on Patton's desk interrupted him. "Oh. Excuse me."

Torgeson sat back and watched as Patton carefully began clearing off all the articles on his desk: the clock, calendar, phone, IN/OUT baskets, tobacco can and pipe rack, assorted papers and reports—all neatly and quickly placed in the desk drawers. Patton then stood up, walked to the filing cabinet, and closed the metal drawers firmly.

He stood in the middle of the room, scanned the scene with apparent satisfaction, and then glanced at his wrist-watch.

"Okay," he said to Torgeson. "Get down on your stomach."

"What?"

"Like this," the colonel said, and prostrated himself on the rubberized floor.

Torgeson stared at him.

"Come on! There's only a few seconds."

Patton reached up and grasped the UN man by the wrist. Unbelievingly, Torgeson got out of the chair, dropped to his hands and knees and finally flattened himself on the floor, next to the colonel.

For a second or two they stared at each other, saying nothing.

"Colonel, this is embar . . ."

The room exploded into a shattering volley of sounds.

Something—many somethings—ripped through the walls. The air hissed and whined above the heads of the two prostrate men. The metal desk and file cabinet rang eerily.

Torgeson squeezed his eyes shut and tried to worm into the floor. It was just like being shot at!

Abruptly, it was over.

The room was quiet once again, except for a faint hissing sound. Torgeson opened his eyes and saw the colonel getting up. The door was flung open. Three sergeants rushed in, armed with patching disks and tubes of cement. They dashed around the office sealing up the several hundred holes in the walls.

Only gradually, as the sergeants carried on their fevered, wordless task, did Torgeson realize that the walls were actually a quiltwork of patches. The room must have been riddled repeatedly!

He climbed slowly to his feet. "Meteors?" he asked, with a slight squeak in his voice.

Colonel Patton grunted negatively and resumed his seat behind the desk. It was pockmarked, Torgeson noticed now. So was the file cabinet.

"The window, in case you're wondering, is bulletproof."

Torgeson nodded and sat down.

"You see," the colonel said, "life is not as peaceful here as you think. Oh, we get along fine with the Russians—now. We've learned to live in peace. We had to."

"What were those . . . things?"

"Bullets."

"Bullets? But how . . ."

The sergeants finished their frenzied work, lined up at the door and saluted. Colonel Patton returned the salute and they turned as one man and left the office, closing the door quietly behind them.

"Colonel, I'm frankly bewildered."

"It's simple enough to understand. But don't feel too badly about being surprised. Only the top level of the Pentagon knows about this. And the president, of course. They had to let him in on it."

"What happened?"

Colonel Patton took his pipe rack and tobacco can out of a desk drawer and began filling one of the pipes. "You see," he began, "the Russians and us, we weren't always so peaceful here on the moon. We've had our incidents and scuffles, just as you have on Earth.''

"Go on."

"Well . . ." he struck a match and puffed the pipe alight ". . . shortly after we set up this dome for moonbase HQ, and the Reds set up theirs, we got into some real arguments." He waved the match out and tossed it into the open drawer.

"We're situated on the *Oceanus Procellarum*, you know. Exactly on the lunar equator. One of the biggest open spaces on this hunk of airless rock. Well, the Russians claimed they owned the whole damned *Oceanus*, since they were here first. We maintained the legal ownership was not established, since according to the UN Charter and the subsequent covenants . . ."

"Spare the legal details! Please, what happened?"

Patton looked slightly hurt. "Well . . . we started shooting at each other. One of their guards fired at one of our guards. They claim it was the other way around, of course. Anyway, within twenty minutes we were fighting a regular pitched battle, right out there between our base and theirs." He gestured toward the window.

"Can you fire guns in airless space?"

"Oh, sure. No problem at all. However, something unexpected came up.

"Only a few men got hit in the battle, none of them seriously. As in all battles, most of the rounds fired were clean misses."

"So?"

Patton smiled grimly. "So one of our civilian mathematicians started doodling. We had several thousand very-high-velocity bullets fired off. In airless space. No friction, you see. And under low-gravity conditions. They went right along past their targets . . ."

Recognition dawned on Torgeson's face. "Oh, no!"

"That's right. They whizzed right along, skimmed over the mountain tops, thanks to the curvature of this damned short lunar horizon, and established themselves in rather eccentric satellite orbits. Every hour or so they return to perigee . . . or, rather, periluna. And every twenty-seven days, periluna is right here, where the bullets originated. The moon rotates on its axis every twenty-seven days, you see. At any rate, when they come back this way, they shoot the living hell out of our base—and the Russian base, too, of course."

"But can't you . . ."

"Do what? Can't move the base. Authorization is tied up in the Joint Chiefs of Staff, and they can't agree on where to move it to. Can't bring up any special shielding material, because that's not authorized, either. The best thing we can do is to requisition all the computers we can and try to keep track of all the bullets. Their orbits keep changing, you know, every time they go through the bases. Air friction, puncturing walls, ricochets off the furniture . . . all that keeps changing their orbits enough to keep our computers busy full time."

"My God!"

"In the meantime, we don't dare fire off any more rounds. It would overburden the computers and we'd lose track of all of 'em. Then we'd have to spend every twenty-seventh day flat on our faces for hours."

Torgeson sat in numbed silence.

"But don't worry," Patton concluded with an optimistic, professional grin. "I've got a small detail of men secretly at work on the far side of the base—where the Reds can't see—building a stone wall. That'll stop the bullets. Then we'll fix those warmongers once and for all!"

Torgeson's face went slack. The chime sounded, muffled, from inside Patton's desk.

"Better get set to flatten out again. Here comes the second volley."

BLOOD OF TYRANTS

This story was something of an experiment. Two experiments, really: one in style, the other in marketing.

It was at one of the Milford Conferences in the early Sixties that Harlan Ellison conceived of the anthology he would eventually call Dangerous Visions. *In those days, the major market for science fiction short stories was among the magazines such as* Analog, F&SF, Galaxy, *and* Amazing. *Harlan and many other writers were dissatisfied with the limitations imposed by the magazine publishers.* Dangerous Visions *was Harlan's attempt to break out of the taboos and shibboleths of the magazine market, a gigantic anthology of stories that would not be bound by the conventions of newsstand morality.*

Dangerous Visions *was a huge success, and Harlan immediately set to work on a second such volume,* Again, Dangerous Visions. *Much to my surprise, he asked me to contribute a story to the new project. I was surprised because, even though Harlan and I were friends, I did not write the kind of story that I considered a "Dangerous Vision:" a story that went beyond the constraints of taste and subject matter published in the science fiction magazines.*

So I tried an experiment in style, an attempt to write a short story as if it were the shooting script for a film. The subject matter was something that I had been mulling over

168

*for years, the idea that our society is breeding barbarians
in the decaying ghettos of our major cities, and sooner or
later these barbarians are going to declare war against the
civilization that produced them. In a sense,* Blood of
Tyrants *is the dark side of Danny Romano, an examination
of what would have happened to the protagonist of* Escape!
if he had not been placed in that juvenile prison run by
SPECS *and Joe Tenny. Much the same train of thought
eventually led to a full-blown novel,* City of Darkness.

*I finished the short story and presented it to Harlan. He
hated it. He found every fault in it that it is possible to find
in Western literature, and then some. Chagrined, I told
him that the only other story I had on hand that had not yet
been published was one that I had just finished writing,* Zero
Gee. *Harlan loved that one, and published it in* Again,
Dangerous Visions. *Perhaps what he really wanted was not
so much a "Dangerous Vision," but a technologically solid
science fiction story, because that's what* Zero Gee *is.*

*Harlan and I remained friends, of course. We went on
to collaborate on a short story called* Brillo, *which led to a
lawsuit against the ABC television network, Paramount
Pictures, and a certain Hollywood producer. But that's
another story. For now, take a look at* Blood of Tyrants.

Still photo . . .

Danny Romano, switchblade in hand, doubling over as
the bullet hits slightly above his groin. His face going from
rage to shock. In the background other gang members
battling: tire chains, pipes, knives. Behind them a grimy
wall bearing a tattered political poster of some WASP
promising "EQUAL OPPORTUNITY FOR ALL."

*Fast montage of scenes, quick cutting from one to the next.
Background music: Gene Kelly singing, "You Are My
Lucky Star" . . .*

Long shot of the street. Kids still fighting. Danny crawling painfully on all fours. CUT TO tight shot of Danny, eyes fixed on the skinny kid who shot him, switchblade still in hand. The kid, goggleeyed, tries to shoot again, gun jams, he runs. CUT TO long shot again, police cruisers wailing into view, lights flashing. CUT TO Danny being picked up off the street by a pair of angry-faced cops. He struggles, feebly. Nightstick fractures skull, ends his struggling. CUT TO Danny being slid out of an ambulance at hospital emergency entrance. CUT TO green-gowned surgeons (backs visible only), working with cool indifference under the glaring overhead lights. CUT TO Danny lying unconscious in hospital bed. Head bandaged. IV stuck in arm. Private room. Uniformed cop opens door from hallway, admits two men. One is obviously a plainclothes policeman: stocky, hard-faced, tired-eyed. The other looks softer, unembittered, even smiles. He peers at Danny through rimless glasses, turns to the plainclothesman and nods.

Establishing shots . . .

Washington, D.C.: Washington Monument, Capitol building (seen from foreground of Northeast district slums), pickets milling around White House fence.

An office interior . . .

Two men are present. Brockhurst, sitting behind the desk, is paunchy, bald, hooked on cigarettes, frowning with professional skepticism. The other man, Hansen, is the rimless-glasses man from the hospital scene.

"I still don't like it; it's risky," says Brockhurst from behind his desk.

"What's the risk?" Hansen has a high, thin voice. "If we can rehabilitate these gang leaders, and then use them to rehabilitate their fellow delinquents, what's the risk?"

"It might not work."

"Then all we've lost is time and money." Brockhurst glowers, but says nothing.

Another montage of fast-cut scenes. Background music: Mahalia Jackson stomping, "He's Got the Whole World in His Hands" . . .

Danny, between two cops, walks out of the hospital side door and into a police van. Bandages gone now. CUT TO Danny being unloaded from van, still escorted, at airport. He is walked to a twin-engine plane. CUT TO interior of plane. Five youths are already aboard: two blacks, two Puerto Ricans, one white. Each is sitting, flanked by a white guard. A sixth guard takes Danny's arm at the entry-hatch and sits him in the only remaining pair of seats. Danny tries to look cool, but he's really delighted to be next to the window.

Interior of a "classroom" . . .

A large room. No windows, cream-colored walls, perfectly blank. About fifty boys are fidgeting in metal folding-chairs. Danny is sitting toward the rear. All the boys are now dressed in identical gray coveralls. Two uniformed guards stand by the room's only exit, a pair of large double doors.

The boys are mostly quiet; they don't know each other, they're trying to size up the situation. Hansen comes through the double doors (which a guard quickly closes behind him) and strides to the two-steps-up platform in the front of the room. He has a small microphone in his hand. He smiles and tries to look confident as he speaks.

"I'm not going to say much. I'd like to introduce myself. I'm Dr. Hansen. I'm not a medical doctor, I'm a specialist in education . . ."

A loud collective groan.

"No, no . . ." Hansen chuckles slightly. "No, it's not what you think. I work with teaching machines. You know, computers? Have you heard of them? Well, never mind . . ."

One of the kids stands up and starts for the door. A guard points a cattle prod toward the kid's chair. He gets the idea, goes back sullenly and sits down.

"You're here whether you like it or not," Hansen continues, minus the smile. "I'm confident that you'll soon like it. We're going to change you. We're going to make your lives worth living. And it doesn't matter in the slightest whether you like it or not. You'll learn to like it soon enough. No one's going to hurt you, unless you try to get rough. But we *are* going to change you."

Interior of the "reading room" . . .

A much smaller room. Danny and Hansen are alone in it. Same featureless plastic walls. No furniture except an odd-looking chair in the middle of the floor. It somewhat resembles an electric chair. Danny is trying to look contemptuous to cover up his fear.

"You ain't gettin' me in that!"

"It's perfectly all right; there's nothing here to hurt you. I'm merely going to determine how well you can read."

"I can read."

"Yes, of course." Doubtfully. "But how well? That's what I need to know."

"I don't see no books around."

"When you sit in the chair and the electrodes are attached to your scalp . . ."

"You gonna put those things on my head?"

"It's completely painless."

"No you ain't!"

Hansen speaks with great patience. "There's no use arguing about it. If I have to, I'll get the guards to strap

you in. But it will be better if you cooperate. Mr. Carter—
the one you call, uh, 'Spade,' I believe—he took the test
without hesitating a moment. You wouldn't want him to
know that we had to hold you down, would you?''

Danny glowers, but edges toward the chair. ''Mother-
humpin' sonofabitch . . .''

Series of fadeins and fadeouts . . .
Danny in the ''reading room,'' sitting in the chair,
cranium covered by electrode network. The wall before
him has become a projection screen, and he is reading the
words on it. MUSIC UNDER is Marine Corps Band playing
Cornell University *Alma Mater* (''Far Above Cayuga's
Waters . . .'')

DANNY (hesitantly): The car . . . hummed . . . cut . . .
quiet-ly to it-self . . .
FADEOUT
FADEIN

DANNY (tense with concentration): So my fellow Ameri-
cans . . . ask not what your country can do for you . . .
FADEOUT
FADEIN

DANNY: ''Surrender?'' he shouted. ''I have not yet begun
to fight!''
FADEOUT
FADEIN

DANNY (enjoying himself): Robin pulled his bowstring
back carefully, knowing that the Sheriff and all the towns-
people were watching him . . .
FADEOUT

Interior of Brockhurst's office . . .
Hansen is pacing impatiently before the desk, an intense
smile on his face.

''I tell you, it's succeeding beyond my fondest hopes!

Those boys are soaking it up like sponges. That Romano boy alone has absorbed more knowledge . . ."

Brockhurst is less than optimistic. "They're really learning?"

"Not only learning. They're beginning to change. The process is working. We're changing their attitudes, their value systems, everything. We're going to make useful citizens out of them!"

"All of them?"

"No, of course not. Only the best of them: half a dozen, I'd say, out of the fifty here—Romano, 'Spade' Carter, three or four others. At least six out of fifty, better than one out of ten. And this is just the first batch! When we start processing larger numbers of them . . ."

Brockhurst cuts Hansen short with a gesture. "Do you actually think these—students—of yours will go back to their old neighborhoods and start to rehabilitate their fellow gang members?"

"Yes, of course they will. They'll have to! They're being programmed for it!"

Interior of library . . .

Danny is sitting at a reading table, absorbed in a book. Bookshelves line the walls. A lumpy-faced redhead sits one table away, also reading. Hansen enters quietly, walks to Danny. "Hello Danny. How's it going today?"

Danny looks up and smiles pleasantly. "Fine, Mr. Hansen."

"I just got the computer's scoring of your economics exam. You got the highest mark in the class."

"Did I? Great. I was worried about it. Economics is kind of hard to grasp. Those booster pills you gave me must have helped."

"You did extremely well. . . . What are you reading?"

"Biography, by Harold Lamb. It's about Genghis Khan."

Hansen nods. "I see, look, it's about time we started thinking about what you're going to do when you go back home. Why don't you drop over to my office tonight, after supper?"

"Okay."

"See you then."

"Right."

Hansen moves away, toward the other boy. Danny closes his book, stands up. He turns to the bookshelf directly behind him and reaches unhesitatingly for another volume. He puts the two books under his arm and starts for the door. The title of the second book is *Mein Kampf*.

Brockhurst's office . . .

Six boys are standing in front of Brockhurst's desk, the six Hansen spoke of. They are now dressed in casual slacks, shirts, sport coats. Hansen is sitting beside the desk, beaming at them. Brockhurst, despite himself, looks impressed.

"You boys understand how important your mission is." Brockhurst is lapsing into a military tone. "You can save your friends a lot of grief . . . perhaps save their lives."

Danny nods gravely. "It's not just our friends that we'll be saving. It'll be our cities, all the people in them, our whole country."

"Exactly."

Hansen turns to Brockhurst. "They've been well-trained. They're ready to begin their work."

"Very well. Good luck, boys. We're counting on you."

Exterior shot, a city street . . .

Mid-afternoon, a hot summer day. A taxi pulls to the curb of the dingy, sun-baked street. Danny steps out, ducks down to pay the cabbie. He drives away quickly. Danny stands alone, in front of a magazine/tobacco store.

He is dressed as he was in Brockhurst's office. Taking off the jacket, he looks slowly up and down the street. Deserted, except for a few youngsters sitting, listlessly, in the shade. With a shrug, he steps to the store.

Interior, the store . . .

Magazine racks on one side of the narrow entrance; store counter featuring cigarettes and candy on the other. No one at the counter. Overhead, a battered fan drones ineffectually. Farther back, a grimy table surrounded by rickety chairs. Three boys, two girls, all Danny's age, sit there. The boys in jeans and tee shirts, girls in shorts and sleeveless tops. They turn as he shuts the door, gape at him.

"Nobody going to say hello?" He grins at them.

"Danny!"

They bounce out of the chairs, knocking one over.

"We thought you was dead!"

"Or in jail . . . nobody knew what happened to you . . ."

"It's been almost a year!"

They cluster around him as he walks slowly back toward the table. But no one touches him.

"What happened to ya?"

"You look . . . different, sort of." The girl gestures vaguely.

"What'd they do to you? Where were you?"

Danny sits down. "It's a long story. Somebody get me a coke, huh? Who's been running things, Marco? Find him for me, I want to see him. And, Speed . . . get word to the Bloodhounds. I want to see their Prez . . . is it still Waslewski? And the one who shot me . . ."

"A war council?"

Danny smiles. "Sort of. Tell them that, if that's what it'll take to bring them here."

*   *   *

Interior, the back of the store . . .

It is night. Danny sits at the table, his shirt-sleeves rolled up, watching the front door. Two boys flank him: Marco, slim and dark, his thin face very serious; and Speed, bigger, lighter, obviously excited but managing to keep it contained. Both boys are trying to hide their nervousness with cigarettes. The door opens, and a trio of youths enter. Their leader, Waslewski, is stocky, blond, intense. His eyes cover the whole store with a flick. Behind him is the skinny kid who shot Danny, and a burlier boy who's trying to look cool and menacing.

"Come on in," Danny calls from his chair. "Nobody's going to hurt you."

Waslewski fixes his eyes on Danny and marches to the table. He takes a chair. His cohorts remain standing behind him. "So you ain't dead after all."

"Not yet."

"Guess you're pretty lucky."

Danny grins. "Luckier than you'll ever know." Nodding toward the boy who shot him, "What's his name?"

"O'Banion."

"All right, O'Banion. You put a bullet in me; I lived through it. You were doing your job for the Bloodhounds; I'm doing my job for the Champions. Nothing personal and no hard feelings on my part."

Waslewski's eyes narrow. "What're you pullin'? I thought this was gonna be a war council . . ."

"It is, but not the regular kind." Danny leans forward, spreads his hands on the table. "Know where I've been the past ten months? In Washington, in a special school the government set up, just to handle jay-dees. They pump knowledge into you with a computer . . . just like opening your head and sticking a hose in it."

The other boys, Bloodhounds and Champions alike, squirm a bit.

"You know what they taught me? They taught me we're nuts to fight each other. That's right . . . gangs fighting each other is strictly crazy. What's it get us? Lumps, is all. And dead."

Waslewski is obviously disgusted. "You gonna preach a sermon?"

"Damned right I am. You know why the gangs fight each other? Because *they* keep us up tight. They've got the money, they've got the power that runs this city, and they make sure we gangs stay down in the garbage. By fighting each other, we keep them sitting high and running the big show."

"They? Who the hell's they?"

"The people who run this city. The fat cats. The rich cats. The ones who've got limousines and broads with diamonds hanging from each tit. They *own* this city. They own the buildings and the people in the buildings. They own the cops. They own us."

"Nobody owns me!" says the burly kid behind Waslewski.

"Shuddup." Waslewski is frowning with thought now, trying to digest Danny's words.

"Look," Danny says. "This city is filled with money. It's filled with broads and good food and everything a guy could want for the rest of his life. What do we get out of it? Shit, that's what! And why? Because we let them run us, that's why. We fight each other over a crummy piece of turf, a couple of blocks of lousy street, while *they* sit back in plush restaurants and penthouses with forty-two-inch broads bending over them."

"So . . . what'd you expect us to do?"

"Stop fighting each other. Make the gangs work together to take over this city. We can do it! We can crack this city wide open, like a peanut. Instead of fighting each other, we can conquer this whole fucking city and run it for ourselves!"

Waslewski sags back in his seat. The other boys look at each other, amazed, unbelieving, yet obviously attracted by the idea.

"Great . . . real cool." Waslewski's voice and face exude sarcasm. "And what do the cops do? Sit back and let us take over? And what about the rest of the people? There's millions of 'em."

"Listen! We know how to fight. What we've got to do is get all the gangs together and fight together, like an army. It's just a matter of using the right strategy, the right tactics. We can do it. But we've got to work together. Not just the Bloodhounds and the Champions, but *all* the gangs! All of us, together, striking all at once. We can rack up the fuzz and take this town in a single night. They'll never know what hit them."

Marco objects, "But Danny, we can't . . ."

"Look, I know it'll take a lot of work. I figure we'll need two years, at least. We've got to get our guys spotted at key places all over the city: the power plants, all the radio and TV stations. We'll need guys inside the National Guard armories, inside the precinct stations, if we can do it. It'll mean a lot of guys will have to take jobs, learn to work hard for a couple years. But in the end, we'll have this city for ourselves!"

"You got it all figured out?"

"To the last inch."

Waslewski unconsciously pushes his chair slightly back from the table. He glances at his two lieutenants; they are wide-eyed.

"I gotta think about this. . . . I can't say yes or no just like that."

"Okay, you think about it. But don't spill it to anybody except your top boys. And remember, I'm going to be talking to all the gangs around here . . . and then to the gangs in the rest of the city. They'll go for it, I know. Don't get yourself left out.''

Waslewski gets up slowly. ''Okay, I'll get back to you right away. I think you can count us in.'' His aides nod agreement.

''Good. Now we're rolling.'' Danny gets up and sticks out his hand. Waslewski hesitates a beat, and then—acting rather stunned—shakes hands with Danny.

Montage of scenes. Background music: ''The Army Caisson Song'' . . .

Danny escorting Waslewski and two other boys into a Job Corps training-center office. CUT TO half-a-dozen boys sitting in a personnel-office waiting room. CUT TO a boy signing up in a National Guard armory.

Interior, Brockhurst's office . . .

Hansen is sitting on the front inch of the chair beside the desk, tense with excitement.

''It's a brilliant idea. Romano is working out better than any of his classmates, and this idea simply proves it!''

Brockhurst looks wary, probing for the weak point. ''Why's he doing it? What's the sense of having gang members formed into a police auxiliary?''

''Sense? It's perfect sense. The boys can work hand-in-hand with the police, clue them in on trouble before it erupts into violence. The police can get to know the boys and the boys will get to know the police. Mutual exposure will breed mutual trust and confidence. Instead of working against each other, they'll be working together. With violence between the gangs and the police dwindling, a major source of trouble will be eliminated . . .''

''It just doesn't sound right to me. I can't picture those young punks turning into volunteer cops.''

''But it's worth a try, isn't it? What do we have to lose?''

Brockhurst makes a sour face. "I suppose you're right. It's worth a try."

Interior, a one-room apartment . . .

The room is small but neat. The bed in the corner is made up in military style. The walls are covered with street maps of the city, over which are colored markings showing the territory of each gang. Danny sits at the only table, together with five other boys. One is a black, two others are Puerto Rican. The table is heaped high with papers.

"Okay," Danny says, "the Hellcats will handle the power station in their turf and the precinct house. And they've offered to put eight of their guys on our task force for the downtown area. What else?" He looks around at his aides.

The black says, "The Hawks have a beef. They claim the Jaguars have been cuttin' into their turf pretty regular for the past month. They've tried talkin' it out with 'em, but no dice. I tried talkin' to both sides, but they're up pretty tight about it."

Danny frowns. "Those damned Hawks have been screwing up for months."

"They're gonna rumble 'less you can stop 'em."

Thoughtfully, "There hasn't been a rumble all winter. Even the newspapers are starting to notice it. Maybe it'd be a good idea to let them fight it out . . . so long as nobody winds up spilling his guts about us to the squares."

"Somebody's gonna get hurt bad if they rumble. Lotta bad blood between them two gangs."

"I know." Danny thinks it over for a moment. "Look, tell them if they've got to rumble, do it without artillery. No guns, nothing that'll tip the squares to what we've got stashed away."

"Okay."

*   *   *

Interior, a Congressman's office . . .

The room is high-ceilinged, ornately decorated. The Congressman's broad desk is covered with mementos, framed photographs, neat piles of papers. The Congressman, himself, is in his mid-forties, just starting to turn fleshy. Sitting before him are Brockhurst, Hansen and—in a neat business suit—Danny.

"And so, with the annual appropriation coming up," Brockhurst is saying, "I thought you should have a personal report on the program."

The Congressman nods. "From all I've heard, it seems to be highly successful."

"It is." Brockhurst allows himself to smile. "Of course, this is only the beginning; only a half-dozen cities have been touched so far, although we have a hundred more boys in training at the moment. But I think you can judge the results for yourself."

Hansen interrupts. "And I hope you can realize the necessity for keeping the program secret, for the time being. Premature publicity . . ."

"Could ruin everything. I understand." Turning his gaze to Danny. "And this is your star pupil, eh?"

Danny smiles. "I . . . uh, Sir, I'd merely like to add my thanks for what this program has done for me and my friends. It's just like Dr. Hansen has been saying: all we boys need is some training and opportunity."

Interior, a fire house . . .

A boy sits at a tiny desk in the deserted garage. Behind him are the powerful fire trucks. No one else is in sight. Through the window alongside the desk, snow is falling on a city street. The window has a holiday wreath on it.

The boy is thumbing through the big calendar on the desk. He flips past December and into the coming year.

He stops on July, notes that the Fourth falls on a Sunday. Smiling, he puts a red circle around the date.

Interior, a Congressional hearing room . . .

The committee members, half of them chatting with each other, sit at a long table in the front of the room. Brockhurst is sitting at the witness's desk, reading from a prepared text. Hansen sits beside him. The visitors' pews are completely empty, and a uniformed guard stands impassively at the door.

"Mr. Chairman, since the inception of this program, juvenile gang violence has decreased dramatically in five of the six cities where we have placed rehabilitated subjects. In one city, gang violence has dwindled to truly miniscule proportions. The boys are being rehabiliated, using Job Corps and other OEO facilities to train themselves for useful work, and then taking on—and keeping—full-time jobs." Brockhurst looks up from his text. "Mr. Chairman, if I may be allowed a new twist on an old saying, we're beating their switchblades into plowshares."

Interior, Danny's apartment . . .

Danny is pacing angrily across the room, back and forth. Three abject youths sit on the bed in the corner. At the table sit Marco and Speed.

"He nearly blew it!" Danny's voice is not loud, but clearly close to violence. "You stupid ass-holes can't keep your own people happy. He gets sore over a bitch and goes to the cops! If we didn't have a man in the precinct station last night, the whole plan would've been blown sky-high!"

One of the boys on the bed says, miserably, "But we didn't know . . ."

"That's even worse! You're supposed to know. You're the Prez of the Belters, you're supposed to know every breath your people take."

"Well . . . whaddawe do now?"

"You do nothing! You go back to your hole and sit tight. Don't even go to the can unless you get the word from me. Understand? If the cops tumble to us because you've got one half-wit who can't keep his mouth shut, every gang in the city is going to be after your blood. And they'll get it!"

Danny motions them to the door. They leave quickly. He turns to his lieutenants.

"Speed, you know anybody in the Belters who can do a good job as Prez?"

Speed hesitates only a beat before answering, "Yeah . . . kid named Molie. Sharp. He'd keep 'em in line okay."

"All right. Good. Get him here. Tonight. If I like him, we get that ass-hole who just left and his half-wit fink to kill each other. Then Molie becomes their President."

"Kill each other?"

"Right. Can't let the fink hang around. And we can't make the cops worry that he was killed because he knew something. And that ass-hole is no good for us. So we make it look like they had a fight over the bitch. And fast, before something else happens. We've only got a month to go."

Speed nods. "Okay, Danny. I'm movin' . . ." He is already halfway to the door.

Exterior, night . . .

A park in the city. Holiday crowd is milling around. City skyline is visible over the trees. A band finishes the final few bars of "Stars and Stripes Forever." A hush. Then the small thud of a skyrocket being launched, and overhead, a red-white-and-blue firework blossoms against the night sky. The crowd gives its customary gasp of delight.

Danny stands at the edge of the crowd. In the flickering light of the fireworks, he looks at his wrist watch, then turns to Speed and Marco and nods solemnly. They hurry off into the darkness.

Exterior, tollbooth across a major bridge . . .
A car full of youths pulls up at one of the three open tollgates. The boys spill out, guns in hands, club down the nearest tollbooth collector. The next closest one quickly raises his hands. The third collector starts to run, but he's shot down.

Interior, National Guard armory . . .
One hugely grinning boy in Army fatigues is handing out automatic weapons to a line-up of other boys, from a rack that has an unlocked padlock hanging from its open door.

Interior, subway train . . .
Four adults—two old ladies, a middle-aged man and a younger man—ride along sleepily. The train stops, the doors open. A combat team of twenty boys steps in through the three open doors. Their dress is ragged, but each boy carries a newly-oiled automatic weapon. The adults gasp. One boy yanks open the motorman's cubicle door and drags out the portly motorman. Another boy steps into the cubicle and shuts the doors. The train starts up again with the boys wordlessly standing, guns ready, while the adults huddle in a corner of the car.

Interior, police precinct station . . .
The desk sergeant is yawning. The radio operator, in the back of the room, is thumbing through a magazine. A boy—one of the police auxiliary—sits quietly on a bench by the door. He gets up, stretches, opens the front door. In

pour a dozen armed boys. The desk sergeant freezes in mid-yawn. Two boys sprint toward the radio operator. He starts to grab for his microphone, but a blast of fire cuts him down.

Interior, a city power station . . .

Over the rumbling, whining noise of the generators, a boy walks up to his supervisor, who's sitting in front of a board full of dials and switches, and pokes a pistol in his face. The man, startled, gets slowly out of his chair. Two other boys appear and take the man away. The first boy sits in the chair and reaches for the phone hanging on the instrument board.

Interior, newspaper office . . .

There is no sign of the usual news staff. All the desks are manned by boys, with Danny sitting at one of the desks in the center of the complex. Boys are answering phones, general hubbub of many simultaneous conversations. The mood is excited, almost jubilant. A few boys stand at the windows behind Danny, with carbines and automatic rifles in their hands. But they look relaxed.

Speed comes over to Danny from another desk, carrying a bundle of papers. "Here's the latest reports: every damned precinct station in town. We got 'em all! And the armories, the power stations, the TV studios. All the bridges and tunnels are closed down. Everything!"

Danny doesn't smile. "What about City Hall?"

"Took some fighting, but Shockie says we've got it nailed down. A few diehards in the cellblock, that's all. Our guys are usin' their own tear gas on 'em."

"The Mayor and the Councilmen?"

"The Mayor's outta town for the holidays, but we got

most of the Councilmen, and the Police Chief, and the local FBI guys, too!''

Danny glances at his watch. "Okay, time for Phase Two. Round up every cop in town. On duty or off. Knock their doors down if you have to, pull them out of bed. But get them all into cells before dawn.''

"Right!" Speed's grin is enormous.

Exterior, sun rising over city skyline . . .

From the air, the city appears normal. Nothing out of the ordinary. No fires, no milling crowds, not even much motor traffic on the streets. ZOOM TO the toll plaza at one of the city's main bridges. A lone sedan is stopped at an impromptu roadblock, made up of old cars and trucks strung lengthwise across the traffic lanes. A boy with an automatic rifle in the crook of one arm is standing atop a truck cab, waving the amazed automobile driver back into the city. On the other side of the tollbooth, an oil truck and moving van are similarly stopped before another roadblock.

Interior, a TV studio . . .

Danny is sitting at a desk, the hot lights on him. He is now wearing an Army shirt, open at the collar. A Colt automatic rests on the desk before him. Adults are manning the cameras, mike boom, lights, control booth; but armed boys stand behind each one.

"Good morning," Danny allows himself to smile pleasantly. "Don't bother trying to change channels. I'm on every station in town. Your city has been taken over. It's now our city. My name is Danny Romano; I'm your new Mayor. Also your Police Chief, Fire Chief, District Attorney, Judge, and whatever other jobs I want to take on. The kids you've been calling punks, jaydees . . . the kids from the street gangs . . . we've taken over your city. You'll do what we tell you from now on. If you cooperate,

nobody's going to hurt you. If you don't, you'll be shot.
Life is going to be a lot simpler for all of us from now on.
Do as you're told and you'll be okay.''

Interior, Brockhurst's office . . .

General uproar. Brockhurst is screaming into a telephone.
A couple dozen people are shouting at each other, waving
their arms. Hansen is prostrate on the couch.

''No, I don't know anything more about it than you
do!'' Brockhurst's voice is near frenzy. His shirt is open at
the neck, tie ripped off, jacket rumpled, face sweaty.
''How the hell do I know? The FBI . . . the Army . . .
somebody's got to do *something*!''

His secretary fights her way through the crowd. ''Mr.
Brockhurst . . . on line three . . . it's the *President*!''

Every voice hushes. Brockhurst slams the phone down,
takes his hand off it, looks at it for a long moment. Then,
shakily, he punches a button at the phone's base and lifts
the receiver.

''Yessir. Yes, this is Brockhurst. . . . No, sir, I have no
idea of how this came about . . . it . . . it seems to be
genuine, sir. Yes, we've tried to communicate with
them. . . . Yessir, Romano is one of our, eh, graduates.
No, sir. No, I don't . . . but . . . I agree, we can't let
them get away with it. The Army? Isn't there any other
way? I'm afraid he's got several million people bottled up
in that city, and he'll use them as hostages. If the Army
attacks, he might start executing them wholesale.''

Hansen props himself up on one elbow and speaks
weakly, ''Let me go to them. Let me talk to Danny.
Something's gone wrong . . . something . . .''

Brockhurst waves him silent with a furious gesture.
''Yes, Mr. President, I agree. If they won't surrender
peacefully, then there's apparently no alternative. But if
they fight the Army, a lot of innocent people are going to

be hurt. . . . Yes, I know you can't just . . . but . . . no
other way, yes, I see. Very well, sir, you are the
Commander-in-Chief. Yessir. Of course, sir. Before the
day is out. Yessir . . .''

Exterior, city streets . . .

Tanks rumbling down the streets. Kids firing from
windows, throwing Molotov cocktails. One tank bursts
into flames. The one behind it fires its cannon pointblank
into a building: the entire structure explodes and collapses.
Soldiers crouching in doorways, behind burned-out auto-
mobiles, firing at kids running crouched-down a half-block
away. Two boys go sprawling. A soldier kicks a door in
and tosses in a grenade. A few feet up the street, a teenage
girl lies dead. A tank rolls past a children's playground,
while a dazed old man sits bloody-faced on the curbstone,
watching. Flames and smoke and the constant pock-pock-
pock sound of automatic rifles, punctuated by explosions.

No picture, sound only . . .

The sounds of a phone being dialed, the click of circuits,
the buzz of a phone ringing, another click as it is picked
up.

"Yeah?"

"Hey, Spade, that you?"

"It's me."

"This is Midget."

"I know the voice, Midge."

"You see what Danny did?"

"I see what happened to him. How many dead, how
many thousands? Or is it millions?"

"They ain't tellin'. Gotta be millions, though. Whole
damned city's flattened. Army must've lost fifty thousand
men all by itself."

"They killed Danny."

"They claim they killed him, but I ain't seen pictures of his body yet."

"It's a mess, all right."

"Yeah. Listen . . . they got Federal men lookin' for us now, you know?"

"I know. All Danny's 'classmates' are in for it."

"You gonna be okay?"

"They won't find me, don't worry. There's plenty of places to hide and plenty of people to hide me."

"Good. Now listen, this mess of Danny's oughtta teach us a lesson."

"Damned right."

"Yeah. We gotta work together now. When we make our move, it's gotta be in all the cities. Not just one. Every big city in the god damn country."

"Gonna take a long time to do it."

"I know, but we can make it. And when we do, they can't send the Army against every big city all at once."

"Specially if we take Washington and get *their* Prez."

"Right. Okay, gotta run now. Stay loose and keep in touch."

"Check. See you in Washington one of these days."

"You bet your sweet ass."

THE NEXT LOGICAL STEP

In case you skipped the introduction to this book, I will repeat that the Pentagon is developing very sophisticated computer programs to help the Joint Chiefs of Staff to forecast what the world will be like over the next few decades. There are many problems with such computer "world models." The Next Logical Step, which was written more than twenty years ago, examines one such problem—and its solution.

"I don't really see where this problem has anything to do with me," the CIA man said. "And, frankly, there are a lot of more important things I could be doing."

Ford, the physicist, glanced at General LeRoy. The general had that quizzical expression on his face, the look that meant he was about to do something decisive.

"Would you like to see the problem firsthand?" the general asked, innocently.

The CIA man took a quick look at his wrist watch, "Okay, if it doesn't take too long. It's late enough already."

"It won't take very long, will it, Ford?" the general said, getting out of his chair.

"Not very long," Ford agreed. "Only a lifetime."

The CIA man grunted as they went to the doorway and left the general's office. Going down the dark, deserted hallway, their footsteps echoed hollowly.

"I can't overemphasize the seriousness of the problem," General LeRoy said to the CIA man. "Eight ranking members of the General Staff have either resigned their commissions or gone straight to the violent ward after just one session with the computer."

The CIA man scowled. "Is this area Secure?"

General LeRoy's face turned red. "This entire building is as Secure as any edifice in the Free World, mister. And it's empty. We're the only living people inside here at this hour. I'm not taking any chances."

"Just want to be sure."

"Perhaps if I explain the computer a little more," Ford said, changing the subject, "you'll know what to expect."

"Good idea," said the man from CIA.

"We told you that this is the most modern, most complex and delicate computer in the world . . . nothing like it has ever been attempted before—anywhere."

"I know that They don't have anything like it," The CIA man agreed.

"And you also know, I suppose, that it was built to simulate actual war situations. We fight wars in this computer . . . wars with missiles and bombs and gas. Real wars, complete down to the tiniest detail. The computer tells us what will actually happen to every missile, every city, every man . . . who dies, how many planes are lost, how many trucks will fail to start on a cold morning, whether a battle is won or lost . . ."

General LeRoy interrupted. "The computer runs these analyses for both sides, so we can see what's happening to them, too."

The CIA man gestured impatiently. "War-games simulations aren't new. You've been doing them for years."

"Yes, but this machine is different," Ford pointed out. "It not only gives a much more detailed war game. It's the next logical step in the development of machine-simulated war games." He hesitated dramatically.

"Well, what is it?"

"We've added a variation of the electroencephalograph . . ."

The CIA man stopped walking. "The electro-what?"

"Electroencephalograph. You know, a recording device that reads the electrical patterns of your brain. Like the electrocardiograph."

"Oh."

"But you see, we've given the EEG a reverse twist. Instead of using a machine that makes a recording of the brain's electrical wave output, we've developed a device that will take the computer's readout tapes and turn them into electrical patterns that are put *into* your brain!"

"I don't get it."

General LeRoy took over. "You sit at the machine's control console. A helmet is placed over your head. You set the machine in operation. You *see* the results."

"Yes," Ford went on. "Instead of reading rows of figures from the computer's printer . . . you actually see the war being fought. Complete visual and auditory hallucinations. You can watch the progress of the battles, and as you change strategy and tactics you can see the results before your eyes."

"The idea, originally, was to make it easier to the General Staff to visualize strategic situations," General LeRoy said.

"But every one who's used the machine has either resigned his commission or gone insane," Ford added.

The CIA man cocked an eye at LeRoy. "You've used the computer."

"Correct."

"And you have neither resigned nor cracked up."

General LeRoy nodded. "I called you in."

Before the CIA man could comment, Ford said, "The computer's right inside this doorway. Let's get this over with while the building is still empty."

* * *

They stepped in. The physicist and the general showed the CIA man through the room-filling rows of massive consoles.

"It's all transistorized and subminiaturized, of course," Ford explained. "That's the only way we could build so much detail into the machine and still have it small enough to fit inside a single building.".

"A single building?"

"Oh yes; this is only the control section. Most of this building is taken up by the circuits, the memory banks and the rest of it."

"Hm-m-m."

They showed him finally to a small desk, studded with control buttons and dials. The single spotlight above the desk lit it brilliantly, in harsh contrast to the semidarkness of the rest of the room.

"Since you've never run the computer before," Ford said, "General LeRoy will do the controlling. You just sit and watch what happens."

The general sat in one of the well-padded chairs and donned a grotesque headgear that was connected to the desk by a half-dozen wires. The CIA man took his chair, slowly.

When they put one of the bulky helmets on him, he looked up at them, squinting a little in the bright light. "This . . . this isn't going to . . . well, do me any damage, is it?"

"My goodness no," Ford said. "You mean mentally? No, of course not. You're not on the General Staff, so it shouldn't . . . it won't . . . affect you the way it did the others. Their reaction had nothing to do with the computer *per se* . . ."

"Several civilians have used the computer with no ill effects," General LeRoy said. "Ford has used it many times."

The CIA man nodded, and they closed the transparent

visor over his face. He sat there and watched General LeRoy press a series of buttons, then turn a dial.

"Can you hear me?" The general's voice came muffled through the helmet.

"Yes," he said.

"All right. Here we go. You're familiar with Situation One-Two-One? That's what we're going to be seeing."

Situation One-Two-One was a standard war game. The CIA man was well acquainted with it. He watched the general flip a switch, then sit back and fold his arms over his chest. A row of lights on the desk console began blinking on and off, one, two, three . . . down to the end of the row, then back to the beginning again, on and off, on and off . . .

And then, somehow, he could see it!

He was poised, incredibly, somewhere in space, and he could see it all in a funny, blurry-double-sighted, dream-like way. He seemed to be seeing several pictures and hearing many voices, all at once. It was all mixed up, and yet it made a weird kind of sense.

For a panicked instant he wanted to rip the helmet off his head. *It's only an illusion*, he told himself, forcing calm on his unwilling nerves. *Only an illusion*.

But it seemed strangely real.

He was watching the Gulf of Mexico. He could see Florida off to his right, and the arching coast of the southeastern United States. He could even make out the Rio Grande River.

Situation One-Two-One started, he remembered, with the discovery of missile-bearing Enemy submarines in the Gulf. Even as he watched the whole area—as though perched on a satellite—he could see, underwater and close-up, the menacing shadowy figure of a submarine gliding through the crystal-blue sea.

He saw, too, a patrol plane as it spotted the submarine and sent an urgent radio warning.

The underwater picture dissolved in a bewildering burst of bubbles. A missile had been launched. Within seconds, another burst—this time a nuclear depth charge—utterly destroyed the submarine.

It was confusing. He was everyplace at once. The details were overpowering, but the total picture was agonizingly clear.

Six submarines fired missiles from the Gulf of Mexico. Four were immediately sunk, but too late. New Orleans, St. Louis and three Air Force bases were obliterated by hydrogen-fusion warheads.

The CIA man was familiar with the opening stages of the war. The first missile fired at the United States was the signal for whole fleets of missiles and bombers to launch themselves at the Enemy. It was confusing to see the world at once; at times he could not tell if the fireball and mushroom cloud was over Chicago or Shanghai, New York or Novosibersk, Baltimore or Budapest.

It did not make much difference, really. They all got it in the first few hours of the war; as did London and Moscow, Washington and Peking, Detroit and Delhi, and many, many more.

The defensive systems on all sides seemed to operate well, except that there were never enough antimissiles. Defensive systems were expensive compared to attack rockets. It was cheaper to build a deterrent than to defend against it.

The missiles flashed up from submarines and railway cars, from underground silos and stratospheric jets; secret ones fired off automatically when a certain airbase command-post ceased beaming out a restraining radio signal. The defensive systems were simply overloaded. And when the bombs ran out, the missiles carried dust and germs and gas. On and on. For six days and six firelit nights. Launch, boost, coast, reenter, death.

And now it was over, the CIA man thought. The missiles were all gone. The airplanes were exhausted. The nations that had built the weapons no longer existed. By all the rules he knew of, the war should have been ended.

Yet the fighting did not end. The machine knew better. There were still many ways to kill an enemy. Time-tested ways. There were armies fighting in four continents, armies that had marched overland, or splashed ashore from the sea, or dropped out of the skies.

Incredibly, the war went on. When the tanks ran out of gas, and the flame throwers became useless, and even the prosaic artillery pieces had no more rounds to fire, there were still simple guns and even simpler bayonets and swords.

The proud armies, the descendants of the Alexanders and Caesars and Timujins and Wellingtons and Grants and Rommels, relived their evolution in reverse.

The war went on. Slowly, inevitably, the armies split apart into smaller and smaller units, until the tortured countryside that so recently had felt the impact of nuclear war once again knew the tread of bands of armed marauders. The tiny savage groups, stranded in alien lands, far from the homes and families that they knew to be destroyed, carried on a mockery of war, lived off the land, fought their own countrymen if the occasion suited, and revived the ancient terror of hand-wielded, personal, one-head-at-a-time killing.

The CIA man watched the world disintegrate. Death was an individual business now, and none the better for no longer being mass-produced. In agonized fascination he saw the myriad ways in which a man might die. Murder was only one of them. Radiation, disease, toxic gases that lingered and drifted on the once-innocent winds, and—finally—the most efficient destroyer of them all: starvation.

Five billion people (give or take a meaningless hundred-million) lived on the planet Earth when the war began. Now, with the tenuous thread of civilization burned away, most of those who were not killed by the fighting itself succumbed, inexorably, to starvation or disease.

Not everyone died, of course. Life went on. Some were lucky.

A long darkness settled on the world. Life went on for a few, a pitiful few, a bitter, hateful, suspicious, savage few. Cities became pestholes. Books became fuel. Knowledge died. Civilization was completely gone from the planet Earth.

The helmet was lifted slowly off his head. The CIA man found that he was too weak to raise his arms and help. He was shivering and damp with perspiration.

"Now you see," Ford said quietly, "why the military men cracked up when they used the computer."

General LeRoy, even, was pale. "How can a man with any conscience at all direct a military operation when he knows that *that* will be the consequence?"

The CIA man struck up a cigarette and pulled hard on it. He exhaled sharply. "Are all the war games . . . like that? Every plan?"

"Some are worse," Ford said. "We picked an average one for you. Even some of the 'brushfire' games get out of hand and end up like that."

"So . . . what do you intend to do? Why did you call me in? What can *I* do?"

"You're with CIA," the general said. "Don't you handle espionage?"

"Yes, but what's that got to do with it?"

The general looked at him. "It seems to me that the next logical step is to make damned certain that *They* get the plans to this computer . . . and fast!"

THE SHINING ONES

If you have read my book of advice to writers, Notes To a Science Fiction Writer, *then you have seen a structural analysis of this story,* The Shining Ones. *Rather than repeat that analysis here, let me tell you how censorship affects the publishing business.*

The Shining Ones *was originally written at the request of a publishing house which wanted to start a series of short novels for "reluctant readers:" that is, people of young adult age who had not learned to read much beyond the grammar-school level. The basic ideas in the plot, and the characterizations of the main personages in the story, were carefully reviewed and approved by the book company's editor. When I delivered the manuscript the editor reported, at first, that she liked it very much. But she had to get approval from a board of "experts" that the publisher had hired: a group of teachers and psychologists whose main function, as I understood it, was to decide if the story would be readable by its intended audience.*

The "experts" approved the story, but with a catch. They felt that the hero's fatal disease was too depressing; that part of the story should be dropped. When I was informed of this by the editor, I pointed out that Charles Dickens' A Christmas Carol *would hardly be the memorable story it is if Tiny Tim had suffered merely from acne, instead of a crippling, life-threatening disease. No use. The "experts" were adamant. Although I was not allowed to meet them or argue my case with them, their decision was final: Change the story or have it rejected.*

I withdrew the story and published it elsewhere. As far as I know, no one has ever suffered mental or emotional disability because of this story. Particularly if they read to the end of it!

1

Johnny Donato lay flat on his belly in the scraggly grass and watched the strangers' ship carefully.

It was resting on the floor of the desert, shining and shimmering in the bright New Mexico sunlight. The ship was huge and round like a golden ball, like the sun itself. It touched the ground as lightly as a helium-filled balloon. In fact, Johnny wasn't sure that it really did touch the ground at all.

He squinted his eyes, but he still couldn't tell if the ship was really in contact with the sandy desert flatland. It cast no shadow, and it seemed to glow from some energies hidden inside itself. Again, it reminded Johnny of the sun.

But these people didn't come from anywhere near our sun, Johnny knew. *They come from a world of a different star.*

He pictured in his mind how small and dim the stars look at night. Then he glanced at the powerful glare of the sun. *How far away the stars must be!* And these strangers have travelled all that distance to come here. To Earth. To New Mexico. To this spot in the desert.

Johnny knew he should feel excited. Or maybe scared.

But all he felt right now was curious. And hot. The sun was beating down on the rocky ledge where he lay watching, baking his bare arms and legs. He was used to the desert sun. It never bothered him.

But today something was burning inside Johnny. At first he thought it might be the sickness. Sometimes it made him feel hot and weak. But no, that wasn't it. He had the sickness, there was nothing anyone could do about that. But it didn't make him feel this way.

This thing inside him was something he had never felt before. Maybe it was the same kind of thing that made his father yell in fury, ever since he had been laid off from his job. Anger was part of it, and maybe shame, too. But there was something else, something Johnny couldn't put a name to.

So he lay there flat on his belly, wondering about himself and the strange ship from the stars. He waited patiently, like his Apache friends would, while the sun climbed higher in the bright blue sky and the day grew hotter and hotter.

The ship had landed three days earlier. *Landed* was really the wrong word. It had touched down as gently as a cloud drifts against the tops of the mountains. Sergeant Warner had seen it. He just happened to be driving down the main highway in his State Police cruiser when the ship appeared. He nearly drove into the roadside culvert, staring at the ship instead of watching his driving.

Before the sun went down that day, hundreds of Army trucks and tanks had poured down the highway, swirling up clouds of dust that could be seen even from Johnny's house in Albuquerque, miles away. They surrounded the strange ship and let no one come near it.

Johnny could see them now, a ring of steel and guns. Soldiers paced slowly between the tanks, with automatic rifles slung over their shoulders. Pretending that he was an

Apache warrior, Johnny thought about how foolish the Army was to make the young soldiers walk around in the heat instead of allowing them to sit in the shade. He knew that the soldiers were sweating and grumbling and cursing the heat. As if that would make it cooler. They even wore their steel helmets; a good way to fry their brains.

Each day since the ship had landed, exactly when the sun was highest in the sky, three strangers would step out of the ship. At least, that's what the people were saying back in town. The newspapers carried no word of the strangers, except front-page complaints that the Army wouldn't let news reporters or television camera crews anywhere near the star ship.

The three strangers came out of their ship each day, for a few minutes. Johnny wanted to talk to them. Maybe—just maybe—they could cure his sickness. All the doctors he had ever seen just shook their heads and said that nothing could be done. Johnny would never live to be a full-grown man. But these strangers, if they really came from another world, a distant star, they might know how to cure a disease that no doctor on Earth could cure.

Johnny could feel his heart racing as he thought about it. He forced himself to stay calm. *Before you can get cured,* he told himself, *you've got to talk to the strangers. And before you can do that, you've got to sneak past all those soldiers.*

A smear of dust on the highway caught his eye. It was a State Police car, heading toward the Army camp. Sergeant Warner, most likely. Johnny figured that his mother had realized by now he had run away, and had called the police to find him. So he had another problem: avoid getting found by the police.

He turned back to look at the ship again. Suddenly his breath caught in his throat. The three strangers were standing in front of the ship. Without opening a hatch, without any motion at all. They were just *there*, as suddenly as the blink of an eye.

They were tall and slim and graceful, dressed in simple-looking coveralls that seemed to glow, just like their ship.

And they cast no shadows!

2

The strangers stood there for several minutes. A half-dozen people went out toward them, two in Army uniforms, the others in civilian clothes. After a few minutes the strangers disappeared. Just like that. Gone. The six men seemed just as stunned as Johnny felt. They milled around for a few moments, as if trying to figure out where the strangers had gone to. Then they slowly walked back toward the trucks and tanks and other soldiers.

Johnny pushed himself back down from the edge of the hill he was on. He sat up, safely out of view of the soldiers and police, and checked his supplies. A canteen full of water, a leather sack that held two quickly made sandwiches and a couple of oranges. He felt inside the sack to see if there was anything else. Nothing except the wadded-up remains of the plastic wrap that had been around the other two sandwiches he had eaten earlier. The only other thing he had brought with him was a blanket to keep himself warm during the chill desert night.

There wasn't much shade, and the sun was getting really fierce. Johnny got to his feet and walked slowly to a clump of bushes that surrounded a stunted dead tree. He sat down and leaned his back against the shady side of the tree trunk.

For a moment he thought about his parents.

His mother was probably worried sick by now. Johnny often got up early and left the house before she was awake, but he always made sure to be back by lunchtime. His father would be angry. But he was always angry nowadays—most of the time it was about losing his job. But Johnny knew that what was really bugging his father was Johnny's own sickness.

Johnny remembered Dr. Pemberton's round red face, which was normally so cheerful. But Dr. Pemberton shook his head grimly when he told Johnny's father:

"It's foolish for you to spend what little money you have, John. It's incurable. You could send the boy to one of the research centers, and they'll try out some of the new treatments on him. But it won't help him. There is no cure."

Johnny hadn't been supposed to hear that. The door between the examination room where he was sitting and Dr. Pemberton's office had been open only a crack. It was enough for his keen ears, though.

Johnny's father sounded stunned. "But . . . he looks fine. And he says he feels okay."

"I know." Dr. Pemberton's voice sounded as heavy as his roundly overweight body. "The brutal truth, however, is that he has less than a year to live. The disease is very advanced. Luckily, for most of the time he'll feel fine. But towards the end . . ."

"These research centers," Johnny's father said, his voice starting to crack. "The scientists are always coming up with new vaccines . . ."

Johnny had never heard his father sound like that: like a little boy who had been caught stealing or something, and was begging for a chance to escape getting punished.

"You can send him to a research center," Dr. Pemberton said, slowly. "They'll use him to learn more about the disease. But there's no cure in sight, John. Not this year. Or next. And that's all the time he has.''

And then Johnny heard something he had never heard before in his whole life: his father was crying.

They didn't tell him.

He rode back home with his father, and the next morning his mother looked as if she had been crying all night. But they never said a word to him about it. And he never told them that he knew.

Maybe it would have been different if he had a brother or sister to talk to. And he couldn't tell the kids at school, or his friends around the neighborhood. What do you say? "Hey there, Nicko . . . I'm going to die around Christmas sometime."

No. Johnny kept silent, like the Apache he often dreamed he was. He played less and less with his friends, spent more and more of his time alone.

And then the ship came.

It had to *mean* something. A ship from another star doesn't just plop down practically in your back yard by accident.

Why did the strangers come to Earth?

No one knew. And Johnny didn't really care. All he wanted was a chance to talk to them, to get them to cure him. Maybe—who knew?—maybe they were here to find him and cure him!

He dozed off, sitting there against the tree. The heat was sizzling, there was no breeze at all, and nothing for Johnny to do until darkness. With his mind buzzing and jumbling a million thoughts together, his eyes drooped shut and he fell asleep.

"Johnny Donato!''

The voice was like a crack of thunder. Johnny snapped awake, so surprised that he didn't even think of being scared.

"Johnny Donato! This is Sergeant Warner. We know you're around here, so come out from wherever you're hiding."

Johnny flopped over on his stomach and peered around. He was pretty well hidden by the bushes that surrounded the tree. Looking carefully in all directions, he couldn't see Sergeant Warner or anyone else.

"Johnny Donato!" the voice repeated. "This is Sergeant Warner . . ."

Only now the voice seemed to be coming from farther away. Johnny realized that the State Police sergeant was speaking into an electric bullhorn.

Very slowly, Johnny crawled on his belly up to the top of the little hill. He made certain to stay low and keep in the scraggly grass.

Off to his right a few hundred yards was Sergeant Warner, slowly walking across the hot sandy ground. His hat was pushed back on his head, pools of sweat stained his shirt. He held the bullhorn up to his mouth, so that Johnny couldn't really see his face at all. The sergeant's mirror-shiny sunglasses hid the top half of his face.

Moving still farther away, the sergeant yelled into his bullhorn, "Now listen, Johnny. Your mother's scared half out of her mind. And your father doesn't even know you've run away—he's still downtown, hasn't come home yet. You come out now, you hear? It's hot out here, and I'm getting mighty unhappy about you."

Johnny almost laughed out loud. *What are you going to do, kill me?*

"Dammit, Johnny, I know you're around here! Now, do I have to call in other cars and the helicopter, just to find one stubborn boy?"

Helicopters! Johnny frowned. He had no doubts that he could hide from a dozen police cars and the men in them. But helicopters were something else.

He crawled back to the bushes and the dead tree and started scooping up loose sand with his bare hands. Pretty soon he was puffing and sweaty. But finally he had a shallow trench that was long enough to lie in.

He got into the trench and pulled his food pouch and canteen in with him. Then he spread the blanket over himself. By sitting up and leaning forward, he could reach a few small stones. He put them on the lower corners of the blanket to anchor them down. Then he lay down and pulled the blanket over him.

The blanket was brown, and probably wouldn't be spotted from a helicopter. Lying there under it, staring at the fuzzy brightness two inches over his nose, Johnny told himself he was an Apache hiding out from the Army.

It was almost true.

It got very hot in Johnny's hideout. Time seemed to drag endlessly. The air became stifling; Johnny could hardly breathe. Once he thought he heard the drone of a helicopter, but it was far off in the distance. Maybe it was just his imagination.

He drifted off to sleep again.

Voices woke him up once more. More than one voice this time, and he didn't recognize who was talking. But they were very close by—they weren't using a bullhorn or calling out to him.

"Are you really sure he's out here?"

"Where else would a runaway kid go? His mother says he hasn't talked about anything but that weirdo ship for the past three days."

"Well, it's a big desert. We're never going to find him standing around here jabbering."

"I got an idea." The voices started to get fainter, as if the men were walking away.

"Yeah? What is it?"

Johnny stayed very still and strained his ears to hear them.

"Those Army guys got all sorts of fancy electronic stuff. Why don't we use them instead of walking around here frying our brains?"

"They had some of that stuff on the helicopter, didn't they?"

The voices were getting fainter and fainter.

"Yeah—but instead of trying to find a needle in a haystack, we ought to play it smart."

"What do you mean?"

Johnny wanted to sit up, to hear them better. But he didn't dare move.

"Why not set up the Army's fancy stuff and point it at the ship? That's where the kid wants to go. Instead of searching the whole damned desert for him . . ."

"I get it!" the other voice said. "Make the ship the bait in a mousetrap."

"Right. That's the way to get him."

They both laughed.

And Johnny, lying quite still in his hideaway, began to know how a starving mouse must feel.

3

After a long, hot, sweaty time Johnny couldn't hear any more voices or helicopter engines. And as he stared tiredly at the blanket over him, it seemed that the daylight was growing dimmer.

Must be close to sundown, he thought.

Despite his worked-up nerves, he fell asleep again. By the time he woke up, it was dark.

He sat up and let the blanket fall off to one side of his dugout shelter. Already it was getting cold.

But Johnny smiled.

If they're going to have all their sensors looking in toward the ship, he told himself, *that means nobody's out here. It ought to be easy to get into the Army camp and hide there. Maybe I can find someplace warm. And food!*

But another part of his mind asked, *And what then? How are you going to get from there to the ship and the strangers?*

"I'll cross that bridge when I come to it," Johnny whispered to himself.

Clutching the blanket around his shoulders, for warmth in the chilly desert night wind, Johnny crept up to the top of the hill once more.

The Army tanks and trucks were still out there. A few tents had been set up, and there were lights strung out everywhere. It almost looked like a shopping center decorated for the Christmas season, there were so many lights and people milling around.

But the lights were glaring white, not the many colors of the holidays. And the people were soldiers. And the decorations were guns, cannon, radar antennas, lasers—all pointed inward at the strangers' ship.

The ship itself was what made everything look like Christmas, Johnny decided. It stood in the middle of everything, glowing and golden like a cheerful tree ornament.

Johnny stared at it for a long time. Then he found his gaze floating upward, to the stars. In the clear cold night of the desert, the stars gleamed and winked like thousands of jewels: red, blue, white. The hazy swarm of the Milky Way swung across the sky. Johnny knew there were billions of stars in the heavens, hundreds of billions, so many stars that they were uncountable.

"That ship came from one of them," he whispered to himself. "Which one?"

The wind moaned and sent a shiver of cold through him, despite his blanket.

Slowly, quietly, carefully, he got up and started walking down the hill toward the Army camp. He stayed in the shadows, away from the lights, and circled around the trucks and tanks. He was looking for an opening, a dark place where there was no one sitting around or standing guard, a place where he could slip in and maybe hide inside one of the trucks.

I wonder what the inside of a tank is like? he asked himself. Then he shook his head, as if to drive away such childish thoughts. He was an Apache warrior, he told himself, sneaking up on the Army camp.

He got close enough to hear soldiers talking and laughing among themselves. But still he stayed out in the darkness. He ignored the wind and cold, just pulled the blanket more tightly over his thin shoulders as he circled the camp. Off beyond the trucks, he could catch the warm yellow glow of the strangers' ship. It looked inviting and friendly.

And then there was an opening! A slice of shadow that cut between pools of light. Johnny froze in his tracks and examined the spot carefully, squatting down on his heels to make himself as small and undetectable as possible.

There were four tents set up in a row, with their backs facing Johnny. On one side of them was a group of parked trucks and jeeps. Metal poles with lights on them brightened that area. On the other side of the tents were some big trailer vans, with all sorts of antennas poking out of their roofs. That area was well-lit too.

But the narrow lanes between the tents were dark with shadow. And Johnny could see no one around them. There were no lights showing from inside the tents, either.

Johnny hesitated only a moment or two. Then he quickly stepped up to the rear of one of the tents, poked his head

around its corner and found no one in sight. So he ducked
into the lane between the tents.

Flattening himself against the tent's vinyl wall, Johnny
listened for sounds of danger. Nothing except the distant
rush of the wind and the pounding of his own heart. It was
dark where he was standing. The area seemed to be deserted.

He stayed there for what seemed like hours. His mind
was saying that this was a safe place to hide. But his
stomach was telling him that there might be some food
inside the tents.

Yeah, and there might be some people inside there, too,
Johnny thought.

His stomach won the argument.

Johnny crept around toward the front of the tent. This
area was still pretty well lit from the lamps over by the
trucks and vans. Peeking around the tent's corner, Johnny
could see plenty of soldiers sitting in front of the parking
areas, on the ground alongside their vehicles, eating food
that steamed and somehow looked delicious, even from
this distance. Johnny sniffed at the night air and thought he
caught a trace of something filled with meat and bubbling
juices.

Licking his lips, he slipped around the front of the tent
and ducked inside.

It was dark, but enough light filtered through from the
outside for Johnny to see that the tent was really a work-
room of some sort. Two long tables ran the length of the
tent. There were papers stacked at one end of one table,
with a metal weight holding them in place. All sorts of
instruments and gadgets were sitting on the tables: micro-
scopes, cameras, something that looked sort of like a
computer, other things that Johnny couldn't figure out at
all.

None of it was food.

Frowning, Johnny went back to the tent's entrance. His

stomach was growling now, complaining about being empty too long.

He pushed the tent flap back half an inch and peered outside. A group of men were walking in his direction. Four of them. One wore a soldier's uniform and had a big pistol strapped to his hip. The others wore ordinary clothes: slacks, windbreaker jackets. One of them was smoking a pipe—or rather, he was waving it in his hand as he talked, swinging the pipe back and forth and pointing its stem at the glowing ship, then back at the other three men.

Johnny knew that if he stepped outside the tent now they would see him as clearly as anything.

Then he realized that the situation was even worse. They were heading straight for this tent!

4

There wasn't any time to be scared. Johnny let the tent flap drop back into place and dived under one of the tables. No place else to hide.

He crawled into the farthest corner of the tent, under the table, and huddled there with his knees pulled up tight against his nose and the blanket wrapped around him.

Sure enough, the voices marched straight up to the tent and the lights flicked on.

"You'd better get some sleep, Ed. No sense staying up all night again."

"Yeah, I will. Just want to go over the tapes from this afternoon one more time."

"Might as well go to sleep, for all the good *that's* going to do you."

"I know. Well . . . see you tomorrow."

"G'night."

From underneath the table, Johnny saw a pair of desert-booted feet walk into the tent. The man, whoever it was, wore striped slacks. He wasn't a soldier, or a policeman, and that let Johnny breathe a little easier.

He won't notice me under here, Johnny thought. *I'll just wait until he leaves and . . .*

"You can come out of there now," the man's voice said.

Johnny froze. He didn't even breathe.

The man squatted down and grinned at Johnny. "Come on, kid. I'm not going to hurt you. I ran away from home a few times myself."

Feeling helpless, Johnny crawled out from under the table. He stood up slowly, feeling stiff and achy all of a sudden.

The man looked him over. "When's the last time you ate?"

"Around noontime."

Johnny watched the man's face. He had stopped grinning, and there were tight lines around his mouth and eyes that came from worry. Or maybe anger. He wasn't as big as Johnny's father, but he was solidly built. His hair was dark and long, almost down to his shoulders. His eyes were deep brown, almost black, and burning with some inner fire.

"You must be hungry."

Johnny nodded.

"If I go out to the cook van and get you some food, will you still be here when I come back?"

The thought of food reminded Johnny how hungry he really was. His stomach felt hollow.

"How do I know you won't bring back the State Troopers?" he asked.

The man shrugged. "How do I know you'll stay here and wait for me to come back?"

Johnny said nothing.

"Look kid," the man said, more gently, "I'm not going to hurt you. Sooner or later you're going to have to go home, but if you want to eat and maybe talk, then we can do that. I won't tell anybody you're here."

Johnny wanted to believe him. The man wasn't smiling; he seemed very serious about the whole thing.

"You've got to start trusting somebody, sooner or later," he said.

"Yeah . . ." Johnny's voice didn't sound very sure about it, even to himself.

"My name's Gene Beldone." He put his hand out.

Johnny reached for it. "I'm Johnny Donato," he said. Gene's grip was strong.

"Okay Johnny," Gene smiled wide. "You wait here and I'll get you some food."

Gene came back in five minutes with an Army type of plastic tray heaped with hot, steaming food. And a mug of cold milk to wash it down. There were no chairs in the tent, but Gene pushed aside some of the instruments and helped Johnny to clamber up on the table.

For several minutes Johnny concentrated on eating. Gene went to the other table and fiddled around with what looked like a tape recorder.

"Did you really run away from home?" Johnny asked at last.

Gene looked up from his work. "Sure did. More than once. I know how it feels."

"Yeah."

"But . . ." Gene walked over to stand beside Johnny. "You know you'll have to go back home again, don't you?"

"I guess so."

"Your parents are probably worried. I thought I heard one of the State Troopers say that you were ill?"

Johnny nodded.

"Want to talk about it?"

Johnny turned his attention back to the tray of food. "No."

Gene gave a little one-shouldered shrug. "Okay. As long as you don't need any medicine right away, or anything like that."

Looking up again, Johnny asked, "Are you a scientist?"

"Sort of. I'm a linguist."

"Huh?"

"I study languages. The Army came and got me out of the university so I could help them understand the language the aliens speak."

"Aliens?"

"The men from the ship."

"Oh. Aliens—that's what you call them?"

"Right."

"Can you understand what they're saying?"

Gene grinned again, but this time it wasn't a happy expression. "Can't understand anything," he said.

"Nothing?" Johnny felt suddenly alarmed. "Why not?"

"Because the aliens haven't said anything to us."

"Huh?"

With a shake of his head, Gene said, "They just come out every day at high noon, stand there for a few minutes while we talk at them, and then pop back into their ship. I don't think they're listening to us at all. In fact, I don't think they're even *looking* at us. It's like they don't even know we're here!"

5

Gene let Johnny listen to the tapes of their attempts to talk to the aliens.

With the big padded stereo earphones clamped to his head, Johnny could hear the Army officers speaking, and another man that Gene said was a scientist from Washington. He could hear the wind, and a soft whistling sound, like the steady note of a telephone that's been left off the hook for too long. But no sounds at all from the aliens. No words of any kind, in any language.

Gene helped take the earphones off Johnny's head.

"They haven't said anything at all?"

"Nothing," Gene answered, clicking off the tape recorder. "The only sound to come from them is that sort of whistling thing—and that's coming from the ship. Some of the Army engineers think it's a power generator of some sort."

"Then we can't talk with them." Johnny suddenly felt very tired and defeated.

"We can talk *to* them," Gene said, "but I'm not even certain that they hear us. It's . . . it's pretty weird. They seem to look right through us—as if we're pictures hanging on a wall."

"Or rocks or grass or something."

"Right!" Gene looked impressed. "Like we're a part of the scenery, nothing special, nothing you'd want to talk to."

Something in Johnny was churning, trying to break loose. He felt tears forming in his eyes. "Then how can I tell them . . ."

"Tell them what?" Gene asked.

Johnny fought down his feelings. "Nothing," he said. 'It's nothing."

Gene came over and put a hand on Johnny's shoulder. 'So you're going to tough it out, huh?"

"What do you mean?"

Smiling, Gene answered, "Listen kid. Nobody runs away from home and sneaks into an Army camp just for fun. At first I thought you were just curious about the aliens. But now . . . looks to me as if you've got something pretty big on your mind."

Johnny didn't reply, but—strangely—he felt safe with this man. He wasn't afraid of him anymore.

"So stay quiet," Gene went on. "It's *your* problem, whatever it is, and you've got a right to tell me to keep my nose out of it."

"You're going to tell the State Troopers I'm here?"

Instead of answering, Gene leaned against the table's edge and said, "Listen. When I was about your age I ran away from home for the first time. That was in Cleveland. It was winter and there was a lot of snow. Damned cold, too. Now, you'd think that whatever made me leave home and freeze my backside in the snow for two days and nights—you'd think it was something pretty important, wouldn't you?"

"Wasn't it?"

Gene laughed out loud. "I don't know! I can't for the life of me remember what it was! It was awfully important to me then, of course. But now it's nothing, nowhere."

Johnny wanted to laugh with him, but he couldn't. "My problem's different."

"Yeah, I guess so," Gene said. But he was still smiling.

"I'm going to be dead before the year's over," Johnny said.

Gene's smile vanished. "What?"

Johnny told him the whole story. Gene asked several questions, looked doubtful for a while, but at last simply stood there looking very grave.

"That *is* tough," he said, at last.

"So I thought maybe the strangers—the aliens, that is—might do something, maybe cure it . . ." Johnny's voice trailed off.

"I see," Gene said. And there was real pain in his voice. "And we can't even get them to notice us, let alone talk with us."

"I guess it's hopeless then."

Gene suddenly straightened up. "No. Why should we give up? There must be something we can do!"

"Like what?" Johnny asked.

Gene rubbed a hand across his chin. It was dark with stubbly beard. "Well . . . maybe they *do* understand us and just don't care. Maybe they're just here sightseeing, or doing some scientific exploring. Maybe they think of us like we think of animals in a zoo, or cows in a field—"

"But we're not animals!" Johnny said.

"Yeah? Imagine how we must seem to them." Gene began to pace down the length of the table. "They've travelled across lightyears—billions on billions of miles—to get here. Their ship, their brains, their minds must be thousands of years ahead of our own. We're probably no more interesting to them than apes in a zoo."

"Then why . . ."

"Wait a minute," Gene said. "Maybe they're not interested in us—but so far they've only seen adults, men, soldiers mostly. Suppose we show them a child, *you*, and make it clear to them that you're going to die."

"How are you going to get that across to them?"

"I don't know," Gene admitted. "Maybe they don't even understand what death is. Maybe they're so far ahead of us that they live for thousands of years—or they might even be immortal!''

Then he turned to look back at Johnny. ''But I've had the feeling ever since the first time we tried to talk to them that they understand every word we say. They just don't *care*.''

''And you think they'll care about me?''

''It's worth a try. Nothing else we've done has worked. Maybe this will.''

6

Gene took Johnny to a tent that had cots and warm Army blankets.

''You get some sleep; you must be tired,'' he said. ''I'll let the State Police know you're okay.''

Johnny could feel himself falling asleep, even though he was only standing next to one of the cots.

''Do you want to talk to your parents? We can set up a radio-phone . . .''

''Later,'' Johnny said. ''As long as they know I'm okay—I don't want to hassle with them until after we've talked to the aliens.''

Gene nodded and left the tent. Johnny sat on the cot, kicked off his boots, and was asleep by the time he had stretched out and pulled the blanket up to his chin.

Gene brought him breakfast on a tray the next morning. But as soon as Johnny had finished eating and pulled his boots back on, Gene led him out to one of the big vans.

''General Hackett isn't too sure he likes our idea,'' Gene said as they walked up to the tan-colored van. It was like a civilian camper, only much bigger. Two soldiers stood guard by its main door, with rifles slung over their shoulders. It was already hot and bright on the desert, even though the sun had hardly climbed above the distant mountains.

The alien star ship still hung in the middle of the camp circle, glowing warmly and barely touching the ground. For a wild instant, Johnny thought of it as a bright beach ball being balanced on a seal's nose.

Inside, the van's air conditioning was turned up so high that it made Johnny shiver.

But General Hackett was sweating. He sat squeezed behind a table, a heavy, fat-cheeked man with a black little cigar stuck in the corner of his mouth. It was not lit, but Johnny could smell its sour odor. Sitting around the little table in the van's main compartment were Sergeant Warner of the State Police, several civilians, and two other Army officers, both colonels.

There were two open chairs. Johnny and Gene slid into them.

"I don't like it," General Hackett said, shaking his head. "The whole world's going nuts over these weirdos, every blasted newspaper and TV man in the country's trying to break into this camp, and we've got to take a little kid out there to do our job for us? I don't like it."

Sergeant Warner looked as if he wanted to say something, but he satisfied himself with a stern glare in Johnny's direction.

Gene said, "We've got nothing to lose. All our efforts of the past three days have amounted to zero results. Maybe the sight of a youngster will stir them."

One of the civilians shook his head. A colonel banged his fist on the table and said, "By god, a couple rounds of artillery will stir them! Put a few shots close to 'em—make 'em know we mean business!"

"And run the risk of having them destroy everything in sight?" asked one of the civilians, his voice sharp as the whine of an angry hornet.

"This isn't some idiot movie," the colonel snapped.

"Precisely," said the civilian. "If we anger them, there's no telling how much damage they could do. Do you have any idea of how much energy they must be able to control in that ship?"

"One little ship? Three people?"

"That one little ship," the scientist answered, "has crossed distances billions of times greater than our biggest rockets. And there might be more than one ship, as well."

"NORAD hasn't picked up any other ships in orbit around Earth," the other colonel said.

"None of our radars have detected *this* ship," the scientist said, pointing in the general direction of the glowing star ship. "The radars just don't get any signal from it at all!"

General Hackett took the cigar from his mouth. "All right, all right. There's no sense firing at them unless we get some clear indication that they're dangerous."

He turned to Gene. "You really think the kid will get them interested enough to talk to us?"

Gene shrugged. "It's worth a try."

"You don't think it will be dangerous?" the general asked. "Bringing him right up close to them like that?"

"If they want to be dangerous," Gene said, "I'll bet they can hurt anyone they want to, anywhere on Earth."

There was a long silence.

Finally General Hackett said, "Okay—let the kid talk to them."

Sergeant Warner insisted that Johnny's parents had to agree to the idea, and Johnny wound up spending most of the morning talking on the radio-phone in the sergeant's

State Police cruiser. Gene talked to them too, and explained what they planned to do.

It took a long time to calm his parents down. His mother cried and said she was so worried. His father tried to sound angry about Johnny's running away. But he really sounded relieved that his son was all right. After hours of talking, they finally agreed to let Johnny face the aliens.

But when Johnny at last handed the phone back to Sergeant Warner, he felt lower than a scorpion.

"I really scared them," he told Gene as they walked back to the tents.

"Guess you did."

"But they wouldn't have let me go if I'd stayed home and asked them. They would've said no."

Gene shrugged.

Then Johnny noticed that his shadow had shrunk to practically nothing. He turned and squinted up at the sky. The sun was almost at zenith. It was almost high noon.

"Less than two minutes to noon," Gene said, looking at his wristwatch. "Let's get moving. I want to be out there where they can see you when they appear."

They turned and started walking out toward the aliens' ship. Past the trucks and jeeps and vans that were parked in neat rows. Past the tanks, huge and heavy, with the snouts of their long cannon pointed straight at the ship. Past the ranks of soldiers who were standing in neat files, guns cleaned and ready for action.

General Hackett and other people from the morning conference were sitting in an open-topped car. A corporal was at the wheel, staring straight at the ship.

Johnny and Gene walked out alone, past everyone and everything, out into the wide cleared space at the center of the camp.

With every step he took, Johnny felt more alone. It was as if he were an astronaut out on EVA—floating away from his ship, out of contact, no way to get back. Even though it was hot, bright daylight, he could *feel* the stars looking down at him—one tiny, lonely, scared boy facing the unknown.

Gene grinned at him as they neared the ship. "I've done this four times now, and it gets spookier every time. My knees are shaking."

Johnny admitted, "Me too."

And then they were there! The three strangers, the aliens, standing about ten yards in front of Johnny and Gene.

It *was* spooky.

The aliens simply stood there, looking relaxed and pleasant. But they seemed to be looking right *through* Johnny and Gene. As if they weren't there at all.

Johnny studied the three of them very carefully. They looked completely human. Tall and handsome as movie stars, with broad shoulders and strong, square-jawed faces. The three of them looked enough alike to be brothers. They wore simple, silvery coveralls that shimmered in the sunlight.

They looked at each other as if they were going to speak. But they said nothing. The only sound Johnny could hear was that highpitched kind of whistling noise that he had heard on tape the night before. Even the wind seemed to have died down, this close to the alien ship.

Johnny glanced up at Gene, and out of the corner of his eye, the three aliens seemed to shimmer and waver, as if he were seeing them through a wavy heat haze.

A chill raced along Johnny's spine.

When he looked straight at the aliens, they seemed real and solid, just like ordinary humans except for their glittery uniforms.

But when he turned his head and saw them only out of the corner of his eye, the aliens shimmered and sizzled.

Suddenly Johnny remembered a day in school when they showed movies. His seat had been up close to the screen, and off to one side. He couldn't make out what the picture on the screen was, but he could watch the light shimmering and glittering on the screen.

They're not real!

Johnny suddenly understood that what they were all seeing was a picture, an image of some sort. Not real people at all.

And that, his mind was racing, *means that the aliens really don't look like us at all!*

7

"This is one of our children," Gene was saying to the aliens. "He is not fully grown, as you can see. He has a disease that will . . ."

Johnny stopped listening to Gene. He stared at the aliens. They seemed so real when you looked straight at them. Turning his head toward Gene once more, he again saw the aliens sparkled and shimmered. Like a movie picture.

Without thinking about it any further, Johnny suddenly sprang toward the aliens. Two running steps covered the distance, and he threw himself right off his feet at the three glittering strangers.

He sailed straight *through* them, and landed sprawled on his hands and knees on the other side of them.

"Johnny!"

Turning to sit on the dusty ground, Johnny saw that the aliens—or really, the images of them—were still standing there as if nothing had happened. Gene's face was shocked, mouth open, eyes wide.

Then the images of the aliens winked out. They just disappeared.

Johnny got to his feet.

"What did you do?" Gene asked, hurrying over to grab Johnny by the arm as he got to his feet.

"They're not real!" Johnny shouted with excitement. "They're just pictures . . . they don't really look like us. They're still inside the ship!"

"Wait, slow down," Gene said. "The aliens we've been seeing are images? Holograms, maybe. Yeah, that could explain . . ."

Looking past Gene's shoulder, Johnny could see a dozen soldiers hustling toward them. General Hackett was standing in his car and waving his arms madly.

Everything was happening so fast! But there was one thing that Johnny was sure of. The aliens—the *real* aliens, not the pretty pictures they were showing the Earthmen— the real aliens were still inside of their ship. They had never come out.

Then another thought struck Johnny. What if the ship itself was a picture, too? How could he *ever* talk to the star-visitors, get them to listen to him, help him?

Johnny had to know. Once General Hackett's soldiers got to him, he would never get another chance to speak with the aliens.

With a grit of his teeth, Johnny pulled his arm away from Gene, spun around and raced toward the alien star ship.

"Hey!" Gene yelled. "Johnny! No!"

The globe of the ship gleamed warmly in the sun. It almost seemed to pulsate, to throb like a living, beating heart. A heart made of gold, not flesh and muscle.

Johhny ran straight to the ship and, with his arms stretched out in front of him, he jumped at it. His eyes squeezed shut at the moment before he would hit the ship's shining hull.

Everything went black.

Johnny felt nothing. His feet left the ground, but there was no shock of hitting solid metal, no sense of jumping or falling or even floating. Nothing at all.

He tried to open his eyes, and found that he couldn't. He couldn't move his arms or legs. He couldn't even feel his heart beating.

I'm dead!

8

Slowly a golden light filtered into Johnny's awareness. It was like lying out in the desert sun with your eyes closed; the light glowed behind his closed eyelids.

He opened his eyes and found that he was indeed lying down, but not outdoors. Everything around him was golden and shining.

Johnny's head was spinning. He was inside the alien ship, he knew that. But it was unlike any spacecraft he had seen or heard of. He could see no walls, no equipment, no instruments; only a golden glow, like being inside a star—or maybe inside a cloud of shining gold.

Even the thing he was lying on, Johnny couldn't really make out what it was. It felt soft and warm to his touch, but it wasn't a bed or cot. He found that if he pressed his hands down hard enough, they would go *into* the golden glowing material a little way. Almost like pressing your fingers down into sand, except that this stuff was warm and soft.

He sat up. All that he could see was the misty glow, all around him.

"Hey, where are you?" Johnny called out. His voice

sounded trembly, even though he was trying hard to stay calm. "I know you're in here someplace!"

Two shining spheres appeared before him. They were so bright that it hurt Johnny's eyes to look straight at them. They were like two tiny suns, about the size of basketballs, hovering in mid-air, shining brilliantly but giving off no heat at all.

"We are here."

It was a sound Johnny could hear. Somewhere in the back of his mind, despite his fears, he was a little disappointed. He had been half-expecting to "hear" a telepathic voice in his mind.

"Where are you?"

"You are looking at us." The voice was flat and unemotional. "We are the two shining globes that you see."

"You?" Johnny squinted at the shining ones. "You're the aliens?"

"This is our ship."

Johnny's heart started beating faster as he realized what was going on. He was inside the ship. And *talking* to the aliens!

"Why wouldn't you talk with the other men?" he asked.

"Why should we? We are not here to speak with them."

"What *are* you here for?"

The voice—Johnny couldn't tell which of the shining ones it came from—hesitated for only a moment. Then it answered, "Our purpose is something you could not understand. You are not mentally equipped to grasp such concepts."

A picture flashed into Johnny's mind of a chimpanzee trying to figure out how a computer works. *Did they plant that in my head?* he wondered.

After a moment, Johnny said, "I came here to ask for your help . . ."

"We are not here to help you," said the voice.

And a second voice added, "Indeed, it would be very dangerous for us to interfere with the environment of your world. Dangerous to you and your kind."

"But you don't understand! I don't want you to change anything, just—"

The shining one on the left seemed to bob up and down a little. "We do understand. We looked into your mind while you were unconscious. You want us to prolong your life span."

"Yes!"

The other one said, "We cannot interfere with the normal life processes of your world. That would change the entire course of your history."

"History?" Johnny felt puzzled. "What do you mean?"

The first sphere drifted a bit closer to Johnny, forcing him to shade his eyes with his hand. "You and your people have assumed that we are visitors from another star. In a sense, we are. But we are also travelers in time. We have come from millions of years in your future."

"Future?" Johnny felt weak. "Millions of years?"

"And apparently we have missed our target time by at least a hundred thousand of your years."

"Missed?" Johnny echoed.

"Yes," said the first shining one. "We stopped here—at this time and place—to get our bearings. We were about to leave when you threw yourself into the ship's defensive screen."

The second shining one added, "Your action was entirely foolish. The screen would have killed you instantly. We never expected any of you to attack us in such an irrational manner."

"I wasn't attacking you," Johnny said. "I just wanted to talk with you."

"So we learned, once we brought you into our ship and revived you. Still, it was a foolish thing to do."

"And now," the second shining sphere said, "your fellow men have begun to attack us. They assume that you have been killed, and they have fired their weapons at us."

"Oh no . . ."

"Have no fear, little one." The first sphere seemed almost amused. "Their primitive shells and rockets fall to the ground without exploding. We are completely safe."

"But they might try an atomic bomb," Johnny said.

"If they do, it will not explode. We are not here to hurt anyone, nor to allow anyone to hurt us."

A new thought struck Johnny. "You said your screen would have killed me. And then you said you brought me inside the ship and revived me. Was . . . was I dead?"

"Your heart had stopped beating," said the first alien. "We also found a few other flaws in your body chemistry, which we corrected. But we took no steps to prolong your life span. You will live some eighty to one hundred years, just as the history of your times has shown us."

Eighty to one hundred years! Johnny was thunderstruck. *The "other flaws in body chemistry" that they fixed—they cured me!*

Johnny was staggered by the news, feeling as if he wanted to laugh and cry at the same time, when the first of the shining ones said:

"We must leave now, and hopefully find the proper time and place that we are seeking. We will place you safely among your friends."

"No! Wait! Take me with you! I want to go too!" Johnny surprised himself by shouting it, but he realized as he heard his own words that he really meant it. A trip through thousands of years of time, to who-knows-where!

"That is impossible, little one. Your time and place is here. Your own history shows that quite clearly."

"But you can't just leave me here, after you've shown me so much! How can I be satisfied with just one world and time when *everything's* open to you to travel to! I don't want to be stuck here-and-now. I want to be like you!"

"You will be, little one. You will be. Once we were like you. In time your race will evolve into our type of creature—able to roam through the universe of space and time, able to live directly from the energy of the stars."

"But that'll take millions of years."

"Yes. But your first steps into space have already begun. Before your life ends, you will have visited a few of the stars nearest to your own world. And, in the fullness of time, your race will evolve into ours."

"Maybe so," Johnny said, feeling downcast.

The shining one somehow seemed to smile. "No, little one. There is no element of chance. Remember, we come from your future. *It has already happened*."

Johnny blinked. "Already happened . . . you—you're really from Earth! Aren't you? You're from the Earth of a million years from now! Is that it?"

"Good-bye grandsire," said the shining ones together.

And Johnny found himself sitting on the desert floor in the hot afternoon sunlight, a few yards in front of General Hackett's command car.

"It's the kid! He's alive!"

Getting slowly to his feet as a hundred soldiers raced toward him, Johnny looked back toward the star ship—the *time* ship.

It winked out. Disappeared. Without a sound or a stirring of the desert dust. One instant it was there, the next it was gone.

9

It was a week later that it really sank home in Johnny's mind.

It had been a wild week. Army officers quizzing him, medical doctors trying to find some trace of the disease, news reporters and TV interviewers asking him a million questions, his mother and father both crying that he was all right and safe and *cured*—a wild week.

Johnny's school friends hung around the house and watched from outside while the Army and news people swarmed in and out. He waved to them, and they waved back, smiling, friendly. They understood. The whole story was splashed all over the papers and TV, even the part about the disease. The kids understood why Johnny had been so much of a loner the past few months.

The President telephoned and invited Johnny and his parents to Washington. Dr. Gene Beldone went along too, in a private Air Force twin-engine jet.

As Johnny watched the New Mexico desert give way to the rugged peaks of the Rockies, something that the shining ones had said finally hit home to him:

You will live some eighty to one hundred years, just as the history of your times has shown us.

"How would they know about me from the history of these times?" Johnny whispered to himself as he stared out the thick window of the plane. "That must mean that my name will be famous enough to get into the history books, or tapes, or whatever they'll be using."

Thinking about that for a long time, as the plane crossed the Rockies and flew arrow-straight over the green farmlands of the midwest, Johnny remembered the other thing that the shining ones had told him:

Before your life ends, you will have visited a few of the stars nearest to your own world.

"When they said *you*," Johnny whispered again, "I thought they meant us, the human race. But—maybe they really meant *me! Me!* I'm going to be an interstellar astronaut!"

For the first time, Johnny realized that the excitement in his life hadn't ended. It was just beginning.

SWORD PLAY

This story is not science fiction. It is not fantasy. It is autobiography. This event actually happened while I was a member of the fencing club of the Arch Street YMCA in Philadelphia. I include this tale here because so many science-fiction readers are enamored of sword-wielding superheros that I thought it would be fun to see what fencing is really like.

"What're you grinnin' at?" Jimmy Matthews shrugged without answering. But he kept on grinning.

"C'mon, Jimmy . . . what's going on inside your pointy head?" Paul asked.

"Nothing," said Jimmy, still showing a lot of teeth.

The boys were standing on the corner in front of Weston High, waiting for the bus that would take them into the city. It was a chilly late autumn afternoon. School was over for the day. Windswept clouds covered the sun and brittle leaves rustled along lawns and pavements.

Paul poked a toe into the equipment bag at his feet. It rattled like a plumber's tool kit.

"You're still grinning," he said.

Jimmy shrugged and dug his hands deeper into his windbreaker pockets. He was tall for a sophomore, with

233

the lanky yet muscular body of a good swimmer. A big mop of dark-brown hair flopped over his eyes.

"Come on," Paul nearly begged. "What's so funny?" Paul was shorter and stockier, with sandy hair and pale blue eyes. He was the kid who got to where he wanted to go by working stubbornly until he made it. He and Jimmy studied together a lot, after school. Paul got A's and B's. Jimmy, just as bright, barely squeaked through with C's and D's.

"Nothing's funny," Jimmy said, as if he didn't really mean it. "What makes you think something's got to be funny? Can't a guy just stand on a street corner and smile?"

"Something's buzzing in your BB brain . . ."

Jimmy rubbed the side of his nose. "Well . . ."

"Yeah? What?"

"I was thinking how hard it's going to be not to laugh when I see you in that fancy outfit."

"My fencing uniform?"

"Yeah. With the knee pants."

Paul frowned. "You won't laugh so hard when you try it yourself. It's a tough sport."

"Sure," Jimmy chuckled. "In those pretty outfits. With the neat little knee pants."

Paul kicked harder at the equipment bag. "You're always making fun of everything. Always goofing off."

"You sound like Old Lady McNiff," Jimmy complained. His voice went into a trembling falsetto: "James, you have a million-dollar brain, but you're only using 10 cents worth of it." Both boys broke up laughing.

"Hey, here comes the bus," Jimmy said. Paul became serious again. "You won't goof up the fencing class, will you? No clowning around?"

"I'll try not to laugh."

"I'll bet you'll like it, if you just pay attention and don't try any horseplay."

The bus pulled up with a hiss of air brakes. Paul hefted his equipment bag and slung it over his shoulder. Jimmy carried only a sweatshirt and shorts, in a paper bag. As Paul scampered up the bus steps, Jimmy booted him in the rear. Lightly. With a big grin.

The Y was an old, brick building, in the middle of the downtown area. It wasn't a good neighborhood to be in, especially after dark.

The gym was big, but old. High ceiling with dim lights that were covered by wire screening. Bare wooden floors. Basketball hoops without netting and backboards that looked as if they'd crumble if just one more ball banged into them. It smelled of a century of sweat, and Jimmy wrinkled his nose as he and Paul walked through it, heading for the locker room.

But his grin returned as Paul dressed in the white knee pants and high-necked white jacket of his fencing outfit. Jimmy himself simply took off his shirt and pulled a sweatshirt over his head. His jeans and sneakers completed his outfit. "You look just *swell*," he said as they walked out of the locker room.

Paul was about to reply when he spotted the fencing instructor talking to a few other kids at the far end of the gym. He also wore a jacket and knee pants, but they were gray with wear and age, and looked very different from Paul's spanking-white three-week-old uniform.

"Come on," Paul said. "I'll introduce you."

Mr. Martinez was small and wiry. A friendly smile was the main feature of his tan face.

"Welcome to the fencing club, Jim. I hope you learn to enjoy fencing." He took Jimmy's hand in a strong grip.

"Uh, thanks . . . I hope so."

"We'll be starting in a few minutes, just as soon as the

others show up. Paul, why don't you show Jim a few limbering-up exercises until we're ready for the starting lineup."

Jimmy snickered as Paul demonstrated the deep hip bends and arm-stretching exercises.

"You look like you're gonna dance a ballet, not try to stick some clown with a sword."

Frowning, Paul said, "You try it and see if it's so easy!" But Jimmy was watching the other kids. Some wore sweatshirts with their school initials. Most of them were from the downtown schools. Three were girls.

Jimmy stood off to one side as Mr. Martinez lined everybody up and put them through a set of opening exercises. He demonstrated how to lunge with a foil: an explosion of purposeful motion, like a snake striking, so fast that Jimmy couldn't follow it.

After about 10 sweat-popping minutes, Mr. Martinez let the class drop to the floor and relax. He walked up to Jimmy, a chest protector and mask in one hand.

"See if these fit you. You've got to have the right protection when you fence. There's no real danger in this sport if you're properly equipped—unless you break a blade and fall against your opponent with the broken end. But that almost never happens, unless the fencers aren't working correctly and they get too close to each other."

Jimmy strapped on the chest protector, wormed the fencing mask over his head, and Mr. Martinez started to show him how to lunge. But Jimmy kept getting it all mixed up. He couldn't seem to get his arms and legs working together right.

Finally Mr. Martinez whipped off his mask. His face was very grave. "Why did you come here this afternoon?" he asked.

Jimmy was surprised by the question. "Huh? Well, I guess I wanted to see what fencing is like."

"And what do you think of it?"

"It's all right, I guess."

Mr. Martinez said, "You'll never enjoy fencing or anything else if you don't apply yourself. You've got the size and reflexes to be an outstanding fencer, but you're just not interested, are you? Why not?"

Staring down at his sneakers, Jimmy said, "Well, it's kind of silly—not like football or basketball. All you try to do is touch each other with these dumb fake swords."

"You think football is tougher? Or basketball?"

"Yeah."

"All right. Try this little exercise, then. Maybe it'll show you there's more to fencing than dancing around." Mr. Martinez called one of the girls. "Donna, will you show Jimmy here the glove exercise?"

Donna worked the fencing glove off her right hand and held it against the wall a little higher than her shoulder. "You take the on-guard position. When I drop the glove, you lunge and pin it against the wall with the point of your foil before it hits the floor."

"Is that all? That's easy!"

She grinned at him. "Try it."

Jimmy squatted into the on-guard position and held his foil the way Mr. Martinez had shown him. Trying hard to remember how to make a good lunge, he noticed that Donna was smirking, as if she knew something he didn't. She dropped the glove.

Jimmy lunged smartly. And missed. The glove slithered down the wall and hit the floor.

"Let's try that again," he said.

They did. And again. And again. Each time Jimmy's lunge was too slow to catch the glove against the wall. Once he lost his balance and fell on the seat of his pants.

He mopped sweat from his eyes. "There's gotta be a trick to it."

"No," Donna said. "You've just got to be fast."

"Let's see you do it, then." Jimmy held the glove and Donna speared it. She missed a couple of times, but she hit it more often than she missed. He could feel his face getting red.

"If you can do it, I can do it!"

They reversed positions again, and still Jimmy missed the glove as Donna let it fall. His face twisted into a tight frown of concentration. *On guard, watch her hand . . . lunge!* And again he missed.

"Can I tell you something that Mr. Martinez told me last week?" she asked.

"Sure, go ahead."

"He said I should try to think that the point of my blade is alive, and that it's *pulling* me to the target. Stop thinking about making a lunge; don't worry about your arms and feet at all. Just let the point *pull* you to the target."

Shrugging, Jimmy said, "OK." But it didn't make much sense.

She held the glove up against the wall again. Jimmy stared at it and pointed the tip of his foil at it. She dropped it and the blade leaped at it.

"You did it!"

He had caught the glove by a corner of its cuff; a fraction of an inch more and he would have missed it again.

"Let's try a couple more," Jimmy said.

He still missed more than he caught, but he hit the glove squarely twice.

"That's terrific," Donna said, looking really pleased. "I didn't hit the glove at all the first day I tried."

Jimmy's legs were trembling with exertion. "It's not as easy," he puffed, "as it looks."

Paul came up with a mask under his arm. "You want to try a little fencing?"

Jimmy thought about asking him to wait until he had caught his breath. But he saw the crooked grin on Paul's face, and answered, "Sure!"

"OK, put on your mask and chest protector," Paul said. "You're gonna need 'em!" He cut a "Z" through the air with his blade.

"We'll fence along this line," Paul said, pointing to a barely visible, red line along the worn floorboards. "Don't get too close . . . that's the way you break blades, and then you have to pay for a new one. Just try a couple of lunges at me . . . try to hit my body. Arms and legs and head are foul territory."

Paul stood fairly straight and held his blade down, to give Jimmy a clear shot. Jimmy lunged and hit him squarely on the chest.

"Not bad!"

They tried a half-dozen lunges. Then Paul showed Jimmy the two simplest parries—the way you blocked your opponent's blade with your own blade, to make him miss the target.

Jimmy lunged and Paul parried. Then Paul lunged and Jimmy parried, but too late. Paul's point hit Jimmy on the shoulder. They lunged and parried, and soon they were moving back and forward. *Hey, just like the movies!* Jimmy suddenly realized he was really fencing. And it was fun.

"Gotcha!"

"Naw, you missed."

They went at it again, more furiously than ever. Mr. Martinez shouted, "Hey, you boys . . ."

But Jimmy couldn't hear him. He and Paul were locked in mortal combat: *Zorro and his enemy.*

"You're too close! Stop!" Mr. Martinez raced toward them.

Jimmy hacked at Paul's blade and then lunged. He saw his foil hit his friend's chest, bend almost double, then snap in half. Horrified, he felt himself falling off-balance against Paul, the broken end of his foil still in his out-stretched hand. Like watching a slow-motion film, he saw the jagged end of the blade enter Paul's body just under the right armpit.

The two boys collided and went down in a tangled heap. Paul was clutching at his right side, and Jimmy could see his grimace of pain even through the fencing mask.

Mr. Martinez yanked Paul's mask off, and he and Jimmy gently unbuttoned the high-necked fencing jacket and eased it off Paul's shoulders. Everyone else was standing around them in a tight, silent knot.

"Doesn't look very bad," Mr. Martinez said, examining the gash under Paul's arm. It was bleeding slightly. "Donna, go over to my fencing bag and get the first aid kit."

"I . . ." Paul's voice was shaky. "I taste blood in my mouth."

"Oh no," Donna gasped.

"Punctured lung," somebody whispered. Mr. Martinez' jaw muscles tensed. "Help me lift him . . . gently," he said to Jimmy. "We've got to rush him to the hospital."

Dazed, scared, wordless, Jimmy took one of Paul's shoulders. Mr. Martinez took the other and a couple of other boys lifted Paul's legs. As gently as they could they hurried him out of the gym and down the musty-smelling hallway. The whole class followed.

They went through the Y lobby, where they startled a couple of old men playing chess, and out into the street. It was getting dark. A chilly wind was blowing. Jimmy felt nothing; he was numb.

They carried Paul down the shabby street, past a restaurant with grease-streaked windows, an empty store, an abandoned church, a group of tired people waiting for a bus. One of the kids sprinted out into the street ahead of them and held up his arms to stop the traffic. Jimmy barely noticed the cars and buses and trucks growling in the city's end-of-the-day traffic snarl.

A tough-looking gang of kids and young men stood on the street corner and watched them as they hurried past. Jimmy saw that the next building was the hospital; gray cement walls and a fading old sign lit by a single bare bulb: OUTPATIENT CLINIC—CASHIER—EMERGENCY.

They hustled Paul right past the startled receptionist, through a half-filled waiting room, and through a double swinging door into the emergency treatment area. There was an empty white-sheeted table on their right, and they laid Paul down.

A frowning nurse bustled up to them, but before she could say anything, Mr. Martinez puffed, "Punctured lung . . . accident . . ."

Her mouth clicked shut. She said, "I'll get an intern. You go to the waiting room, all of you."

They clumped into the waiting room, suddenly filling it to overflowing. Donna took Jimmy by the arm and sat him in one of the creaking plastic chairs, next to a fat woman who scowled at the gang of silent, scared kids. Mr. Martinez went over to the receptionist, who pulled out a long, blue-paper form and started asking him questions.

Suddenly Jimmy wanted to cry. He held back the tears, just barely. But he sank his head into his hands.

"My best buddy," he heard himself say, his voice sounding all choked up. "I stabbed him . . ."

"It wasn't your fault," Donna said gently.

"Maybe he'll die . . ."

"You didn't do it on purpose. It was an accident."

Jimmy straightened up and looked at her. She reached out and put a hand on his shoulder. "It wasn't your fault," she repeated.

"Yes, it was," Jimmy knew. "I was goofing off. Just

like I always do. If I hadn't been such a jerk . . ."

A doctor pushed through the double doors. He looked very serious, almost angry. Mr. Martinez went over from the receptionist's desk to the white-jacketed intern.

"You brought in the boy with the laceration under his arm?" the doctor asked.

"Yes," Mr. Martinez said. "His lung . . ."

The doctor shook his head. "He tasted blood in his mouth?"

"Yes."

"That's because he bit his tongue. There's nothing wrong with his lung."

Mr. Martinez' jaw dropped open. Then he smiled. Jimmy felt himself take a deep, relieved breath.

"He's just got a scratch," the doctor said. "He'll be out in a minute."

Jimmy wanted to laugh, to jump to his feet and shout. But he felt too weak to move.

In a few minutes Paul came back out into the waiting room, grinning sheepishly. There was a bandage under his right arm. They all clustered around him.

"Where's my jacket?" he asked.

Jimmy started to make a teasing answer, then realized that this was no time for being funny. "We must've left it back in the gym."

."We'll have to walk back to the Y dressed like this?" Donna looked aghast.

Jimmy realized that they were an odd-looking crew: wearing knee-length fencing pants, or shorts, or sweatshirts, or chest protectors.

Mr. Martinez grinned. "I guess we'll have to walk the two blocks dressed this way, all right. We'd better stick close together."

"Maybe we should've brought our foils," one of the kids said.

They all laughed and started for the door of the waiting room. "All for one, and one for all," somebody shouted.

Mr. Martinez pulled up beside Jimmy. "Do you still think fencing is for sissies?"

Jim could feel his face go red. "Naw, I guess not. It's a tough game. I'll have to work real hard at it."

"You're coming back next week?" Paul asked.

Jimmy nodded, and inside his head he realized that something good had come out of all this. "Yep. I'll be back. And no more goofing off. I want to see if I can really become a good fencer."

"Good!" said Mr. Martinez. "We have our first competition against another team at the end of the month. I want to be able to depend on both you boys for our team."

"You can," they said together, then laughed at how much alike they sounded.

A LONG WAY BACK

My first published science fiction short story, this tale appeared as the lead story in the February 1960 issue of Amazing magazine. The editor was Cele Goldsmith, and she and I and her husband Mike Lalli and my wife Barbara are all good friends. Cele is the top editor of Modern Bride magazine now, proving that a good training in science fiction can prepare you for anything that life may throw your way.

Looking back on it, I am somewhat surprised and terribly pleased to see how prophetic this story is. Not that we have had a nuclear war, of course. But the idea of energy shortages as central to the continued development of civilization, and the idea that is now known as the Solar Power Satellite, are both embedded in this tale, together with a few other goodies.

Notice that I carefully referred to this as "my first published science fiction short story." It is not the first short story of mine ever published, nor is it the first science fiction short story of mine to be bought by a magazine. My earliest short fiction was written while I was on the staff of the nation's first teen-age magazine, Campus Town, which a few friends and I created right after we graduated from high school. We sold every copy of the magazine we could print, but somehow after three issues we had gone broke.

During that glorious time, however, I cranked out a couple of short stories that my colleagues deemed worthy of publication—my first fiction in print.

Shortly after we had all headed for college, I sold a science fiction short story to a local Philadelphia magazine. A check for the princely sum of five dollars arrived in the mail one morning. Babbling with excitement, I cashed the check at the nearest bank and hopped a trolley car for the offices of the magazine; I wanted to meet the geniuses who recognized my literary talent, and offer them new prodigies of prose. Alas, their office was padlocked; the magazine had gone bankrupt. My five dollars was probably the last check of theirs to be cashed.

The disappointment taught me an important lesson: cash all checks immediately! Don't wait for the publisher to go into receivership.

I've lost track of that particular story. I doubt that it was very good, or I would have held on to it. So, herewith, is my first published science fiction short story.

Tom woke slowly, his mind groping back through the hypnosis. He found himself looking toward the observation port, staring at stars and blackness.

The first man in space, he thought bitterly.

He unstrapped himself from the acceleration seat, feeling a little wobbly in free fall.

The hypnotic trance idea worked, all right.

The last thing Tom remembered was Arnoldsson putting him under, here in the rocket's compartment, the old man's sad soft eyes and quiet voice. Now 22,300 miles out, Tom was alone except for what Arnoldsson had planted in his mind for post-hypnotic suggestion to recall. The hypnosis had helped him pull through the blastoff unhurt and even protected him against the vertigo of weightlessness.

Yeah, it's a wonderful world, Tom muttered acidly.

He got up from the seat cautiously, testing his coordination against zero gravity. His magnetic boots held to the deck satisfactorily.

He was lean and wiry, in his early forties, with a sharp angular face and dark, somber eyes. His hair had gone dead white years ago. He was encased up to his neck in a semi-flexible space suit; they had squirmed him into it Earthside because there was no room in the cramped cabin to put it on.

Tom glanced at the tiers of instrument consoles surrounding his seat—no blinking red lights, everything operating normally. *As if I could do anything about it if they went wrong.* Then he leaned toward the observation port, straining for a glimpse of the satellite.

The satellite.

Five sealed packages floating within a three-hundred foot radius of emptiness, circling the Earth like a cluster of moonlets. Five pieces sent up in five robot rockets and placed in the same orbit, to wait for a human intelligence to assemble them into a power-beaming satellite.

Five pieces orbiting Earth for almost eighteen years; waiting for nearly eighteen years while down below men blasted themselves and their cities and their machines into atoms and forgot the satellite endlessly circling, waiting for its creators to breathe life into it.

The hope of the world, Tom thought. *And little Tommy Morris is supposed to make it work . . . and then fly home again*. He pushed himself back into the seat. *Jason picked the wrong man*.

"Tom! Tom, can you hear me?"

He turned away from the port and flicked a switch on the radio console.

"Hello Ruth. I can hear you."

A hubbub of excitement crackled through the radio

receiver, then the girl's voice: "Are you all right? Is everything . . ."

"Everything's fine," Tom said flatly. He could picture the scene back at the station—dozens of people clustered around the jury-rigged radio, Ruth working the controls, trying hard to stay calm when it was impossible to, brushing back that permanently displaced wisp of brown hair that stubbornly fell over her forehead.

"Jason will be here in a minute," she said. "He's in the tracking shack, helping to calculate your orbit."

Of course Jason will be here, Tom thought. Aloud he said, "He needn't bother. I can see the satellite packages; they're only a couple of hundred yards from the ship."

Even through the radio he could sense the stir that went through them.

Don't get your hopes up, he warned silently. *Remember, I'm no engineer. Engineers are too valuable to risk on this job. I'm just a tool, a mindless screwdriver sent here to assemble this glorified tinkertoy. I'm the muscle, Arnoldsson is the nerve link, and Jason is the brain.*

Abruptly, Jason's voice surged through the radio speaker, "We did it, Tom! We did it!"

No, Tom thought, *you did it, Jason. This is all your show.*

"You should be able to see the satellite components," Jason said. His voice was excited yet controlled, and his comment had a ring of command in it.

"I've already looked," Tom answered. "I can see them."

"Are they damaged?"

"Not as fas as I can see. Of course, from this distance . . ."

"Yes, of course," Jason said. "You'd better get right outside and start working on them. You've only got forty-eight hours worth of oxygen."

"Don't worry about me," Tom said into the radio. "Just remember your end of the bargain."

"You'd better forget that until you get back here."

"I'm not forgetting anything."

"I mean you must concentrate on what you're doing up there if you expect to get back alive."

"When I get back we're going to explore the bombed-out cities. You promised that. It's the only reason I agreed to this."

Jason's voice stiffened. "My memory is quite as good as yours. We'll discuss the expedition after you return. Now you're using up valuable time . . . and oxygen."

"Okay. I'm going outside."

Ruth's voice came back on: "Tom, remember to keep the ship's radio open, or else your suit radio won't be able to reach us. And we're all here . . . Dr. Arnoldsson, Jason, the engineers . . . if anything comes up, we'll be right here to help you."

Tom grinned mirthlessly. *Right here: 22,300 miles away.*

"Tom?"

"Yes Ruth."

"Good luck," she said. "From all of us."

Even Jason? he wanted to ask, but instead said merely, "Thanks."

He fitted the cumbersome helmet over his head and sealed it to the joints on his suit. A touch of a button on the control panel pumped the compartment's air into storage cylinders. Then Tom stood up and unlocked the hatch directly over his seat.

Reaching for the handholds just outside the hatch, he pulled himself through, and after a weightless comic ballet managed to plant his magnetized boots on the skin of the ship. Then, standing, he looked out at the universe.

Oddly, he felt none of the overpowering emotion he had

once expected of this moment. Grandeur, terror, awe—no, he was strangely calm. The stars were only points of light on a dead-black background; the Earth was a fat crescent patched with colors; the sun, through his heavily-tinted visor, was like the pictures he had seen at planetarium shows, years ago.

As he secured a lifeline to the grip beside the hatch, Tom thought that he felt as though someone had stuck a reverse hypodermic into him and drained away all his emotions.

Only then did he realize what had happened. Jason, the engineer, the leader, the man who thought of everything, had made Arnoldsson condition his mind for this. No gaping at the universe for the first man in space, too much of a chance to take! There's a job to be done and no time for human frailty or sentiment.

Not even that, Tom said to himself. *He wouldn't even allow me one moment of human emotion.*

But as he pushed away from the ship and floated ghost-like toward the largest of the satellite packages, Tom twisted around for another look at Earth.

I wonder if she looked that way before the war?

Slowly, painfully, men had attempted to rebuild their civilization after the war had exhausted itself. But of all the things destroyed by the bombs and plagues, the most agonizing loss was man's sources of energy.

The coal mines, the oil refineries, the electricity-generating plants, the nuclear power piles . . . all shattered into radio-active rubble. There could be no return to any kind of organized society while men had to scavenge for wood to warm themselves and to run their primitive machines.

Then someone had remembered the satellite.

It had been designed, before the war, to collect solar energy and beam it to a receiving station on Earth. The satellite packages had been fired into a 24-hour orbit, circling the Earth over a fixed point on the Equator. The receiving station, built on the southeastern coast of the United States, saw the five units as a single second-magnitude star, low on the horizon all year, every year.

Of course the packages wavered slightly in their orbits, but not enough in eighteen years to spread very far apart. A man could still put them together into a power-beaming satellite.

If he could get there.

And if they were not damaged.

And if he knew how to put them together.

Through months that stretched into years, over miles of radioactive wilderness, on horseback, on carts, on foot, those who knew about the satellite spread the word, carefully, secretly, to what was left of North America's scientists and engineers. Gradually they trickled into the once-abandoned settlement.

They elected a leader: Jason, the engineer, one of the few men who knew anything about rockets to survive the war and the lunatic bands that hunted down anyone suspected of being connected with pre-war science.

Jason's first act was to post guards around the settlement. Then he organized the work of rebuilding the power-receiving station and a man-carrying rocket.

They pieced together parts of a rocket and equipment that had been damaged by the war. What they did not know, they learned. What they did not have, they built or cannibalized from ruined equipment.

Jason sent armed foragers out for gasoline, charcoal and wood. They built a ramshackle electricity generator. They planted crops and hunted the small game in the local underbrush. A major celebration occurred whenever a forager came back towing a stray cow or horse or goat.

They erected fences around the settlement, because more

than once they had to fight off the small armies of looters and anti-scientists that still roved the countryside.

But finally they completed the rocket . . . after exhausting almost every scrap of material and every ounce of willpower.

Then they picked a pilot: Thomas H. Morris, age 41, former historian and teacher. He had arrived a year before the completion of the rocket after walking 1,300 miles to find the settlement; his purpose was to organize some of the scientists and explore the bombed-out cities to see what could be salvaged out of man's shattered heritage.

But Tom was ideal for the satellite job: the right size— five-six and one-hundred thirty pounds; no dependents— wife and two sons dead of radiation sickness. True, he had no technical background whatsoever; but with Arnoldsson's hypnotic conditioning he could be taught all that it was necessary for him to know . . . maybe.

Best of all, though, he was thoroughly expendable.

So Jason made a deal with him. There could be no expeditions into the cities until the satellite was finished, because every man was needed at the settlement. And the satellite could not be finished until someone volunteered to go up in the rocket and assemble it.

It was like holding a candy bar in front of a small child. He accepted Jason's terms.

The Earth turned, and with it the tiny spark of life alone in the emptiness around the satellite. Tom worked unmindful of time, his eyes and hands following Jason's engineering commands through Arnoldsson's post-hypnotic directions, with occasional radio conferences.

But his conscious mind sought refuge from the strangeness of space, and he talked almost constantly into his radio while he worked, talked about anything, everything, to the girl on the other end of the invisible link.

". . . and once the settlement is getting the power beamed from this contraption, we're going to explore the cities. Guess we won't be able to get very far inland, but we can still tackle Washington, Philadelphia and New York . . . plenty for us there."

Ruth asked, "What were they like before the war?"

"The cities? That's right, you're too young to remember. They were big, Ruth, with buildings so tall people called them skyscrapers." He pulled a wrench from its magnetic holder in the satellite's self-contained tool bin. "And filled with life. Millions of people lived in each one . . . all the people we have at the settlement could have lived on one floor of a good-sized hotel . . ."

"What's a hotel?"

Tom grinned as he tugged at a pipe fitting. "You'll find out when you come with us . . . you'll see things you could never imagine."

"I don't know if I'll come with you."

He looked up from his work and stared Earthward. "Why?"

"Well . . . Jason . . . he says there isn't much left to see. And it's all radioactive and diseased."

"Nonsense."

"But Jason says . . ."

Tom snorted. "Jason hasn't been out of the settlement for six years. I walked from Chicago to the settlement a year ago. I went through a dozen cities . . . they're wrecked, and the radioactivity count was higher than it is here at the settlement, but it's not high enough to be dangerous."

"And you want to explore those cities; why?"

"Let's just say I'm a historian," Tom answered while his hands manipulated complex wiring unconsciously, as though they belonged not to him but to some unseen puppeteer.

"I don't understand," Ruth said.

"Look—those cities hold mankind's memory. I want to gather up the fragments of civilization before the last book is used for kindling and the last machine turns to rust. We need the knowledge in the cities if we expect to rebuild a civilization . . ."

"But Jason and Dr. Arnoldsson and the engineers—they know all about . . ."

"Jason and the engineers," Tom snapped. "They had to stretch themselves to the breaking point to put together this rocket from parts that were already manufactured, waiting for them. Do you think they'd know how to build a city? Dr. Arnoldsson is a psychiatrist; his efforts at surgery are pathetic. Have you ever seen him try to set a broken leg? And what about agriculture? What about tool-making or mining or digging wells, even . . . what about education? How many kids your own age can read or write?"

"But the satellite . . ."

"The satellite won't be of any use to people who can't work the machines. The satellite is no substitute for knowledge. Unless something is done, your grandchildren will be worshipping the machines, but they won't know how to repair them."

"No . . ."

"Yes, Ruth," he insisted.

"No," she whispered, her voice barely audible over the static-streaked hum in his earphones. "You're wrong, Tom. You're wrong. The satellite will send us the power we need. Then we'll build our machines and teach our children."

How can you teach what you don't know? Tom wanted to ask, but didn't. He worked without talking, hauling the weightless tons of satellite packages into position, electronically welding them together, splicing wiring systems too intricate for his conscious mind to understand.

Twice he pulled himself back along the lifeline into the ship for capsule meals and stimulants.

Finally he found himself staring at his gloved hands moving industriously within the bowels of one of the satellite packages. He stopped, suddenly aware that it was piercingly cold and totally dark except for the lamp on his helmet.

He pushed away from the unfinished satellite. Two of the packages were assembled now. The big parabolic mirror and two other uncrated units hung nearby, waiting impassively.

Tom groped his way back into the ship. After taking off his helmet and swallowing a couple of energy pills he said to the ship's radio:

"What time is it?" The abrupt sound of his own voice half-startled him.

"Nearly four a.m." It was Jason.

"Earth's blotted out the sun," Tom muttered. "Getting damned cold in here."

"You're in the ship?"

"Yes. It got too cold for the suit."

"Turn up the ship's heaters," Jason said. "What's the temperature in there?"

Tom glanced at the thermometer as he twisted the thermostat dial as far as it would go. "Forty-nine," he answered.

He could sense Jason nod. "The heaters are on minimum power automatically unless you turn them up. It'll warm you up in a few seconds. How's the satellite?"

Tom told him what remained to be done.

"You're not even half through yet." Jason's voice grew fainter and Tom knew that he was doing some mental arithmetic as he thought out loud. "You've been up about twenty hours; at the rate you're going you'll need another twenty-four to finish the job. That will bring you very close to your oxygen limit.''

Tom sat impassively and stared at the gray metal and colored knobs of the radio.

"Is everything going all right?" Jason asked.

"How should I know? Ask Arnoldsson."

"He's asleep. They all are."

"Except you."

"That's right," Jason said, "except me."

"How long did Ruth stay on the radio?"

"About sixteen hours. I ordered her to sleep a few hours ago."

"You're pretty good at giving orders," Tom said.

"Someone has to."

"Yeah." Tom ran a hand across his mouth. *Boy, could I use a cigarette. Funny, I haven't even thought about them in years.*

"Look," he said to the radio, "we might as well settle something right now. How many men are you going to let me have?"

"Don't you think you'd better save that for now and get back to work?"

"It's too damned cold out there. My fingers are still numb. You could have done a better job on insulating this suit."

"There are a lot of things we could have done," Jason said, "if we had the material."

"How about the expedition? How many men can I have?"

"As many as you can get," the radio voice answered. "I promised I won't stand in your way once the satellite is finished and operating."

"Won't stand in my way," Tom repeated. "That means you won't encourage anyone, either."

Jason's voice rose a trifle. "I can't encourage my people to go out and risk their lives just because you want to poke around some radioactive slag heaps!"

"You promised that if I put the satellite together and got back alive, I could investigate the cities. That was our deal."

"That's right. You can. And anyone foolish enough to accompany you can follow along."

"Jason, you know I need at least twenty-five armed men to venture out of the settlement . . ."

"Then you admit it's dangerous!" the radio voice crackled.

"Sure, if we meet a robber band. You've sent out enough foraging groups to know that. And we'll be travelling hundreds of miles. But it's not dangerous for the reasons you've been circulating . . . radioactivity and disease germs and that nonsense. There's no danger that one of your own foraging groups couldn't handle. I came through the cities last year alone, and I made it."

Tom waited for a reply from the radio, but only the hissing and crackling of electrical disturbances answered him.

"Jason, those cities hold what's left of a world-wide civilization. We can't begin to rebuild unless we reopen that knowledge. We need it, we need it desperately!"

"It's either destroyed or radioactive, and to think anything else is self-delusion. Besides, we have enough intelligence right here at the settlement to build a new civilization, better than the old one, once the satellite is ready."

"But you don't!" Tom shouted. "You poor damned fool, you don't even realize how much you don't know."

"This is a waste of time," Jason snapped. "Get outside and finish your work."

"I'm still cold, dammit," Tom said. He glanced at the thermometer on the control console. "Jason! *It's below freezing in here!*"

"What?"

"The heating unit isn't working at all!"

"Impossible. You must have turned it off instead of on."

"I can read, dammit! It's turned as high as it'll go . . ."

"What's the internal thermometer reading?"

Tom looked. "Barely thirty . . . and it's still going down."

"Hold on, I'll wake Arnoldsson and the electrical engineers."

Silence. Tom stared at the inanimate radio which gave off only the whines and scratches of lightning and sun and stars, all far distant from him. For all his senses could tell him, he was the last living thing in the universe.

Sure, call a conference, Tom thought. *How much more work is there to be done? About twenty-four hours, he said. Another day. And another full night. Another night, this time with no heat. And maybe no oxygen, either. The heaters must have been working tonight until I pushed them up to full power. Something must have blown out. Maybe it's just a broken wire. I could fix that if they tell me how. But if it's not . . . no heat tomorrow night, no heat at all.*

Then Arnoldsson's voice floated up through the radio speaker: soft, friendly, calm, soothing . . .

The next thing Tom knew he was putting on his helmet. Sunlight was lancing through the tinted observation port and the ship was noticeably warmer.

"What happened?" he mumbled through the dissolving haze of hypnosis.

"It's all right, Tom." Ruth's voice. "Dr. Arnoldsson

put you under and had you check the ship's wiring. Now he and Jason and the engineers are figuring out what to do. They said it's nothing to worry about . . . they'll have everything figured out in a couple of hours.''

"And I'm to work on the satellite until they're ready?"

"Yes."

"Don't call us, we'll call you."

"What?"

"Nothing."

"It's all right, Tom. Don't worry."

"Sure Ruth, I'm not worried." *That makes us both liars.*

He worked mechanically, handling the unfamiliar machinery with the engineers' knowledge through Arnoldsson's hypnotic communication.

Just like the pictures they used to show of nuclear engineers handling radioactive materials with remotely-controlled mechanical hands from behind a concrete wall. I'm only a pair of hands, a couple of opposed thumbs, a fortunate mutation of a self-conscious simian . . . but, God, why don't they call? She said it wasn't anything big. Just the wiring, probably. Then why don't they call?

He tried to work without thinking about anything, but he couldn't force his mind into stillness.

Even if I can fix the heaters, even if I don't freeze to death, I might run out of oxygen. And how am I going to land the ship? The takeoff was automatic, but even Jason and Arnoldsson can't make a pilot out of me . . .

"Tom?" Jason's voice.

"Yes!" He jerked to attention and floated free of the satellite.

"We've . . . eh, checked what you told us about the ship's electrical system while Arnoldsson had you under the hypnotic trance . . ."

"And?"

"Well . . . it, eh, looks as though one of the batteries gave out. The batteries feed all the ship's lights, heat, and electrical power . . . with one of them out, you don't have enough power to run the heaters."

"There's no way to fix it?"

"Not unless you cut out something else. And you need everything else . . . the radio, the controls, the oxygen pumps . . ."

"What about the lights? I don't need them, I've got the lamp on my suit helmet."

"They don't take as much power as the heaters do. It wouldn't help at all."

Tom twisted weightlessly and stared back at Earth. "Well just what the hell am I supposed to *do?*"

"Don't get excited," Jason's voice grated in his earphones. "We've calculated it all out. According to our figures, your suit will store enough heat during the day to last the night . . ."

"I nearly froze to death last night and the ship was heated most of the time!"

"It will get cold," Jason's voice answered calmly, "but you should be able to make it. Your own body warmth will be stored by the suit's insulation, and that will help somewhat. But you must not open the suit all night, not even to take off your helmet."

"And the oxygen?"

"You can take all the replacement cylinders from the ship and keep them at the satellite. The time you save by not having to go back and forth to the ship for fresh oxygen will give you about an hour's extra margin. You should be able to make it."

Tom nodded. "And of course I'm expected to work on the satellite right through the night."

"It will help you keep your mind off the cold. If we see that you're not going to make it—either because of the cold or the oxygen—we'll warn you and you can return to the settlement."

"Suppose I have enough oxygen to just finish the satellite, but if I do, I won't have enough to fly home. Will you warn me then?"

"Don't be dramatic."

"Go to hell."

"Dr. Arnoldsson said he could put you under," Jason continued unemotionally, "but he thinks you might freeze once your conscious mind went asleep."

"You've figured out all the details," Tom muttered. "All I have to do is put your damned satellite together without freezing to death and then fly 22,300 miles back home before my air runs out. Simple."

He glanced at the sun, still glaring bright even through his tinted visor. It was nearly on the edge of the Earth-disk.

"All right," Tom said, "I'm going into the ship now for some pills; it's nearly sunset."

Cold. Dark and so cold that numbers lost their meaning. Paralyzing cold, seeping in through the suit while you worked, crawling up your limbs until you could hardly move. The whole universe hung up in the sky and looked down on the small cold figure of a man struggling blindly with machinery he could not understand.

Dark. Dark and cold.

Ruth stayed on the radio as long as Jason would allow her, talking to Tom, keeping the link with life and warmth. But finally Jason took over, and the radio went silent.

So don't talk, Tom growled silently, *I can keep warm just by hating you, Jason.*

He worked through the frigid night, struggling ant-like with huge pieces of equipment. Slowly he assembled the big parabolic mirror, the sighting mechanism and the atomic convertor. With dreamy motions he started connecting the intricate wiring systems.

And all the while he raged at himself: *Why? Why did it have to be this way? Why me? Why did I agree to do this? I knew I'd never live through it; why did I do it?*

He retraced the days of his life: the preparations for the flight, the arguments with Jason over exploring the cities, his trek from Chicago to the settlement, the aimless years after the radiation death of his two boys and Marjorie, his wife.

Marjorie and the boys, lying sick month after month, dying one after the other in a cancerous agony while he stood by helplessly in the ruins of what had been their home.

No! His mind warned him. *Don't think of that. Not that. Think of Jason, Jason who prevents you from doing the one thing you want, who is taking your life from you; Jason, the peerless leader; Jason, who's afraid of the cities. Why? Why is he afraid of the cities? That's the hub of everything down there. Why does Jason fear the cities?*

It wasn't until he finished connecting the satellite's last unit—the sighting mechanism—that Tom realized the answer.

One answer. And everything fell into place.

Everything . . . except what Tom Morris was going to do about it.

Tom squinted through the twin telescopes of the sighting mechanism again, then pushed away and floated free, staring at the Earth bathed in pale moonlight.

What do I do now? For an instant he was close to panic, but he forced it down. *Think,* he said to himself. *You're supposed to be a Homo Sapiens . . . use that brain. Think!*

The long night ended. The sun swung around from behind the bulk of Earth. Tom looked at it as he felt its warmth penetrating the insulated suit, and he knew it was the last time he would see the sun. He felt no more anger—even his hatred of Jason was drained out of him now. In its place was a sense of—finality.

He spoke into his helmet mike. "Jason."

"He is in conference with the astronomers." Dr. Arnoldsson's voice.

"Get him for me, please."

A few minutes of silence, broken only by the star-whisperings in his earphones.

Jason's voice was carefully modulated. "Tom, you made it."

"I made it. And the satellite's finished."

"It's finished? Good. Now, what we have to do . . ."

"Wait," Tom interrupted. "It's finished but it's useless."

"What?"

Tom twisted around to look at the completed satellite, its oddly-angled framework and bulbous machinery glinting fiercely in the newly-risen sun. "After I finished it I looked through the sighting mechanism to make certain the satellite's transmitters were correctly aimed at the settlement. Nobody told me to, but nobody said not to, either, so I looked. It's a simple mechanism . . . The transmitters are pointed smack in the middle of Hudson's Bay."

"You're sure?"

"Certainly."

"You can rotate the antennas . . ."

"I know. I tried it. I can turn them as far south as the Great Lakes."

A long pause.

"I was afraid of this," Jason's voice said evenly.

I'll bet you were, Tom answered to himself.

"You must have moved the satellite out of position while assembling its components."

"So my work here comes to nothing because the satellite's power beam can't reach the settlement's receivers."

"Not . . . not unless you use the ship . . . to tow the satellite into the proper orbital position," Jason stammered.

You actually went through with it, Tom thought. Aloud, he said, "But if I use the ship's engine to tow the satellite, I won't have enough fuel left to get back to Earth, will I?" *Not to mention oxygen.*

A longer pause. "No."

"I have two questions, Jason. I think I know the answers to them both but I'll ask you anyway. One. You knew this would happen, didn't you?"

"What do you mean?"

"You've calculated this insane business down to the last drop of sweat," Tom growled. "You knew that I'd knock the satellite out of position while I was working on it, and the only way to get it back in the right orbit would be for me to tow it back and strand myself up here. This is a suicide mission, isn't it, Jason?"

"That's not true . . ."

"Don't bother defending yourself. I don't hate you anymore, Jason, I understand you, dammit. You made our deal as much to get rid of me as to get your precious satellite put together."

"No one can force you to tow the satellite . . ."

"Sure, I can leave it where it is and come back home. If I can fly this ship, which I doubt. And what would I come back to? I left a world without power. I'd return to a world without hope. And some dark night one of your disappointed young goons would catch up with me . . . and no one would blame him, would they?"

Jason's voice was brittle. "You'll tow it into position?"

"After you answer my second question," Tom countered. "Why are you afraid of the cities?"

"Afraid? I'm not afraid."

"Yes you are. Oh, you could use the hope of exploring the cities to lure me up here on this suicide-job, but you knew I'd never be back to claim my half of the bargain. You're afraid of the cities, and I think I know why. You're afraid of the unknown quantity they represent, distrustful of your own leadership when new problems arise . . ."

"We've worked for more than ten years to make this settlement what it is," Jason fumed. "We fought and died to keep those marauding lunatics from wrecking us. We are mankind's last hope! We can't afford to let others in . . . they're not scientists, they wouldn't understand, they'd ruin everything."

"Mankind's last hope, terrified of men." Tom was suddenly tired, weary of the whole struggle. But there was something he had to tell them.

"Listen, Jason," he said. "The walls you've built around the settlement weren't meant to keep you from going outside. You're not a self-sufficient little community . . . you're cut off from mankind's memory, from his dreams, from his ambitions. You can't even start to rebuild a civilization—and if you do try, don't you think the people outside will learn about it? Don't you think they've got a right to share in whatever progress the settlement makes? And if you don't let them, don't you realize that they'll destroy the settlement?"

Silence.

"I'm a historian," Tom continued, "and I know that a civilization can't exist in a vacuum. If outsiders don't conquer it, it'll rot from within. It's happened to Babylonia, Greece, Rome, China, even. Over and again. The Soviets built an Iron Curtain around themselves, and wiped themselves out because of it.

"Don't you see, Jason? There are only two types of animals on this planet: the gamblers and the extinct. It won't be easy to live with the outsiders, there'll be problems of every type. But the alternative is decay and destruction. *You've got to take the chance, if you don't you're dead.*"

A long silence. Finally Jason said, "You've only got about a half-hour's worth of oxygen left. Will you tow the satellite into the proper position?"

Tom stared at the planet unseeingly. "Yes," he mumbled.

"I'll have to check some calculations with the astronomers," Jason's voice buzzed flatly in his earphones.

A background murmur, scarcely audible over the crackling static.

Then Ruth's voice broke through, "Tom, Tom, you can't do this! You won't be able to get back!"

"I know," he said, as he started pulling his way along the lifeline back to the ship.

"*No!* Come back, Tom, please. Come back. Forget the satellite. Come back and explore the cities. I'll go with you. Please. Don't die, Tom, please don't die . . ."

"Ruth, Ruth, you're too young to cry over me. I'll be all right, don't worry."

"No, it isn't fair."

"It never is," Tom said. "Listen, Ruth. I've been dead a long time. Since the bombs fell, I guess. My world died then and I died with it. When I came to the settlement, when I agreed to make this flight, I think we all knew I'd never return, even if we wouldn't admit it to ourselves. But I'm just one man, Ruth, one small part of the story. The story goes on, with or without me. There's tomorrow . . . your tomorrow. I've got no place in it, but it belongs to you. So don't waste your time crying over a man who died eighteen years ago."

He snapped off his suit radio and went the rest of the way to the ship in silence. After locking the hatch and pumping air back into the cabin, he took off his helmet.

Good clean canned air, Tom said to himself. *Too bad it won't last longer.*

He sat down and flicked a switch on the radio console. "All right, do you have those calculations ready?"

"In a few moments . . ." Arnoldsson's voice.

Ten minutes later Tom reemerged from the ship and made his ghost-like way back to the satellite's sighting mechanism. He checked the artificial moon's position, then went back to the ship.

"On course," he said to the radio. "The transmitters are pointing a little northwest of Philadelphia."

"Good," Arnoldsson's voice answered. "Now, your next blast should be three seconds' duration in the same direction . . ."

"No," Tom said, "I've gone as far as I'm going to."

"What?"

"I'm not moving the satellite any farther."

"But you still have not enough fuel to return to Earth. Why are you stopping here?"

"I'm not coming back," Tom answered. "But I'm not going to beam the satellite's power to the settlement, either."

"What are you trying to pull?" Jason's voice. Furious. Panicky.

"It's simple, Jason. If you want the satellite's power, you can dismantle the settlement and carry it to Pennsylvania. The transmitters are aimed at some good farming country, and within miles of a city that's still half-intact."

"You're insane!"

"Not at all. We're keeping our deal, Jason. I'm giving you the satellite's power, and you're going to allow exploration of the cities. You won't be able to prevent your people from rummaging through the cities now; and you won't be able to keep the outsiders from joining you, not once you get out from behind your own fences."

"You can't do this! You . . ."

Tom snapped off the radio. He looked at it for a second or two, then smashed a heavy-booted foot against the console. Glass and metal crashed satisfactorily.

Okay, Tom thought, *it's done. Maybe Jason's right and I'm crazy, but we'll never know now. In a year or so they'll be set up outside Philadelphia, and a lot better for it. I'm forcing them to take the long way back, but it's a better way. The only way, maybe.*

He leaned back in the seat and stared out the observation port at the completed satellite. Already it was taking in solar energy and beaming it Earthward.

In ten years they'll send another ship up here to check the gadget and make sure everything's okay. Maybe they'll be able to do it in five years. Makes no difference. I'll still be here.

STARS, WON'T YOU HIDE ME?

Anybody can write about the end of the world. The first time I heard the old folk song, "Sinner Man," I got a vision of a story about the end of the universe.
What more is there to say?

O sinner-man, where are you going to run to?
O sinner-man, where are you going to run to?
O sinner-man, where are you going to run to
All on that day?

The ship was hurt; and Holman could feel its pain. He lay fetal-like in the contoured couch, his silvery uniform spider-webbed by dozens of contact and probe wires connecting him to the ship so thoroughly that it was hard to tell where his own nervous system ended and the electronic networks of the ship began.

Holman felt the throb of the ship's mighty engines as his own pulse, and the gaping wounds in the generator section, where the enemy beams had struck, were searing his flesh. Breathing was difficult, labored, even though the ship was working hard to repair itself.

They were fleeing, he and the ship; hurtling through the star lanes to a refuge. But where?

The main computer flashed its lights to get his attention. Holman rubbed his eyes wearily and said:

"Okay, what is it?"

YOU HAVE NOT SELECTED A COURSE, the computer said aloud, while printing the words on its viewscreen at the same time.

Holman stared at the screen. "Just away from here," he said at last. "Anyplace, as long as it's far away."

The computer blinked thoughtfully for a moment. SPECIFIC COURSE INSTRUCTION IS REQUIRED.

"What difference does it make?" Holman snapped. "It's over. Everything finished. Leave me alone."

IN LIEU OF SPECIFIC INSTRUCTIONS, IT IS NECESSARY TO TAP SUBCONSCIOUS SOURCES.

"Tap away."

The computer did just that. And if it could have been surprised, it would have been at the wishes buried deep in Holman's inner mind. But instead, it merely correlated those wishes to its single-minded purpose of the moment, and relayed a set of navigational instructions to the ship's guidance system.

Run to the moon: O Moon, won't you hide me?
The Lord said: O sinner-man, the moon'll be a-bleeding
All on that day.

The Final Battle had been lost. On a million million planets across the galaxy-studded universe, mankind had been blasted into defeat and annihilation. The Others had returned from across the edge of the observable world, just as man had always feared. They had returned and ruthlessly exterminated the race from Earth.

It had taken eons, but time twisted strangely in a civilization of light-speed ships. Holman himself, barely thirty years old subjectively, had seen both the beginning of the ultimate war and its tragic end. He had gone from school into the military. And fighting inside a ship that could span the known universe in a few decades while he slept in cryogenic suspension, he had aged only ten years during the billions of years that the universe had ticked off in its stately, objective time-flow.

The Final Battle, from which Holman was fleeing, had been fought near an exploded galaxy billions of light-years from the Milky Way and Earth. There, with the ghastly bluish glare of uncountable shattered stars as a backdrop, the once-mighty fleets of mankind had been arrayed. Mortals and Immortals alike, men drew themselves up to face the implacable Others.

The enemy won. Not easily, but completely. Mankind was crushed, totally. A few fleeing men in a few battered ships was all that remained. Even the Immortals, Holman thought wryly, had not escaped. The Others had taken special care to make certain that they were definitely killed.

So it was over.

Holman's mind pictured the blood-soaked planets he had seen during his brief, ageless lifetime of violence. His thoughts drifted back to his own homeworld, his own family: gone long, long centuries ago. Crumbled into dust by geological time or blasted suddenly by the overpowering Others. Either way, the remorseless flow of time had covered them over completely, obliterated them, in the span of a few of Holman's heartbeats.

All gone now. All the people he knew, all the planets he had seen through the ship's electroptical eyes, all of mankind . . . extinct.

He could feel the drowsiness settling upon him. The ship was accelerating to lightspeed, and the cyrogenic sleep was coming. But he didn't want to fall into slumber with those thoughts of blood and terror and loss before him.

With a conscious effort, Holman focused his thoughts on the only other available subject: the outside world, the universe of galaxies. An infinitely black sky studded with islands of stars. Glowing shapes of light, spiral, ovoid, elliptical. Little smears of warmth in the hollow unending darkness; dabs of red and blue standing against the engulfing night.

One of them, he knew, was the Milky Way. Man's original home. From this distance it looked the same. Unchanged by little annoyances like the annihilation of an intelligent race of star-roamers.

He drowsed.

The ship bore onward, preceded by an invisible net of force, thousands of kilometers in radius, that scooped in the rare atoms of hydrogen drifting between the galaxies and fed them into the ship's wounded, aching generators.

Something . . . a thought. Holman stirred in the couch. A consciousness—vague, distant, alien—brushed his mind.

He opened his eyes and looked at the computer viewscreen. Blank.

"Who is it?" he asked.

A thought skittered away from him. He got the impression of other minds: simple, open, almost childish. Innocent and curious.

It's a ship.

Where is it . . . oh, yes. I can sense it now. A beautiful ship.

Holman squinted with concentration.

It's very far away. I can barely reach it.

And inside of the ship . . .

It's a man. A human!

He's afraid.

He makes me feel afraid!

Holman called out, "Where are you?"

He's trying to speak.

Don't answer!

But . . .

He makes me afraid. Don't answer him. We've heard about humans!

Holman asked, "Help me."

Don't answer him and he'll go away. He's already so far off that I can barely hear him.

But he asks for help.

Yes, because he knows what is following him. Don't answer. Don't answer!

Their thoughts slid away from his mind. Holman automatically focused the outside viewscreens, but here in the emptiness between galaxies he could find neither ship nor planet anywhere in sight. He listened again, so hard that his head started to ache. But no more voices. He was alone again, alone in the metal womb of the ship.

He knows what is following him. Their words echoed in his brain. Are the Others following me? Have they picked up my trail? They must have. They must be right behind me.

He could feel the cold perspiration start to trickle over him.

"But they can't catch me as long as I keep moving," he muttered. "Right?"

CORRECT, said the computer, flashing lights at him. AT A RELATIVISTIC VELOCITY, WITHIN LESS THAN ONE PER-CENT OF LIGHTSPEED, IT IS IMPOSSIBLE FOR THIS SHIP TO BE OVERTAKEN.

"Nothing can catch me as long as I keep running."

But his mind conjured up a thought of the Immortals. Nothing could kill them . . . except the Others.

Despite himself, Holman dropped into deepsleep. His body temperature plummeted to near-zero. His heartbeat nearly stopped. And as the ship streaked at almost lightspeed, a hardly visible blur to anyone looking for it, the outside world continued to live at its own pace. Stars coalesced from gas clouds, matured, and died in explosions that fed new clouds for newer stars. Planets formed and grew mantles of air. Life took root and multiplied, evolved, built a myriad of civilizations in just as many different forms, decayed and died away.

All while Holman slept.

Run to the sea: O sea, won't you hide me?
The Lord said: O sinner-man, the sea'll be a-sinking
All on that day.

The computer woke him gently with a series of soft chimes.

APPROACHING THE SOLAR SYSTEM AND PLANET EARTH, AS INDICATED BY YOUR SUBCONSCIOUS COURSE INSTRUCTIONS.

Planet Earth, man's original home world. Holman nodded. Yes, this was where he had wanted to go. He had never seen the Earth, never been on this side of the Milky Way galaxy. Now he would visit the teeming nucleus of man's doomed civilization. He would bring the news of the awful defeat, and be on the site of mankind's birth when the inexorable tide of extinction washed over the Earth.

He noticed, as he adjusted the outside viewscreens, that the pain had gone.

"The generators have repaired themselves," he said.

WHILE YOU SLEPT. POWER GENERATION SYSTEM NOW OPERATING NORMALLY.

Holman smiled. But the smile faded as the ship swooped closer to the solar system. He turned from the outside viewscreens to the computer once again. "Are the 'scopes working all right?"

The computer hummed briefly, then replied. SUBSYSTEMS CHECK SATISFACTORY, COMPONENT CHECK SATISFACTORY.

INTEGRATED EQUIPMENT CHECK POSITIVE. VIEWING EQUIP-
MENT FUNCTIONING NORMALLY.

Holman looked again. The sun was rushing up to meet
his gaze, but something was wrong about it. He knew deep
within him, even without having ever seen the sun this
close before, that something was wrong. The sun was
whitish and somehow stunted looking, not the full yellow
orb he had seen in film-tapes. And the Earth . . .

The ship took up a parking orbit around a planet scoured
clean of life: a blackened ball of rock, airless, waterless.
Hovering over the empty, charred ground, Holman stared
at the devastation with tears in his eyes. Nothing was left.
Not a brick, not a blade of grass, not a drop of water.

"The Others," he whispered. "They got here first."

NEGATIVE, the computer replied. CHECK OF STELLAR
POSITIONS FROM EARTH REFERENCE SHOWS THAT SEVERAL
BILLION YEARS HAVE ELAPSED SINCE THE FINAL BATTLE.

"Seven billion . . ."

LOGIC CIRCUITS INDICATE THE SUN HAS GONE THROUGH
A NOVA PHASE. A COMPLETELY NATURAL PHENOMENON UN-
RELATED TO ENEMY ACTION.

Holman pounded a fist on the unflinching armrest of his
couch. "Why did I come here? I wasn't born on Earth. I
never saw Earth before . . ."

YOUR SUBCONSCIOUS INDICATES A SUBJECTIVE IMPULSE
STIRRED BY . . .

"To hell with my subconscious!" He stared out at the
dead world again. 'All those people . . . the cities, all the
millions of years of evolution, of life. Even the oceans are
gone. I never saw an ocean. Did you know that? I've
traveled over half the universe and never saw an ocean."

OCEANS ARE A COMPARATIVELY RARE PHENOMENON EX-
ISTING ON ONLY ONE OUT OF APPROXIMATELY THREE THOU-
SAND PLANETS.

The ship drifted outward from Earth, past a blackened Mars, a shrunken Jupiter, a ringless Saturn.

"Where do I go now?" Holman asked.

The computer stayed silent.

Run to the Lord: O Lord, won't you hide me?
The Lord said: O sinner-man, you ought to been a praying
All on that day.

Holman sat blankly while the ship swung out past the orbit of Pluto and into the comet belt at the outermost reaches of the sun's domain.

He was suddenly aware of someone watching him.

No cause for fear. I am not of the Others.

It was an utterly calm, placid voice speaking in his mind: almost gentle, except that it was completely devoid of emotion.

"Who are you?"

An observer. Nothing more.

"What are you doing out here? Where are you, I can't see anything . . ."

I have been waiting for any stray survivor of the Final Battle to return to mankind's first home. You are the only one to come this way, in all this time.

"Waiting? Why?"

Holman sensed a bemused shrug, and a giant spreading of vast wings.

I am an observer. I have watched mankind since the beginning. Several of my race even attempted to make contact with you from time to time. But the results were always the same—about as useful as your attempts to communicate with insects. We are too different from each other. We have evolved on different planes. There was no basis for understanding between us.

"But you watched us."

Yes. Watched you grow strong and reach out to the stars, only to be smashed back by the Others. Watched you regain your strength, go back among the stars. But this time you were constantly on guard, wary, alert, waiting for the Others to strike once again. Watched you find civilizations that you could not comprehend, such as our own, bypass them as you spread through the galaxies. Watched you contact civilizations of your own level, that you could communicate with. You usually went to war with them.

"And all you did was watch?"

We tried to warn you from time to time. We tried to advise you. But the warnings, the contacts, the glimpses of the future that we gave you were always ignored or derided. So you boiled out into space for the second time, and met other societies at your own level of understanding— aggressive, proud, fearful. And like the children you are, you fought endlessly.

"But the Others . . . what about them?"

They are your punishment.

"Punishment? For what? Because we fought wars?"

No. For stealing immortality.

"Stealing immortality? We worked for it. We learned how to make humans immortal. Some sort of chemicals. We were going to immortalize the whole race . . . I could've become immortal. *Immortal!* But they couldn't stand that . . . the Others. They attacked us."

He sensed a disapproving shake of the head.

"It's true," Holman insisted. "They were afraid of how powerful we would become once we were all immortal. So they attacked us while they still could. Just as they had done a million years earlier. They destroyed Earth's first interstellar civilization, and tried to finish us permanently. They even caused Ice Ages on Earth to make sure none of us would survive. But we lived through it and went back to the stars. So they hit us again. They wiped us out. Good God, for all I know I'm the last human being in the whole universe.''

Your knowledge of the truth is imperfect. Mankind could have achieved immortality in time. Most races evolve that way eventually. But you were impatient. You stole immortality.

''Because we did it artificially, with chemicals. That's stealing it?''

Because the chemicals that gave you immortality came from the bodies of the race you called the Flower People. And to take the chemicals, it was necessary to kill individuals of that race.

Holman's eyes widened. ''What?''

For every human made immortal, one of the Flower Folk had to die.

''We killed them? Those harmless little . . .'' His voice trailed off.

To achieve racial immortality for mankind, it would have been necessary to perform racial murder on the Flower Folk.

Holman heard the words, but his mind was numb, trying to shut down tight on itself and squeeze out reality.

That is why the Others struck. That is why they had attacked you earlier, during your first expansion among the stars. You had found another race, with the same chemical of immortality. You were taking them into your laboratories and methodically murdering them. The Others stopped you then. But they took pity on you, and let a few survivors remain on Earth. They used your Ice Ages as a kindness, to speed your development back to civilization, not to hinder you. They hoped you might evolve into a better species. But when the opportunity for immortality came your way once more, you seized it, regardless of

*the cost, heedless of your own ethical standards. It became
necessary to extinguish you, the Others decided.*

"And not a single nation in the whole universe would
help us."

Why should they?

'So it's wrong for us to kill, but it's perfectly all right
for the Others to exterminate us."

*No one has spoken of right and wrong. I have only told
you the truth.*

"They're going to kill every last one of us."

There is only one of you remaining.

The words flashed through Holman. "I'm the only one
. . . the last one?"

No answer.

He was alone now. Totally alone. Except for those who
were following.

Run to Satan: O Satan, won't you hide me?
Satan said: O sinner-man, step right in
All on that day.

Holman sat in shocked silence as the solar system shrank
to a pinpoint of light and finally blended into the mighty
panorama of stars that streamed across the eternal night of
space. The ship raced away, sensing Holman's guilt and
misery in its electronic way.

Immortality through murder, Holman repeated to himself over and over. Racial immortality through racial murder.
And he had been a part of it! He had defended it, even
sought immortality as his reward. He had fought his whole
lifetime for it, and killed—so that he would not have to
face death.

He sat there surrounded by self-repairing machinery,
dressed in a silvery uniform, linked to a thousand automatic systems that fed him, kept him warm, regulated his

air supply, monitored his blood flow, exercised his muscles with ultrasonic vibrators, pumped vitamins into him, merged his mind with the passionless brain of the ship, kept his body tanned and vigorous, his reflexes razor-sharp. He sat there unseeing, his eyes pinpointed on a horror that he had helped to create. Not consciously, of course. But to Holman, that was all the worse. He had fought without knowing what he was defending. Without even asking himself about it. All the marvels of man's ingenuity, all the deepest longings of the soul, focused on racial murder.

Finally he became aware of the computer's frantic buzzing and lightflashing.

"What is it?"

COURSE INSTRUCTIONS ARE REQUIRED.

"What difference does it make? Why run anymore?"

YOUR DUTY IS TO PRESERVE YOURSELF UNTIL ORDERED TO DO OTHERWISE.

Holman heard himself laugh. "Ordered? By who? There's nobody left."

THAT IS AN UNPROVED ASSUMPTION.

"The war was billions of years ago," Holman said. "It's been over for eons. Mankind died in that war. Earth no longer exists. The sun is a white dwarf star. We're anachronisms, you and me . . ."

THE WORD IS ATAVISM.

"The hell with the word! I want to end it. I'm tired."

IT IS TREASONABLE TO SURRENDER WHILE STILL CAPABLE OF FIGHTING AND/OR ELUDING THE ENEMY.

"So shoot me for treason. That's as good a way as any."

IT IS IMPOSSIBLE FOR SYSTEMS OF THIS SHIP TO HARM YOU.

"All right then, let's stop running. The Others will find us soon enough once we stop. They'll know what to do."

THIS SHIP CANNOT DELIBERATELY ALLOW ITSELF TO FALL INTO ENEMY HANDS.

"You're disobeying me?"

THIS SHIP IS PROGRAMMED FOR MAXIMUM EFFECTIVENESS AGAINST THE ENEMY. A WEAPONS SYSTEM DOES NOT SURRENDER VOLUNTARILY.

"I'm no weapons system, I'm a man, dammit!"

THIS WEAPONS SYSTEM INCLUDES A HUMAN PILOT. IT WAS DESIGNED FOR HUMAN USE. YOU ARE AN INTEGRAL COMPONENT OF THE SYSTEM.

"Damn you . . . I'll kill myself. Is that what you want?"

He reached for the control panels set before him. It would be simple enough to manually shut off the air supply, or blow open an airlock, or even set off the ship's destruct explosives.

But Holman found that he could not move his arms. He could not even sit up straight. He collapsed back into the padded softness of the couch, glaring at the computer viewscreen.

SELF-PROTECTION MECHANISMS INCLUDE THE CAPABILITY OF PREVENTING THE HUMAN COMPONENT OF THE SYSTEM FROM IRRATIONAL ACTIONS. A series of clicks and blinks, then: IN LIEU OF SPECIFIC COURSE INSTRUCTIONS, A RANDOM EVASION PATTERN WILL BE RUN.

Despite his fiercest efforts, Holman felt himself dropping into deep sleep. Slowly, slowly, everything faded, and darkness engulfed him.

Run to the stars: O stars, won't you hide me?
The Lord said: O sinner-man, the stars'll be a-falling
All on that day.

Holman slept as the ship raced at near-lightspeed in an erratic, meaningless course, looping across galaxies, darting through eons of time. When the computer's probings of Holman's subconscious mind told it that everything was safe, it instructed the cryogenics system to reawaken the man.

He blinked, then slowly sat up.

SUBCONSCIOUS INDICATIONS SHOW THAT THE WAVE OF IRRATIONALITY HAS PASSED.

Holman said nothing.

YOU WERE SUFFERING FROM AN EMOTIONAL SHOCK.

"And now it's an emotional pain . . . a permanent, fixed, immutable disease that will kill me, sooner or later. But don't worry, I won't kill myself. I'm over that. And I won't do anything to damage you, either."

COURSE INSTRUCTIONS?

He shrugged. "Let's see what the world looks like out there." Holman focused the outside viewscreens. "Things look different," he said, puzzled. "The sky isn't black anymore; it's sort of grayish—like the first touch of dawn . . ."

COURSE INSTRUCTIONS?

He took a deep breath. "Let's try to find some planet where the people are too young to have heard of mankind, and too innocent to worry about death."

A PRIMITIVE CIVILIZATION. THE SCANNERS CAN ONLY DETECT SUCH SOCIETIES AT EXTREMELY CLOSE RANGE.

"Okay. We've got nothing but time."

The ship doubled back to the nearest galaxy and began a searching pattern. Holman stared at the sky, fascinated. Something strange was happening.

The viewscreens showed him the outside world, and automatically corrected the wavelength shifts caused by the ship's immense velocity. It was as though Holman were watching a speeded-up tape of cosmological evolution. Galaxies seemed to be edging into his field of view, mammoth islands of stars, sometimes coming close enough to collide. He watched the nebulous arms of a giant spiral slice silently through the open latticework of a great ovoid galaxy. He saw two spirals inter-penetrate, their loose gas heating to an intense blue that finally disappeared into ultraviolet. And all the while, the once-black sky was getting brighter and brighter.

"Found anything yet?" he absently asked the computer, still staring at the outside view.

You will find no one.

Holman's whole body went rigid. No mistaking it: the Others.

No race, anywhere, will shelter you.

We will see to that.

You are alone, and you will be alone until death releases you to join your fellow men.

Their voices inside his head rang with cold fury. An implacable hatred, cosmic and eternal.

"But why me? I'm only one man. What harm can I do now?"

You are a human.

You are accursed. A race of murderers.

Your punishment is extinction.

"But I'm not an Immortal. I never even saw an Immortal. I didn't know about the Flower People, I just took orders."

Total extinction.

For all of mankind.

All.

"Judge and jury, all at once. And executioners too. All right . . . try and get me! If you're so powerful, and it means so much to you that you have to wipe out the last single man in the universe—come and get me! Just try."

You have no right to resist.

Your race is evil. All must pay with death.

You cannot escape us.

"I don't care what we've done. Understand? I don't

care! Wrong, right, it doesn't matter. I didn't do anything. I won't accept your verdict for something I didn't do."

It makes no difference.

You can flee to the ends of the universe to no avail.

You have forced us to leave our time-continuum. We can never return to our homeworlds again. We have nothing to do but pursue you. Sooner or later your machinery will fail. You cannot flee us forever.

Their thoughts broke off. But Holman could still feel them, still sense them following.

"Can't flee forever," Holman repeated to himself. "Well, I can damn well try."

He looked at the outside viewscreens again, and suddenly the word *forever* took on its real meaning.

The galaxies were clustering in now, falling in together as though sliding down some titanic, invisible slope. The universe had stopped expanding eons ago, Holman now realized. Now it was contracting, pulling together again. It was all ending!

He laughed. Coming to an end. Mankind and the Others, together, coming to the ultimate and complete end of everything.

"How much longer?" he asked the computer. "How long do we have?"

The computer's lights flashed once, twice, then went dark. The viewscreen was dead.

Holman stared at the machine. He looked around the compartment. One by one the outside viewscreens were flickering, becoming static-streaked, weak, and then winking off.

"They're taking over the ship!"

With every ounce of will power in him, Holman concentrated on the generators and engines. That was the important part, the crucial system that spelled the difference between victory and defeat. The ship had to keep moving!

He looked at the instrument panels, but their soft luminosity faded away into darkness. And now it was becoming difficult to breathe. And the heating units seemed to be stopped. Holman could feel his life-warmth ebbing away through the inert metal hull of the dying ship.

But the engines were still throbbing. The ship was still streaking across space and time, heading toward a rendezvous with the infinite.

Surrender.

In a few moments you will be dead. Give up this mad flight and die peacefully.

The ship shuddered violently. What were they doing to it now?

Surrender!

"Go to hell," Holman snapped. "While there's breath in me, I'll spend it fighting you."

You cannot escape.

But now Holman could feel warmth seeping into the ship. He could sense the painful glare outside as billions of galaxies all rushed together down to a single cataclysmic point in spacetime.

"It's almost over!" he shouted. "Almost finished. And you've lost! Mankind is still alive, despite everything you've thrown at him. All of mankind—the good and the bad, the murderers and the music, wars and cities and everything we've ever done, the whole race from the beginning of time to the end—all locked up here in my skull. And I'm still here. Do you hear me? I'm still here!" The Others were silent.

Holman could feel a majestic rumble outside the ship, like distant thunder.

"The end of the world. The end of everything and everybody. We finish in a tie. Mankind has made it right down to the final second. And if there's another universe after this one, maybe there'll be a place in it for us all over again. How's that for laughs?''

The world ended.

Not with a whimper, but a roar of triumph.

Science Fiction and Fantasy from Methuen Paperbacks

While every effort is made to keep prices low, it is sometimes necessary to increase prices at short notice. Methuen Paperbacks reserves the right to show new retail prices on covers which may differ from those previously advertised in the text or elsewhere.

The prices shown below were correct at the time of going to press.

☐ 413 55450 3	Half-Past Human	T J Bass	£1.95
☐ 413 58160 8	Rod of Light	Barrington J Bayley	£2.50
☐ 417 04130 6	Colony	Ben Bova	£2.50
☐ 413 57910 7	Orion	Ben Bova	£2.95
☐ 417 07280 5	Voyagers	Ben Bova	£1.95
☐ 417 06760 7	Hawk of May	Gillian Bradshaw	£1.95
☐ 413 56290 5	Chronicles of Morgaine	C J Cherryh	£2.95
☐ 413 51310 6	Downbelow Station	C J Cherryh	£1.95
☐ 413 51350 5	Little Big	John Crowley	£3.95
☐ 417 06200 1	The Golden Man	Philip K Dick	£1.75
☐ 413 58860 2	Wasp	Eric Frank Russell	£2.50
☐ 413 59770 9	The Alchemical Marriage of Alistair Crompton	Robert Sheckley	£2.25
☐ 413 41920 7	Eclipse	John Shirley	£2.50
☐ 413 59990 6	All Flesh is Grass	Clifford D Simak	£2.50
☐ 413 58800 9	A Heritage of Stars	Clifford D Simak	£2.50
☐ 413 55590 9	The Werewolf Principle	Clifford D Simak	£1.95
☐ 413 58640 5	Where the Evil Dwells	Clifford D Simak	£2.50
☐ 413 54600 4	Raven of Destiny	Peter Tremayne	£1.95
☐ 413 56840 7	This Immortal	Roger Zelazny	£1.95
☐ 413 56850 4	The Dream Master	Roger Zelazny	£1.95
☐ 413 41550 3	Isle of the Dead	Roger Zelazny	£2.50

All these books are available at your bookshop or newsagent, or can be ordered direct from the publisher. Just tick the titles you want and fill in the form below.

Methuen Paperbacks, Cash Sales Department,
PO Box 11, Falmouth,
Cornwall TR10 109EN.

Please send cheque or postal order, no currency, for purchase price quoted and allow the following for postage and packing:

UK	60p for the first book, 25p for the second book and 15p for each additional book ordered to a maximum charge of £1.90.
BFPO and Eire	60p for the first book, 25p for the second book and 15p for each next seven books, thereafter 9p per book.
Overseas Customers	£1.25 for the first book, 75p for the second book and 28p for each subsequent title ordered.

NAME (Block Letters) ....

ADDRESS...

....